This is Not a
Love Story

Also by Keren David

When I was Joe

Almost True

Lia's Guide to Winning the Lottery

Another Life

Salvage

This is Not a Love Story

KEREN DAVID

www.atombooks.net

ATOM

First published in Great Britain in 2015 by Atom

3 5 7 9 10 8 6 4 2

A CIP catalogue record for this book
is available from the British Library.

ISBN 978-0-349-00140-1

Typeset in Palatino Light by M Rules
Printed and bound in Great Britain by
Clays Ltd, St Ives plc

Papers used by Atom are from well-managed forests
and other responsible sources.

MIX
Paper from
responsible sources
FSC® C104740

Atom
An imprint of
Little, Brown Book Group
Carmelite House
50 Victoria Embankment
London EC4Y 0DZ

An Hachette UK Company
www.hachette.co.uk

www.atombooks.net

For Jenny, she who must be obeyed. Mostly.

PART 1: Now

Chapter 1

Theo

Amsterdam

Love is not necessarily a good thing. You generally end up getting hurt, or hurting someone else. Or both.

Like last night.

I'm talking about emotional stuff, just to be clear. Maybe actual physical injury would be a lot easier. Not in a *Fifty Shades* kind of way, obviously. Just, well, if Kitty had punched me in the jaw last night, I wouldn't feel so guilty.

My hangover is making my head hurt like crazy, so the after-punch would just add to the pain. And I would have a legitimate reason to avoid her today. I have to do it though. Talk to her. Before things develop any further.

The morning after a break-up is the worst. Trust me, I'm an expert. This is the second time this month. When someone dumps you, it's heartbreaking and insulting and horrible, sure, but being the one who breaks up is almost as bad. You have all the guilt and shame and embarrassment, and you can't blame anyone else. You're the person who killed love.

It's especially bad when you've broken up with Kitty, who is not just a really great person; she's a really great person with five thousand subscribers on YouTube.

I've screwed up big time.

Right now I'm lying on a sofa in the living room of a flat in Amsterdam Old South, which is the equivalent of Notting Hill in London or New York's Upper West Side, somewhere that normal people don't live, all blingy boutiques and posh restaurants. The flat is huge and cool, packed with stuff designed to show off the wealth of the guy who rents it, my friend Lucy's dad. He's an international lawyer, so Lucy gets the place to herself a lot.

My dad runs a furniture company, so I know that the uncomfortable sofa that I'm lying on came all the way from Milan. I can also predict that Lucy's dad is not going to be all that happy about the beer stains on his Eames armchair and the splashes of vomit on the Brink & Campman rug. But that's what happens when you piss off on a romantic weekend in Marrakech with your glamorous actress girlfriend and leave your daughter all alone.

It's early morning and the light is filtering in through flimsy curtains. The trams arriving at the stop right outside announce themselves with a clanging bell and their very own distinctive swooshing noise. Sleep is impossible, just as I'm drifting off another tram arrives.

When the third tram clangs, I accept defeat. Amazingly, no

one else has been woken by the noise. There are five other people sleeping in here, and one of them is Ethan, slumped on the floor, right next to my sofa, his long blond hair hiding his face. I think about waking him up. He's been a good listener in the past. But there's something unpredictable about Ethan, his mood turns like a windmill. I'm not sure he's the right person to talk to about Kitty anyway. I've never been able to work out their relationship. The first time I saw them together, I thought they were a couple.

There's no sign of Kitty, but that's no surprise: she was avoiding me after what happened. She's probably gone home, and is sleeping in her own bed. That's what I should do, but I've told the cousins that I live with that I'll be out for the weekend. They're newlyweds. They won't want me turning up unexpectedly.

And besides, I've got a lot on my mind.

I swing my feet off the cold leather, relieved that I seem to be wearing all my clothes. The room smells of stale beer, sweat and vomit, overlaid with the disinfectant that Lucy used to scrub the rug. I need fresh air, or I'll be throwing up as well.

I find my shoes, creep down the stairs, and let myself out into the cold morning. My bike's chained up outside and I undo it, fingers fumbling with the lock. Then I ride off, bumping over the tramlines, straight ahead, right and then left, down a green, shadowy path into the Vondelpark.

I love cycling. It's been the big discovery of my three months in Amsterdam that you don't need to feel that you're taking your life in your hands every time you get on to a bicycle, like you do in London where you virtually need full body armour to be safe on a bike. Here, cycling feels like flying and there's something liberating about getting around without having to wait for buses or trains or people to give you a lift.

There are quite a few cafés in the Vondelpark, but my favourite one is hidden away on an island in the middle of the lake. It looks like an old-fashioned flying saucer – round and white with blue edges and totally out of place among the trees, as though it's crashed down to ground and adapted to life on Earth by selling coffee and apple cake. In the summer you sit outside, under the trees. Now it's frosty November and the café is warm and cosy inside.

I order a milky coffee – *koffie verkeerd*, the Dutch call it, or 'wrong coffee', presumably because at some point in history it was considered wrong to put milk in your coffee. Now everyone drinks it, so wrong is right.

I feel a bit better after the coffee. My head has stopped throbbing and it's taken away that metallic taste in my mouth. But when my phone rings, I wince at the noise. It's Kitty. I do the brave thing and answer.

It's not Kitty. It's Lucy. 'Is Kitty with you? She's not here.' Her voice is accusing – or am I just feeling guilty?

'How come you're using her phone then?' I ask.

'She's left it here. And her knitting and stuff.'

'She must've gone home,' I say, although it seems really odd. Kitty never goes anywhere without her phone, because she's always taking pictures and loading them online. She's got quite a following for her AmsterKit Tumblr and Instagram accounts, and her vlog is getting more popular every time she posts. Am I going to feature on that vlog? She wouldn't spill personal stuff like that online – or would she? She's certainly posted a load of coupley pictures of us over the last month or so. Will she feel she has to announce that we've split up?

She never goes anywhere without her knitting either, it's typical Kitty to have brought it along to the party. You might think it's a bit of an old person's hobby, but it's not, partly because no grandmas I know do knitting – my Grandma Sarah is into Pilates and Booba Dora is big in the world of charity committees. Kitty always says that knitting is calming, and she knits enough to put a normal person into a coma.

'I'm on my way,' I tell Lucy. A prickle of worry makes me shiver, but I shrug it off – of course Kitty's OK. She's probably doing exactly what I am, having a coffee somewhere.

Except, I don't remember seeing her at the end of the party at all. And she was pretty upset with me. And why would she leave her stuff behind? I step up the pace, making for the pathway out of the park.

When I get back to Lucy's, Ethan is unlocking his bike right outside the front door.

'Hey,' I say. 'You OK?'

He keeps his head down, concentrating on the lock. 'I'm fine. You?'

'Yeah … bit of a hangover … I must've had more than I thought …'

He gets the lock undone, straightens up and looks me in the eye. I take an involuntary step backwards.

'Kitty—' I say, but he interrupts. I don't catch what he says, and we both stumble into silence. He shrugs and gets on to his bike. I stack mine on to the rack and unwind my lock. I can't help noticing Kitty's bike next to it. It's unmistakable, decorated with a string of plastic roses and a pink-checked seat cover.

'See you later?' asks Ethan.

'Yeah, maybe, I'll see how it goes,' I say, and press Lucy's doorbell. Luckily someone buzzes me in right away.

'Did you find Kitty?' Lucy greets me.

'No, no sign of her. But I didn't go far, just to the Theehuis. Do you think she slept here? Or did she go home?'

Lucy looks at me accusingly, like I should know the answer to this. Fair enough, as far as Lucy's concerned, I should know where my girlfriend slept last night.

'Maybe she's just gone for a walk?' I suggest, feebly.

'In that dress? Those shoes?'

Kitty's dress was low-cut, midnight blue, sprinkled with little diamonds. Not real diamonds, obviously, but they sparkled like a million dollars. The dress clung to her so tightly that she'd been taking tiny steps all night. And she was wearing heels too, shiny greeny-blue ones. She was taller than me in those shoes. I see Lucy's point: Kitty looked beautiful last night – but not half as mobile as normal.

'She must have had stuff to get changed into,' I point out.

Lucy hands me Kitty's bag. 'You look.'

All the other girls have big handbags, but Kitty has a khaki backpack, like one a kid would take to school. She's hung it with multi-coloured pom-poms – a look that got so much social media approval that she posted a pom-pom-making tutorial on YouTube. Inside the bag I find jeans, a T-shirt and hoodie, her make-up and some canvas shoes. Plus her keys, her purse, a box of aspirin, her knitting bag and phone, head-phones and gum.

Lucy gets right in there. 'You two had a row or something?'

'Or something,' I say. 'She'll come back for her stuff. When she does, get her to ring me, OK? I'm going home for a shower.' Never mind interrupting the newlyweds. I need to escape Lucy's accusing eye.

'What something? You're meant to be the perfect couple.'

'Oh, give me a break, Lucy. No one's perfect all the time.'

Lucy narrows her eyes at me, but she changes the subject. 'You're not going to let us down this afternoon, are you? Ethan's already upset Alice.'

'What? How?'

'It's today! The parade!'

Alice is lying on the sofa I slept on, a towel over her eyes. At this she sits bolt upright. 'I can't believe you've forgotten!'

'I haven't forgotten!' I object, although actually I had. 'I just thought I'd go home, have a shower ...'

'You can have a shower here, we've got three bathrooms,' says Lucy.

'Ethan very rudely told me that I'm insulting Dutch culture by protesting,' says Alice. 'So that's him out. Kitty's disappeared somewhere. If you duck out on me, Theo, I'll never forgive you.'

The thing about being exiled from your home, about cutting off contact with your friends, is that you end up investing loads in new friends that you've known for five minutes. Kitty being the main one, obviously, but Alice and Lucy and the rest of them are very important to me, because they are all I've got. I had literally hundreds of friends and near-friends back home in London. I'm totally not used to feeling alone.

'Kitty won't have gone far,' I say, more confidently than I feel. 'You know her. She's probably just gone for a walkabout. Taking pictures.'

'Without her phone?'

'She's got a camera as well.'

'So she went off with just her camera, leaving the rest of her stuff behind? Including her bike?'

'I'll go and look for her,' I volunteer.

'Well, if you see her before we do, tell her she's got to come to the parade, OK? On the Henrikkade at midday. We'll hang around in the meantime in case she comes back.'

'I bet she will,' I assure Alice. Kitty was the main person to share her protest plans, discussing them enthusiastically over mint tea and spice biscuits in the café next to our college. The rest of us backed Alice with varying degrees of commitment. I've signed up in theory, but right now I just want to try and find Kitty so we can talk before the parade.

I cycle twice round the Vondelpark, checking each of the cafés. Maybe she had some money in a pocket to buy breakfast. No Kitty. Then I head east to the Pijp district where Kitty lives with her mum in a modern block, just behind the Heineken Experience. A whole exhibition devoted to beer. Kitty dragged me along there one day after college and made a short film about it, the end of which is her drinking beer and gagging. That vlog got two thousand hits.

I lock up my bike outside their building and press the doorbell, but no one answers. I stand around, waiting until someone comes out. Then I duck inside before the door slams shut behind them.

I go up the stairs, all seven floors. There is a lift but I'm too nervy to wait for it. I thump at her door. 'Kitty?' I call, cautiously, but no one's there. Not Kitty, or her mum. The silence feels deliberate, full of tears and hurt feelings, and I don't stay there long.

Maybe she was so upset at the party that her mum came to pick her up? Maybe they've gone off somewhere? If I cycle around, perhaps I can find her. She might not want to talk to me, but at least I won't be worrying about her.

So I embark on a Kitty-hunt, cycling randomly through Amsterdam, looking for a tall girl with dark curly hair cascading past her shoulders. If she's still wearing her party dress, she'll stand out immediately. But I guess she at least grabbed some shoes from the stack down by Lucy's front door, because no one could walk far in those heels. I'm more and more certain that she must have gone home and got changed there. She'll probably turn up to Alice's protest after all.

I check the flea market at the Waterlooplein and the little farm on the Prinseneiland, and I cycle the length of the Singel to the flower market and then down the Spiegelstraat because Kitty loves the antique shops with their amber necklaces and blue and white porcelain and dark wooden carvings all the way from Indonesia. 'Sometimes I wish I had all the money in the world,' she told me once, 'so I could buy all this gorgeous stuff, but mostly it's enough to know that it's there and I'm happy just taking pictures.'

Then I look in her favourite cafés too, the juice place on the Utrechtestraat and the Café de Jaren with its waterside terrace, and the amazing shop on the Staalstraat where you can buy chocolates in every flavour imaginable – thyme, pepper, rhubarb, lemongrass. We've got a pact to try every one before we leave Amsterdam.

I wheel my bike down the Staalstraat, checking in all the shops. She's not in the second-hand art bookshop, or the sweet shop where they have sticks of rock with pictures of flowers and fruit running through them. She isn't looking at cutting-edge furniture by Dutch designers. She's not in the toy shop. Kitty bought Alice a fluffy owl from here for her birthday. Today, the stuffed animals stare at me, passing judgement. *Where's Kitty? Why did you make her cry?*

It's nearly time for the parade, so I'd better get to our meeting point. Hopefully Kitty will be there. I cross over the little bridge, where people have attached padlocks all the way up the chains that lift the bridge if a boat needs to pass underneath. Love locks, they're called, and each one has the name of a couple written on with marker pen. *Theo and Sophie*, I'd have written, just a few months ago. *Theo and Kitty* would have worked in the last few weeks. Now … well … these padlocks are bad for the bridge's structure anyway. The city council clears them away regularly.

I pause on the bridge, because Kitty loves the view down the canal towards the church. 'Of all the canals in the whole of

Amsterdam, this is my favourite,' she says, and then she laughs because its name is the most difficult to pronounce. Groenburg-wal, it's called, pronounced something like *Hroonburchvall*. The G makes a rough, rasping sound that trips up most English speakers. I don't find it so difficult, because I learned Hebrew up to my bar mitzvah three years ago, and it has exactly that throat-clearing noise, but Dutch vowels have, so far, defeated me. There's a sound – *ij* – which is somewhere between *I* and *ay*. I never get it right.

It doesn't matter, though, because everyone here speaks English.

I get out my phone and check Kitty's Instagram account. I'm kind of shocked to see our selfie, taken at the beginning of the party. She's so happy, that wide, sweet smile. How could you not love that smile? And I do love Kitty. I do.

Just not enough.

Chapter 2

Theo

Amsterdam

There's a big crowd already jostling for places at the waterfront when I get there, even though the boat isn't due to arrive for another hour. It takes me a bit of time to find them, and I see right away that Kitty hasn't turned up. There's just Lucy, Alice and a few others from college.

Alice is arguing with Finn. Everyone knows that Alice will win, because she always does. 'You just don't get it,' he's saying. 'No one sees it the way you do.'

'Yeah, because everyone here is whiter than white,' she retorts.

'It's not about colour. No one notices that.'

'Oh, please! Can you hear yourself?'

I interrupt them. 'Where's Kitty? Didn't she come back?'

'No. And she hasn't turned up either. We thought you might have found her,' says Alice. 'Anyway, look, we can't wait for her. We've got to go and join the protesters.'

'Alice, there's a handful of protesters and about thirty thousand people who think this is the best day of the year,' says Finn. He's lived here for five years and Alice suspects he's gone native, despite his Canadian accent.

'Look,' I can't let it go, 'it's just that Kitty hasn't posted any pictures since the party ... I think it's a bit odd ...'

'She's probably just sleeping it off. And I've got her phone, remember?' says Lucy.

'I know, but where is she? What if she's with someone dodgy?'

They look at me. I know what they're thinking. Why would Kitty leave with a stranger when she's meant to be going out with Theo?

'I'm sorry, but we have to do this protest,' says Alice. 'We'll look for her afterwards. What Finn doesn't understand is that it's a matter of right and wrong.' She's holding a big carrier bag. 'I've got the placards in here ... Well, they're not placards really. Bits of cardboard, with slogans written on them.'

Finn looks. 'Slogans in English. Alice, you can't do this.'

Alice purses her lips and glares at him. 'I'll do it on my own if necessary.'

'You think you're standing up for minority rights. They think you're an American cultural colonialist.'

'Well, that's kind of ironic!' spits Alice. She's African-American and one of those people who knows all that stuff about which words are unacceptable and what you're meant to think about everything, which is OK, but she doesn't always get it that British people do things differently. Or Dutch people. Or anyone.

To be honest, if I'd met her in London I'd probably have avoided her, because I'm not so into politics. It's actually good for me that I've made friends with someone like her: it's expanded my worldview a lot. Although, as Kitty has pointed out several times, while we seem to be a diverse group, everyone's either rich or comfortably middle-class. No poor people in our expat world.

'Come on!' says Alice. 'The boat is due soon! We need to get in position.'

The parade is to mark St Nicholas's arrival in Amsterdam, an annual event. There are hundreds of families here, parents bringing their kids to see the saint disembark from a ship, get on to a horse and proceed through Amsterdam. St Nick, generally known as Sinterklaas, is a bishop in flowing white robes, he has a long white beard, and his horse is white too. He's accompanied by his friend and servant – 'slave', insists Alice – known, not very delightfully, as Zwarte Piet. Black Pete.

Black Pete looks like those old golliwog toys that kids used to have in England before people realised that they were totally offensive. He has big red lips. The cake shops are full of grotesque marzipan black faces. The supermarkets sell chocolate Piets.

It's like those old books in which every Jew is untrustworthy and has a hooked nose, and you're not meant to be insulted because, you know, those times were different. The 1920s and 30s and before, when anti-Semitism was just part of being normal, for non-Jewish people, that is.

Today, it seems like no one in Amsterdam got the memo

explaining that caricatures of black people are not nice. Black Petes are everywhere – Dutch men and women in curly wigs, boot-polished skin, red lips, as well as brightly coloured satin knickerbockers and jaunty hats sprouting feathers. They're giving out sweets and biscuits to children. It's excruciating, it's eye-popping, and for Alice, one of the few actual, real live black people present, it's clearly painful. Finn trying to persuade her that Zwarte Piet is loved by the Dutch – 'My little sister calls him "Smart Pete"' – only adds to her pain. I totally support her for wanting to protest, but I'm a bit nervous about the reaction we'll get, as everyone seems to be really happy and enjoying themselves.

I take a placard and appeal to Alice. 'It's just – shouldn't we try and find Kitty? She wasn't at her flat. It seems weird that she's not here either, and she hasn't come back for her stuff.'

'I think Kitty left the party early,' says Jane. 'Did you guys have a row or something?'

'No,' I say, too quickly.

'She looked a bit . . . I don't know. Upset.'

'We were out on the balcony. Then she went back inside. I looked for her but I couldn't find her. Look, guys, it was a diffi-cult night. We were talking about . . . you know, us, and I think . . . well, it wasn't really the best conversation . . . but it wasn't really a row . . . not, you know, an argument.'

'So what actually happened?' starts Lucy, but the music drowns her out and the crowd is shouting and it's time for our protest to begin.

'Come on!' says Alice. So we follow her, pushing through the crowd.

A smiling Zwarte Piet on rollerblades tries to give her some candy, but she stomps past. I accept a handful, because I haven't eaten anything all day. Mixed in with the sweets are spice biscuits. I can just about see that if you ignored the total hideous racism, this would be quite a fun occasion for little kids. Finn and Jane are quietly walking away from us.

The crowd is twenty deep at least. The other protesters – a small, proud group – are right over the other side. As the galleon sails in and Sinterklaas waves to the crowd, Alice raises her placard high and shouts, 'Racist exploitation! Zwarte Piet stinks!'

But her voice gets lost in the children's shouts of 'Sint! Sint!' and – no less adoring – 'Piet! Piet!' and the only response she gets is from a mother in an anorak, who frowns and says, 'If you don't understand Dutch cultural traditions, you should stay away.'

'Screw your traditions!' shouts Alice, and Lucy looks anxiously at me.

'Show some respect!' says the lady. 'Go back to America!'

'Show some respect yourself!' Alice looks like she's about to explode. 'This whole parade, it's an insult! Zwarte Piet stinks! Come on, Theo, come on, Lucy!'

So, just to show willing, I lift up my placard and yell, 'Zwarte Piet stinks!' and unfortunately the crowd shifts at that point and the corner of the cardboard bashes the face of a tiny kid, hoisted on his dad's shoulders.

'Oi!' says the angry dad, as the child screams, and everyone's looking at us; the crowd is turning, children are pointing.

The little boy is wailing in his mum's arms now, his cheek bleeding, and his dad, who is about seven feet tall, is roaring abuse in our direction.

Lucy squeaks, 'We need to get out of here,' but the dad growls, 'You're going nowhere,' and there's a heavy hand gripping my shoulder.

'What the hell?' I say.

'You're coming with me,' says someone in Dutch, and it's a cop. I see Alice and Lucy being led away by one of his colleagues.

And that's how we get arrested at the Sinterklaas parade.

Chapter 3

Theo

Amsterdam

Dutch police stations are nicer than the British or American ones I've seen on TV, but it's still boring and a bit worrying – OK, very worrying – being locked up, especially when they separate us. After a couple of hours, a policeman opens the door to my cell and says something in Dutch.

'I don't speak *Nederlands*,' I say. *'Ik kan niet.* Can you speak English?'

'I can speak English, *eikeltje*, I just choose not to. Right, your friend has apologised for you, so run away and don't insult the Dutch nation again.'

I could say something about freedom of speech and the Dutch history of tolerance and all that, but I don't. Something tells me it wouldn't go down well. Besides, when we get to the foyer, Alice is doing all that for me.

'Racism and unlawful arrest ... restricting our right to protest ... I'm going straight to the American consulate ...'

'Look, miss, I'd keep that pretty little mouth shut if I were you,' says the policeman, and Alice is so outraged by his sexism that she actually stops talking.

Then a side door opens and Ethan comes out, holding some papers. What the hell is he doing here? He looks at us, unsmiling, and shakes hands with the policeman. They exchange a few words in Dutch. I can feel my face burning with embarrassment.

'Why is Ethan here?' I whisper to Lucy.

'I called him. I thought he could talk to them ... he speaks Dutch. I didn't want my dad finding out ...'

'*Tot ziens*,' says the policeman, and we're free to go. Ethan doesn't say a word until we're out on the street and two blocks away from the police station. Then he makes his feelings clear.

'What did you think you were doing? Getting arrested? Hurting some kid?'

'It was a total accident!'

'You were lucky the boy's parents didn't get involved. The police got you out of there just in time.'

'It was an important cause,' says Alice. 'What matters more, speaking out against tyranny, or saving ourselves?'

'Zwarte Piet is not tyranny.' As Ethan says it, two six-feet-tall Piets whizz past us on a tandem. I think one is a girl.

'He's a symbol of slavery!'

'Everyone loves him! He's a role model! He's Sinterklaas's friend!'

Ethan is avoiding looking at me, that's for sure. I don't know if I'm relieved or not.

'Look, never mind all this,' says Lucy. 'What about Kitty?'

'Do you think she's OK?' I ask. 'I'm really worried ...'

'Where is Kitty?' asks Ethan. 'Too sensible to get involved with your idiotic protest, eh?'

'I knew you were an insensitive pig, but I never realised you were actually a racist!' yells Alice.

'I'm not a racist.' Ethan sounds bored.

'Just a pig then. I should have guessed.'

Alice is near to tears. Then a tram draws up, and before we can stop her she's swung on to it and the doors are shutting.

'Quick, follow that tram,' drawls Ethan.

'Oh, shut up, Ethan,' snaps Lucy. 'Why do you have to be a prick?'

Ethan rolls his eyes. 'What's your problem? I just rescued you from the police. Now you're calling me names.'

I wonder if there was anything going on between Alice and Ethan? She did seem more upset with him than I'd have expected.

'Have you heard from Kitty?' I ask him. 'It's just that she left her bag and phone and money at Lucy's, and we haven't seen her. I went round to her flat and she wasn't there. I suppose her mum picked her up or something, but it seems strange.'

'Her mum's in Paris,' he says. 'She's gone away with my dad.'

I stare at him and he stares back at me, and Lucy asks, 'So where is Kitty then?'

'She'll be OK,' says Ethan. 'Don't worry. She's a big girl. She's probably back at your flat, Lucy, waiting for you.'

'What if she isn't?' demands Lucy. 'What do we do then? If her mum's not around it's our responsibility.'

'I'll ring her mum if you want,' says Ethan. 'I doubt they've seen much of Paris. I've got the hotel number. But I shouldn't think it's necessary.

'I don't think you're taking this seriously enough,' says Lucy. 'No one's seen Kitty all day. We've got her house keys and her money and her phone.'

Ethan gestures in the direction of the police station. 'Want to tell your new friends about it?'

'No,' she says, 'I'm going back to the flat first. You'd better come with me.' I'm relieved that Lucy doesn't want to revisit the cops.

'I left my bike at Centraal Station,' I say.

'OK, go and pick it up and then meet me at home,' orders Lucy. 'You coming, Ethan?'

'I've got things to do.'

I'm completely convinced that Kitty *is* there, upset and angry, sitting on Lucy's doorstep, waiting to tell me what she thinks of me. And she doesn't even know the worst of it. I can think of a million places I'd rather be. But I suppose I'd better go back to Lucy's, just to reassure myself that nothing terrible has happened.

'Well, I'll leave you to it,' says Ethan, already astride his bike.

'Where are you going?' says Lucy.

'What's it to you?'

'We might need you. To ring Kitty's mum or –' Lucy swallows. 'Hospitals or the police or something.'

Ethan sighs. 'I'm sure she's fine. I'll be at home. Call me, or come over if you want to. Theo, you know my house, don't you?' He's acting all unconcerned, but he's frowning, and I suspect he's a lot tenser than he's letting on. Ethan's so difficult to read though. Maybe it's because he's sort of Dutch and sort of English and sort of American as well. Or maybe he's tense about something else altogether.

'Yeah,' I say, avoiding Lucy's eye. 'I'll go and check her flat again, if you want. Maybe a neighbour had some keys.'

'Come to mine first and then we'll go together and if she's not in either of those places we're coming straight over to yours, Ethan, OK? And you'd better be there.' Lucy's voice is a little shaky. I don't blame her. It's just so unlike Kitty to go to ground, to stop communicating, that it feels as though she's died. I wish I hadn't had that thought, but now I have it won't go away.

'OK,' says Ethan. 'Hopefully I won't see you.' He rides off, before we can even double-check his address.

'I can't stand him,' says Lucy. 'He's really sneery and I never know what he's thinking. I always get the impression he's laughing at me behind my back. And he's really working that sexy, long-hair messy sort of look, but I'd hate to get involved with him. You could never trust him. Honestly, if it weren't for Kitty, I wouldn't have invited him.'

I feel that I should stand up for Ethan. 'He can be nice,' I tell her. 'He's a good listener.'

'Is he? Do tell,' she says, but luckily her tram comes then and I walk to the station thinking about Ethan and Kitty and all the rest of it, until I find my bike and unwind the chain and cycle south towards Lucy's neighbourhood.

Kitty isn't at Lucy's. And when we go to her flat again there's still no answer.

'Let's go to Ethan's,' says Lucy. 'It's near here. Just round the corner.'

Neither of us knows the Pijp, apart from the street market that runs through it, but Lucy has GPS on her phone and remembers the street name. She wants to take Art History at university, which gives her a real advantage in finding her way around Amsterdam because most of the streets are named after artists, and if you know one, say, Italian painter, then you can guess the basic direction to cycle in to find another. The Pijp, Lucy tells me, is full of seventeenth-century Dutch artists and at least one of them specialised in pictures of cows. The one that Ethan's street was named after painted those gloomy dark portraits of people in white lace stick-out collars around their necks.

I know Ethan's house once I get near. I've only been there once, but it was memorable. We chain our bikes to the rack and consult the name on the brass plate by the door. Melinda McCafferty, Ethan's mother. Lucy rings the doorbell, and I breathe in and out and try to stop the shaking feeling inside me.

'Hey.' Ethan appears on the step. He's got changed into black jeans and a black T-shirt, with his hair pulled back. Put a ruff around his neck and he'd fit right into an old masterpiece. 'Managed to stay out of trouble? Didn't get arrested again?'

'Have you heard anything? From Kitty?' demands Lucy.

Ethan stares at me. His mouth is a straight line; his arms folded. 'You didn't find her.'

'If we'd found her we wouldn't be here,' says Lucy. 'You're going to have to call her mum.'

'OK, no sweat,' he says.

Ethan leads the way through to a kitchen – all old-style wooden cupboards but the fridge is big and modern – and asks if we want a drink. I haven't seen this part of the house before, and I look around curiously. There's a spiral staircase in a corner, leading up to a big hole in the ceiling.

'No alcohol,' says Lucy. 'I had enough last night. Have you got any coffee? Or maybe some herbal tea?'

'Take a look,' says Ethan, pushing a wooden box towards her. Inside it's divided into sections, each with a different flavour of tea bag. He puts on the kettle, rinses some mugs, looks in the fridge. 'Beer?' he asks me.

'No, just water,' I tell him.

'You OK?' he adds, his voice deliberately casual. Or just casual. Whatever.

I nod again, avoiding his gaze. 'Yes. And you?'

'Not too bad.'

'That's . . .' I search for the right word, 'good.'

Ethan fills a mug with hot water and puts it in front of Lucy. He opens a plastic box and produces some biscuits, big, crumbly cookies that taste of spice and ginger. They look homemade. My mum makes something similar. I wish I were at home. Amsterdam's gone wrong.

'I know you all think Amsterdam is just a village, but you can't really search the entire city by cycling around. Kitty's probably got some friends you don't know about. Or she's gone to the movies or something. Maybe she's got a secret lover.'

My mouth is dry. 'Thanks for that,' I say.

He glances at me. 'Yeah, well, we all have our private lives. She was on fire last night.'

I prickle with jealousy, but it's true. When someone who usually wears jeans or leggings and DMs turns up to a party in a skin-tight dress, you notice. Although anyone would notice Kitty any time. She just draws the eye.

'Did she bring a change of clothes?' asks Ethan.

'Yes, but she left them behind,' says Lucy. 'All her spare clothes were in her bag.'

'Maybe she borrowed some of your stuff?'

'I'm half her size.'

Lucy is one of those scrawny, tiny girls, so that wasn't half as bitchy as it sounds. Kitty would just laugh anyway, and pat Lucy on the head. Kitty has no problem with being six feet tall; in fact, she'd told me she felt slightly cheated of her special status when she realised that the Dutch were the tallest nation on Earth.

'Your dad lives with Saskia Albers, doesn't he? She's around the same height as Kitty. Maybe Kitty got changed in their room, borrowed some clothes from Saskia? Her dress and shoes are probably under the bed.'

'How do you know Saskia?' asks Lucy.

'Everyone in the Netherlands knows her. She's famous.'

It must be a bummer being a Dutch celebrity. If the Dutch had hung on to America then people like Saskia would be world-famous. But New Amsterdam turned into New York and Dutch became kind of useless. And I'm thinking about this so that I don't have to imagine Kitty getting in a car with a stranger or hitching a ride somewhere on someone's bike, and then having an accident. Maybe her mum already has bad news about her? She wouldn't tell us, would she?

'Calling Kitty's mum should be our last resort,' I say. 'We don't want to worry her unnecessarily.'

Ethan stretches, arms up high. 'Oh, I'm sure she won't mind us interrupting whatever's going on. She's probably regretting going away with my dad. He's quite dull, you know.'

'It's not a joke,' snaps Lucy. She looks at her phone. 'It's 3pm. Kitty's been missing all day and possibly most of the night.'

'We need to call the hospitals,' I say. 'Kitty might be there. She's got health problems.'

'What problems?' Lucy's frowning at me.

'I once had to take her to hospital,' I admit. 'She was fine, but she said she had this thing ... something to do with asthma.'

Ethan frowns. 'I think my dad said something about her having check-ups on her heart. You know, because of her dad.'

'I don't know,' I tell him. 'What check-ups?'

'It's probably nothing,' he says. 'Just in case. I don't know the English word. *Voorzorg.*'

I can't put the thoughts together. I don't want to say it out loud. *Kitty might have had a heart attack. She might have had an asthma attack. She might have fallen in a canal. She might be dead.*

And if she is – it's my fault.

PART 2: Then

Chapter 4

Kitty

London

Mum got the offer of a transfer to Amsterdam in April. We avoided talking about it while I was doing my exams. That meant a lot of sentences left hanging in mid-air, a lot of 'if's and 'maybe's and 'we'll talk about it soon's. But while we weren't discussing it, all around me, conversations hummed and crackled – Mum and Rachel, Mum and Grandma, Mum on the phone to her friend Paul who had moved to Amsterdam six months ago. I did my best to stay focused on revision – Geography, Textiles, English, horrible Maths, Spanish, Art, the dreaded Double Science – but I also did a lot of internet browsing of things to do and see in Amsterdam. Museums. Coffee shops. Cafés. Markets.

So, when we finally got around to talking, I was ready.

We came out of Great Ormond Street Hospital, where I'd been going almost all my life – ever since my dad died when I was five, anyway, which was as much of my life as I could remember – and we walked a bit in silence until we found our usual after-hospital café.

'Phew,' said Mum. 'I'm glad that's over.'

'Me too,' I said, stirring my camomile tea.

Life is frightening when you have a potentially unreliable heart. Something could go wrong at any moment. Every time I go to the hospital I worry that the doctors might find something and insist on opening up my chest on the spot. That wouldn't be good, although sudden death would be worse. And it doesn't matter how much Mum and the doctors pretend that it's all routine and OK and nothing bad is going to happen. My dad dropped dead sitting on the sofa watching the FA Cup Final ten days after my fifth birthday. After that, I grew up expecting the worst. The regular check-ups confirmed that everyone else was similarly pessimistic.

Tottenham had just scored, so at least he died happy.

'Cheer up, sweetheart.' Mum smiled at me. 'Dr Nathan was very pleased with you. And she said there was no reason not to consider Amsterdam; there are excellent doctors there. So, we really need to make a decision now. I've stalled them long enough.'

'Them' meant her employers, a huge media company. They wanted her to be European Sales Manager. It was a huge boost to her career. She was really happy about it, I could tell, although she was pretending to be as neutral as Switzerland in the Second World War.

'You're really keen, aren't you?'

'Well, it is a promotion. And a new challenge. And it's very near – only an hour on the plane – and Rachel could easily get a ferry over from Newcastle.'

'Yeah, right, when she has time for us.'

Mum rolled her eyes at me and I knew I was being unfair. Rachel is my sister – half-sister officially. She's four years older than me, in her second year studying Law at the University of Newcastle. I missed her like crazy, and her other family too. Without a father of my own, I'd sort of adopted her dad, and called him my Uncle Marcus, even though that was a bit weird because he and Mum basically got divorced after she fell in love with my dad. I know, it's complicated. 'I felt terrible,' Mum once told me, 'because Marcus is lovely, and Rachel was only little and it was such a mess. But Justin was The One. There was nothing I could do about it.'

Uncle Marcus scooped me up when Mum had her Misery Year. He included me in everything he did with Rachel and it was all fun stuff – the zoo and the aquarium, bowling and movies. But, four years ago, he'd got married again and moved to Tel Aviv and I hadn't even been to visit yet.

Mum was still going on about Amsterdam. 'They'd pay our rent – we'd get an expat package – and we could finally finish doing up the Ruin.'

Dad bought our house as a total renovation job. He'd got as far as putting in new electrics, when his heart gave out. 'One of the worst things,' Mum always said, 'was that I could never mourn in peace. The builders were there for the first six months, so I couldn't have a private cry without a drill going off. And for six weeks I couldn't even make myself a cup of tea because we didn't have a kitchen.' She managed to get the basics done, but never completed the job. So we still have flowery wallpaper and swirly carpets that probably date back to the 1970s.

'What about your support system?' I ask. Mum's been seeing Valerie-My-Counsellor for ten years, and she's also got a yoga teacher, a reiki consultant and an occasional aromatherapist.

'I've been talking to Valerie about the possible move. She thinks it might shift a psychic block. Amsterdam is full of holistic healers. It could be just what we need. A new stage of our lives.'

'I don't need a new stage of my life,' I said, more certainly than I felt.

'But it's a natural one, isn't it? Finishing GCSEs. And you're not sure about college here, are you? Now that Martine's going off to stage school, and with Riley and Esther getting into the grammar school.'

'All right, all right,' I said. I didn't need reminding that my friendship group – solid since nursery school – was splitting up. Martine had achieved her dream of a place at stage school, and started going out with a boy who'd been in *EastEnders*, while Riley and Esther had finally admitted that they fancied each other, just at the point when they both got offers from the highly selective sixth-form college and I didn't. They'd promised that nothing would ever affect our friendship, but you can't help noticing when you're with two people and only one person isn't holding hands with anyone.

It wasn't that I especially minded being single; it was just that I didn't like being single on my own.

'Amsterdam does look nice,' I said, cautiously. It looked

gorgeous, for a weekend away. I hadn't been able to stretch my imagination to actually living there.

'Your friends could come and stay ... There's a tutorial college that teaches A-levels ...'

'I haven't even decided which subjects I'm taking,' I pointed out.

'Well, we'll sign you up, and then if the GCSE results are no good, you can have a year off to retake and decide what you want to do. No sweat. I don't want to put any pressure on you.'

No one ever wants to put pressure on me, because of my heart. Not Mum, not Grandma, not the school. Rachel used to get told off for protesting. 'There's nothing actually wrong with her!' she'd say. 'You treat her like she's a china doll!'

Rachel always knew she wanted to be a lawyer, and used to boast about how stressful it would be. I had no idea about my future, so many things seemed to be off limit; I just couldn't wait to give up most of my school subjects.

'Maybe I could do Art and English. And I don't think I'd hate Sociology.'

'That sounds like a plan!' Mum beamed at me.

I scrambled for my knitting. It's a great hobby for stressful situations and just the prospect of moving abroad was an entire cardigan's worth of anxiety. A really complicated Arran cardigan too.

'Only if you're sure,' said Mum, looking anxious. She knew how to read my craft activities. Knitting was OK, but embroidery meant a compulsory reiki session.

'When would we have to go?' I asked.

'They want me to start in September. You get your exam results at the end of August. So we'd go then, stay with Paul for a few days, find somewhere to live ...'

I knitted furiously. An entire row of Rachel's birthday present, a cherry-red beret.

'Amsterdam's beautiful, Kitty. You'll love it. And Paul has already been checking out flats for us, so it won't take long at all to find somewhere nice.'

'We don't speak Dutch,' I pointed out.

'According to Paul, everyone there speaks English. And I'd learn, anyway. We could both learn. It'd be an adventure.'

I thought about Amsterdam. Sex and drugs and works of art. Canals and windmills and clogs. Anne Frank, hiding in the attic. It would certainly make a change from north London.

'Paul says Amsterdam is great for anyone interested in art or photography,' said Mum. 'And Ethan, his son, is just a bit older than you.'

Paul, Paul, Paul. Mum had always insisted that he was just a friend, but she did talk about him a lot. They'd met when she went on a course in 'unleashing your creativity'. Paul was the teacher.

They definitely fancied each other, and went out for lots of drinks, supposedly to discuss her ideas for writing a book. She wrote a few chapters of the novel, but nothing developed with Paul except a friendship. He was newly divorced from his second wife and Mum was nervous, and then he had to move to Amsterdam. He had a son living there, from his first marriage. This Ethan was nearly 18, but his mum was going off working in some war zone and she asked Paul to come and live in their house while she was away. That was six months ago, and there was no sign of him coming home. I knew Mum missed him so I was sure she was keen on this move in part because of Paul.

I knew nothing much about the son except what I remembered Mum telling me when Paul moved – moody, difficult, independent, although also 'very creative'.

'Ethan would be a ready-made friend for you,' Mum said, somewhat optimistically, with a dreamy look on her face. 'I've seen pictures of him, Kitty, he's tall and blond and really quite nice-looking.'

'Mum, that is so inappropriate! Do not start matchmaking! You're such a Jewish mother!' She is too, even though we hardly ever go to synagogue, she never makes chicken soup (she's a vegetarian) and she only occasionally lights candles on a Friday night. It's the protective way she tries to organise my life.

'I am not match-making! And I thought I'd brought up you girls to reject sexist stereotypes!'

'Let's concentrate on you and Paul.'

She blushed, but shook her head. 'We're strictly friends. And apparently Ethan is a handful, anyway. Not right for you, Kitty.'

'That's for me to decide,' I said, annoyed that she'd got me to contradict myself.

Mum smiled. 'So, you're up for it then? You'll come to Amsterdam?'

I took a deep breath. I wasn't sure at all. But then I looked at her dimples, her smile, the way her shoulders had relaxed.

'Let's go for it,' I said.

Chapter 5

Kitty

London

Mum said I could have a party to say goodbye to all my London friends. 'The house will be pretty empty,' she pointed out, 'it's the perfect time to fill it with teenagers. It doesn't matter how much damage they do, the builders are starting as soon as we leave.'

I considered the offer for, ooh, about five minutes. Obviously I wasn't going to have a party. I wasn't that sort of person. There were only about twenty people at school who'd know my name. If I had a party it'd be embarrassingly well behaved, quiet and empty.

Instead I invited my best friends over for afternoon tea, and styled it with a lacy tablecloth and vintage teacups picked up from the charity shop. I baked scones and a Victoria sponge, hulled strawberries, made a centrepiece of pink roses and forget-me-nots and wore a vintage summer dress with a daisy print.

'Oh, Kitty! I'm going to miss you, babes!' Esther pulled me into a hug. 'Look at this table! It's so pretty!'

'Don't cry!' Martine had a big gift bag with her. 'Look! Presents for you!'

Riley and Martine's *EastEnders* boy got stuck into the scones while the girls pulled presents out of my bag.

First an assortment of London tourist souvenirs. A plastic Beefeater pencil holder. A London bus keyring. A mug with Prince George's photo on it. The Underground map on a mouse mat. A Union Jack case for my phone.

'For when you get homesick,' said Esther, 'although we're all sure you'll be far too busy to even spare us a thought, stuck here in boring Palmers Green.'

'I love Palmers Green,' I said, mournfully, and they all started laughing.

'Amsterdam is infinitely cooler than north London,' said Martine. 'You're going to forget all about Palmers Green.'

'Never!' I told her. 'Ooh! Books!'

Romances, of course. My friends knew me well. One historical, one contemporary, one classic – 'Oh wow! *Love Story!* I've never actually read it! Or even seen the film. I just know that line – *"Love means never having to say you're sorry."*'

'My mum said it was brilliant,' said Esther doubtfully. 'It sounds a bit miserable to me. The girl gets ill ... I'm warning you, Kitty ...'

'It's OK! I can cope with fictional death and illness! I actually love it when people die!' I hugged the book to me.

'Are you taking all your books with you?' asked Riley. 'Because that's a lot of books.'

I shook my head. Mum was being quite strict about how

much stuff I could take. I was allowed two boxes for books, photos, pictures, bedding, and another three for clothes. Everything else was going into storage in a warehouse in Tottenham. The entire house was being painted white inside and out and a team of Polish builders were putting in a new bathroom and tarting up the kitchen. Mum had contacted Roger, Dad's old colleague, to sort it all out. 'It's a very desirable house,' he'd told Mum. 'Don't worry about a thing, we'll find the right tenants and look after it for you.'

My dad and Roger were estate agents. Some people get all sniffy and horrible about estate agents, acting like they are all liars and thieves, and making jokes about them. I find that quite offensive really. I know my dad chose his profession because he loved houses and he cared about people, and he wanted to find the right place for the right person, so they could have their ideal home. One of my earliest memories is of my dad showing me round a house and explaining to me how the tattered carpets could be taken away, and the walls painted the colour of vanilla ice cream, and how everything would be light and bright and perfect. That house turned into our house, but Dad died before even one floor could be sanded, and we'd never managed to complete his vision of how it could be.

And now we were leaving and strangers would be moving in.

We ate the cake and strawberries and I drank peppermint tea while the others poured coke and lemonade into my teacups. 'More presents,' said Martine. 'Open this one.'

It was a small flowery bag filled with make-up. Mascara, lipstick, blusher and various pencils. I protested. 'But I don't wear make-up!'

'This is a new start, Kitty,' said Martine. 'You are going to go to Amsterdam with a new image.'

'But I don't want a new image!'

'Just let me make you up,' she pleaded. 'Go on. I'll show you what to do.'

'Oh … I don't know …' I could never be bothered with make-up and all that sort of stuff, because it was such a faff and I wasn't all girly and pretty like Mum or Rachel. They were fine-boned and fair-haired, with big blue eyes and small features. I'd inherited Dad's dark curly hair, except his was short and mine was out of control; I'd got his broad shoulders and his hazel eyes, his heavy eyebrows (I learned to pluck really early) and big mouth.

Plus, I am tall, like an overgrown weed. I look strong and confident and independent and healthy. So did he. Appearances can lie.

'It won't take long,' said Martine, and because she'd been asking for months and I wasn't going to see her for ages, I agreed. I closed my eyes and tried not to giggle as soft brushes tickled my skin. And then tried not to cry when she applied eye-liner and mascara. 'There,' she said. 'How does that look?'

I went and looked in the mirror of the downstairs loo. I had to admit I liked what she'd done. My big mouth actually looked better coated in dark red, and my eyes were enormous. I looked at least eighteen, stylish and like someone who could stand up for herself.

I loved the idea of going to Amsterdam looking like this. I could imagine this girl meeting someone, falling in love – everything I'd ever dreamed of.

So far my romantic dreams had definitely been all about fictional heroes. The boys at school just couldn't match up, only a few of them were taller than my shoulder. I fantasised about meeting someone tall and gorgeous, moody but caring, intense and passionate, with high cheekbones and intellectual depth. A perfect love, like the one my parents had experienced, the love that was ripped away when my father died.

In real life, my romantic history consisted of 1) kissing Riley when we were both twelve – we agreed not to try it again, and 2) last year I'd had a few dates with a basketball player I'd met at a party. Harry was a nice guy, and I had managed to find some common ground in that we both liked Coen brothers films and acapella music. Plus he was six-feet-four. But when we kissed on date three, his jaw sort of locked, and that made me think of a skeleton's fixed grin and it totally put me off him. So we never made it to date four.

Amsterdam would be different; I knew it. The Netherlands was the country with the tallest people in the world. In this land of giants, no one would know me as the girl who might drop dead at any minute. I'd keep my heart check-ups secret, I'd paint on red lipstick and I'd put it all on Instagram to show my old friends just how much I'd changed.

'I love it,' I told Martine, and she danced a little victory jig. 'Can you teach me how to do it myself?'

Chapter 6

Theo

London

'I'm sending you away,' my dad announced, as though I were a parcel and he could dispatch me via a courier service.

I put down my knife and fork. Friday night dinner had stopped being my favourite meal a while ago, because it's the time when the whole family comes together, and right then we couldn't talk without having a row. Ever since the rumours about me got louder and louder and in the end Dad asked me outright and everything changed.

'You're sending me away? What the actual hell?'

'Don't swear, Theo, not at the dinner table,' said Mum faintly.

'*Hell* is not swearing,' I pointed out, quite reasonably.

Dad thumped his hand on the table. 'Don't argue with your mother!' he roared. 'It's Friday night! Show some respect!'

'I wasn't arguing! I was just saying! *Hell* is just a perfectly normal word. It's not even a concept that you believe in.'

Simon, sitting across from me, caught my eye and shook his

head, just a tiny gesture, but it was enough to shut me up. Simon was the expert at reading Dad's moods, because he'd been working in the family business for a year. My dad is like a dormant volcano; he doesn't explode much, but when he does it's spectacular and scary. His last sustained series of massive eruptions had been when my oldest brother Jonathan decided to chuck in university, move to Jerusalem, grow a beard, call himself Yonatan and become a religious maniac. Dad had a lot to say about that. But eventually he came round to it, and even became a bit of a frummer himself and so I had every reason to hope he'd accept my right to fall in love.

The rows would have been worse, but we were all trying to control ourselves because Mum was ill. She'd been to consultants, she'd had tests and scans, but all the doctors were useless and no one could explain why she was so tired all the time, why her hair was falling out and her joints aching, why she was losing weight and spent most days lying on the sofa. My Auntie Mimi had cooked this meal, and Simon had warmed it up: chicken soup, roast chicken, potato kugel, vegetables, just like every Friday night. It didn't taste anything like as good as Mum's cooking though. She wasn't even trying to eat it.

'Theo, you need to get out of London,' said Mum. 'This person—'

'She's got a name!'

'It's an infatuation, it's totally wrong.'

I didn't answer, because I didn't want to shout at her, so I put my head down and concentrated on eating.

Dad bellowed, 'You're breaking our hearts! Your mother – she doesn't need this worry!'

'It's not *about* Mum! It's private! Just forget you ever found out about it!'

'How can we forget?' said Mum. 'It's not possible.'

'OK, then, if you'd just meet her. Sophie's great, Mum, Dad, honestly – you'd really like her.'

Simon scratched his head. He didn't need to say anything; I could tell he thought I was an idiot.

Mum shook her head. 'I love you so much, darling. But I can't take the stress of policing your life to keep you away from her.' Mum said 'her' in the same tone of voice she'd have used to say 'nuclear warfare' or 'Class-A drugs'.

'Don't talk about Sophie like that!'

Mum shook her head. 'I can't cope with this. I'm going to lie down.'

Dad and I watched in silence as Simon helped Mum climb the stairs. I hated the doctors who let her suffer like this. All those tests, and no answers. How incompetent could they be?

Sophie had made the last few months bearable for me. No one ever acknowledged that Mum could die from this unknown disease that seemed to be getting worse every day. It was the great unspoken, the last taboo, the gigantic elephant invisibly charging around the room, breaking the knick-knacks on the mantelpiece and leaving great big muddy footprints all over the thick-pile cream carpet. For a while, Sophie was my own little elephant in the room, a much nicer elephant, a cute baby elephant that totally distracted me from the other one, the out-of-control raging beast.

'Theo, you can see the state your mother's in. I have to think of her welfare.'

'So I get sent away? Is that what Mum wants? So she doesn't have to have anything to do with me?' I could see how much I was upsetting my parents. But I had feelings too. 'I don't even know where you're sending me.' I was assuming Israel, either to Jerusalem to stay with my brother, or the kibbutz near Haifa with Auntie Shira. What about school? How would I do A-levels? Surely Dad didn't intend to send me to some religious seminary?

'Send him to New York,' said Simon, coming back into the room. 'You'd like that, Theo. I could go as well and head up our American office.'

'We don't have an American office,' said Dad. 'And you've got a lot to learn before I let you establish one. Theo's going to Amsterdam.'

'Amsterdam?' I echoed, immediately imagining myself living in a windmill, wearing clogs, eating cheese and smoking weed.

'Amsterdam,' said Dad. 'It's only an hour's flight from here. We can come out to see you when your mum is feeling better.'

Is she ever going to get better? The question was hanging in the air but I couldn't ask it.

'It's a cool place, Amsterdam,' said Simon. 'Alex is really happy there.'

My dad's plan became clear.

'I'm going to stay with Alex and Chani?'

'And what's wrong with that? Alex is your cousin.'

'They got married, like, five minutes ago!' Not only would I be in a different country, I'd be the biggest third wheel in the history of vehicular transport.

'So what? They have room in their house and they'll be happy to show you around. Alex will be a good influence.'

My cousin Alex was the golden boy in our family. Auntie Mimi's second son, he'd never caused anyone any trouble. Head boy, captain of the football team, top grades, his First at university, his career in computing, his marriage to the lovely Chani ... He was charming and well behaved and just religious enough. Every Jewish parent's dream, our Alex.

'What about school?' I said. 'What about my A-levels? I'm predicted really good grades! I've already been picked out for Oxbridge tutoring!'

'Don't talk to me about that school,' said Dad. 'You can't seriously think I'd let you go back there?'

'Why not? It's so unfair. Look, if you could just forget you ever found out about it ... '

'Theo, everyone is talking about you. The whole community. It's a scandal. You need to go away, give everyone a chance to find something else to gossip about.'

'I don't care about gossips,' I said, although I did. No one should have known about Sophie. But we were the subject of whispers at school for a good few months, and then Jack Pollard saw us at the cinema. A cinema in south London too, I mean how unlikely is that? And he told his mates, and they told their mates, and eventually someone said something to Mum's second cousin once removed, who told my auntie, who told my parents. And although Dad had denied it to everyone he could – he even phoned up the rabbi and asked for advice – the rumours went on rumbling around. I'd told Sophie and she'd agreed that we'd stop seeing each other for a bit until it all died down. Or until I was 18 and I could escape my Dad's domestic dictatorship.

'*Why* do I have to go away?'

'We're thinking about you, Theo. It'll be easier for you.'

'I can decide what's best for me!' I yelled.

Simon started clearing the table. Dad just sat there and shook his head. He wasn't shouting any more. Maybe I was making progress.

'We're living in the twenty-first century, not the Dark Ages. What are you going to do when I'm eighteen and I'm with Sophie? Sit shiva for me like I'd died?'

'Theo, you're not eighteen yet and until then you'll do as you're told.' Dad's voice was dismissive, as though I were about six years old.

'So, you don't care about my education?'

'There's a tutorial college in Amsterdam where you can take your A-levels, Alex says, but if you prefer to sit out the year,' Dad shrugged, 'that's up to you. I just want you to give up this ... this ... abomination.'

'It's not an abomination! What sort of a word is that? If you'd just meet her – she's not like you think—'

'Theo,' said Dad, 'don't argue with me. Just do as I ask.'

'This is a joke, isn't it? You're sending me to the sex and drugs capital of Europe!'

'Maybe it'll distract you,' said Dad, without the glimmer of a smile.

I glared at him. How dare he make stupid jokes? But he would probably prefer me to spend every day smoking weed in a brothel than be happy for ever with Sophie.

'I'm not going,' I said. But I knew that I'd have to. My dad is the boss of more than the family business. It was just about OK keeping a secret from him. Outright disobedience was beyond me.

'When I'm eighteen, I'll do whatever I want,' I told him with all the defiance I could muster.

'I know that very well,' he said. 'But until then, I make the decisions. This is not a love story, some romantic movie, Theo. Don't get any silly ideas. And go and help your brother with the washing-up.'

He picked up his *Jewish Chronicle*. There was no point arguing. So I bit my tongue and thought, just under two years. Twenty months. Only eighty weeks until Sophie and I can be together.

Because, when I turned eighteen, it wouldn't matter that she used to be my teacher.

Chapter 7

Kitty

Amsterdam

Paul was waiting for us at Schiphol Airport, clutching two shiny helium balloons and a cake box. All around us, people were meeting and greeting. I nearly barged into a guy wheeling a massive suitcase, just like mine. He glanced at me then turned away.

'Welcome to Amsterdam!' said Paul, hugging Mum with the arm that wasn't carrying baked goods. The balloons bobbed and swayed. 'It's so wonderful that you're here! Jacqui! Kitty!'

'Hey, Paul,' I said, manoeuvring our trolley around a runaway toddler. 'Do you want to put that box on top of the suitcases?'

'Better not, it's a fruit flan – local speciality – and I wouldn't want it to get squashed. Here you are,' he handed us both a balloon, 'that's a local custom too.' I looked around. I saw one other person with a balloon and that was a little girl aged about four. Oh, well, Paul had only lived here for a few months. He probably hadn't got the hang of things yet.

'You're going to stay with us until you find a flat,' he said. 'Plenty of room, it's no problem. You can get to know the city, decide where you want to be.'

'That's so kind of you, Paul,' said Mum.

Paul didn't have a car, so we had to go down an escalator to the station and drag our suitcases on to a train. Accidentally on purpose I let go of my balloon. Mum went on holding hers, like a child leaving a birthday party.

We arrived at Centraal Station, which was like any station anywhere, noisy and ugly and full of people. Paul pointed out the multi-storey bike park – 'I can't wait to get on a bike!' said Mum – then we had to pull our suitcases to a tram stop, climb up into the tram and then get off and pull the cases some more, down dark streets. That is, Mum and Paul pulled the cases. Delicate, fragile me – I'm taller than either of them – carried the cake.

Light glimmered from the windows of houses, and as we walked along we could see into living rooms and huge kitchens. All the flats and houses seemed to be tidy and stylish with bunches of flowers on gleaming wooden tables, ultra-modern furniture and impossibly beautiful people, most of them tall, blonde, supermodel types. Looking through the windows was like flicking through a glossy interiors magazine. I loved it. I wondered if Amsterdam was safe enough for me to go out walking around at night by myself.

'Why don't they draw the curtains?' asked Mum.

'It's a Dutch thing. They have nothing to hide – what you see is what you get. I like it, although it takes some getting used to.'

'Do you draw the curtains at home?' asked Mum.

'My son's lived here for ten years, more or less. He's pretty much Dutch by default. Our curtains stay open.'

He stopped by a door that was right on the pavement – no front garden. Yes, the curtains were open, but the room inside was dark. It seemed quite a small house to me, part of a terrace, but it was hard to see, the street lighting wasn't great.

Paul ushered us in, past a small front room to a large kitchen with a huge window at the back. The fridge and microwave were new; everything else looked as though it hadn't been touched for 100 years. Wooden shelves and cupboards, painted cream. A brick-red tiled floor, blue-grey walls. I liked it at once. It was totally different from any kitchen I'd ever seen in London.

There was a large circular hole in the ceiling, and a spiral stair-case leading up through it. Mum was looking at the suitcases and the hole, and I knew she was wondering how they were going to get up there. She'd been holding her balloon all the way from the airport, but now she let it drift up to the ceiling.

Mum didn't say anything, though, because there was a woman sitting at the kitchen table. She sprang up as we came into the room. 'Jacqui! Kitty! I am so glad to meet you!'

Huh, I thought. Paul had a new girlfriend. I was slightly relieved, but also disappointed for Mum. She'd come all this way and now her hopes of romance were dashed.

'This is Mieke,' said Paul. 'Ethan's teacher.'

Mieke laughed. 'Not his teacher any more,' she said. 'Friend, shall we say? Friend of the family.'

Mieke had short, spiky dark hair and one of those faces that makes you think someone is clever, and not just because of their large black specs. The way she spoke was short and spiky as well. I felt sorry for Ethan. I couldn't imagine anything more ghastly than a parent dating one of your teachers.

'How long is Ethan's mother going to be away?' asked Mum.

Mieke shrugged. 'Who knows? Melinda's spent the last six months in Afghanistan, and she's contracted for another year. When she comes back depends if she thinks she should stay here for a while, or if there is another dangerous place that needs her help.'

'That's Melinda,' said Paul. 'Sometimes I find it extraordinary that she and I were together long enough to have Ethan. She could never settle in London, and Amsterdam is really only a base for her between assignments.'

'Yes, she's a restless spirit,' said Mieke. 'But she does a wonderful job, and helps so many people, so I suppose it is worthwhile. Do, please, come and sit down.'

Mieke seemed very at home in Paul's kitchen, so I guessed that teaching Ethan had been a stepping stone to getting off with his dad. Mum thought so too, I could tell from the big smile on her face, which I recognised as her social armour.

Paul poured us wine, while Mieke served bowls of tomato soup and sliced crusty bread, which spit crumbs all over the pine table.

'Where's Ethan? Did you call him?' said Paul to Mieke. He explained: 'His room is right at the top of the house. He doesn't always hear us.'

'I called, but no answer,' said Mieke, buttering a piece of bread. 'I tried his phone, too.'

'But he knew Jacqui and Kitty were arriving.'

Mieke shrugged. 'He forgot, maybe. He lives in his own world, that one.'

'I'm sorry, ladies,' said Paul. 'Maybe he'll turn up soon.'

'Maybe,' said Mieke, 'but he's not very social.' She smiled at me. 'Don't expect much from him, Kitty. He doesn't like people much.'

A cough interrupted us. A cough from the ceiling. A pair of long legs dangled and then found the stairs. Ethan, it must be, swung down the spiral. For the first time I noticed that there was no banister or railing.

You could see that Paul and Ethan were father and son. Ethan had Paul's grey eyes and craggy nose, but his face was thinner, and his hair was long and fair, tied back in a ponytail, while Paul's was short and black, sprinkled with white. Ethan was tall, I noticed, and his cheekbones promisingly high. I wasn't so keen on his jeans (black and ripped at the knees) or his paint-splattered T-shirt (also black, with a green skull leering at me), but I'd read enough books to know that you should never judge a boy by his clothes. I mentally placed Ethan on my Potential Amsterdam Romance list.

'You must be Jacqui and Kitty,' said Ethan, with an elaborate politeness that was clearly satirical. 'So glad to welcome you to Amsterdam.' He shook hands with Mum and then me. I got a slight electric shock from his touch.

'Were you up there all along?' said Paul. 'Mieke said she shouted up to you.'

'I had company.' Ethan's face dared Paul to ask any more. 'I came downstairs especially to meet our guests,' he added.

'That was nice of you,' said Mum with her eager, peace-maker's smile. I cringed inwardly.

Ethan glanced at Mieke, who was ladling soup into a bowl. 'Yes, it was, wasn't it? Very social of me.'

'Where's your company then?' asked Mieke. 'Do they want to have some soup?'

'Oh, he's gone,' said Ethan.

I was puzzled. Surely we'd have seen anyone coming down the spiral staircase? Clearly Ethan was lying, which was a bit sad. Maybe he had no friends.

'How's the application going?' asked Paul. 'Ethan's thinking of going to art school,' he explained. 'He's very good.'

Mieke plonked a bowl of soup in front of Ethan and said something in Dutch. He replied, also in Dutch, and she made a tutting sound and took a big sip of wine.

'It's going badly,' said Ethan. 'I think maybe I won't bother.'

Paul looked pained. 'I'm sure you could cope, Ethan. Just fill out the forms.'

'I don't want to, OK?'

'It won't be like school,' said Mieke, soothingly.

'I don't want to,' he snapped. 'Leave me alone.'

'What do you teach, Mieke?' said Mum, in a blatant attempt to shift the focus away from Ethan, who was tearing his bread into little bits and chucking them at his soup. 'Do you work in a high school?'

Mieke shook her head. 'No, mostly I work with kids who

aren't in mainstream school. It's called an expertise centre, and it's for kids with behavioural and physical problems. Ethan, I worked with privately, because I was friends with Melinda, and Ethan knew if he cooperated with me he could get his diploma and be allowed to leave school.'

'I never went to school anyway,' said Ethan. 'I don't care what the law says.'

'And you've got your diploma now, so you don't have to go any more,' said Mieke.

'Yeah, and I don't have to be hassled by you.'

'That's fine. You were just a job to me. Just like all those other kids.'

'The crazies and the sickies,' he said. 'I don't know why you bother.'

'Lucky for you I did.'

'So what do you do now?' I asked Ethan, because I couldn't work out whether this was for real, or just banter. Neither of them was smiling anyway.

'Not a lot,' he said. 'This and that. I make some pictures. I clean the house. I paint walls. I go skating. I do a bit of video art. But that's not enough, apparently.'

'Do you put your films on YouTube?' I asked. 'I'm thinking of doing an Amsterdam vlog.'

'Maybe you can collaborate,' said Mum. 'That'd be fun, wouldn't it?'

'I despise social media,' said Ethan. 'Empty people, showing off. Everyone's desperate for approval. I make films for myself.'

'I don't think YouTubers are desperate for approval!'

'Yeah, well, whatever. I don't want people knowing my business.'

This explained why I hadn't been able to find Ethan on Facebook when I was doing my pre-Amsterdam research. Weird, but not totally unprecedented. I decided he was a bit pretentious.

'Are you tempted to follow in your mother's footsteps one day?' asked Mum. 'Humanitarian work?'

Ethan shrugged. 'No way,' he said. 'I'll leave it to my mom to get killed chasing danger. Sorry to disappoint you. I don't really care about other people.'

Paul frowned at his son. 'So, are you excited to be in Amsterdam, Kitty?' he asked.

'Yes, I think so,' I replied, although excited didn't really touch it. I was all churned up inside, scared, anxious, missing my friends and yet super-thrilled at the same time, like I'd won the lottery or been asked out by a member of my favourite band.

'We'll start looking for a flat for you tomorrow,' Paul promised. 'Until then you're very welcome here.'

'Thank you,' said Mum.

Ethan scowled into his soup.

'What will you study, Kitty?' asked Mieke. 'Do you think you will find time for Dutch lessons?'

'I think so,' I said, cautiously, 'although I wasn't very good at Spanish. That's what we did at school.'

'It'll be completely different, hearing it all around you.' Mieke smiled encouragingly. She looked younger and less spiky when she smiled. 'And you can practise with Ethan. Paul can just about manage the basics.'

'Did you always live in this house?' I asked Ethan, in a desperate attempt to make conversation. Mum was talking to Paul about his unfinished novel and I knew from experience that chats about creative writing last ages and are unbearably dull. I mean, obviously it'd be interesting if it was someone like J. K. Rowling talking about how she wrote *Harry Potter*, but my mum and Paul just talk about plot and subplot and characterisation and so on.

'No,' he said. 'I came to Amsterdam when I was little. My mom thought Schiphol was a better airport than Heathrow. And she likes the atmosphere. It's a good place to chill when she's home from wherever. We lived on a houseboat for a while. When she went away I had to go back to London, mostly and stay with Paul.'

'Oh, OK, right.'

'She bought this house last year. I've been doing it up. She stayed a while, said she was going to settle down, but then there was some international disaster, and she's good at those. So she went away and this time Paul came out here. But I'm eighteen soon, and then he can go.'

Paul had half an ear on this conversation; I could tell by the way his eyes flicked from Ethan to Mum and back again. Mieke stacked the soup bowls in the sink and took the cream flan out of its packaging. I wished that Mum and I had spent our first few days in a hotel. I wanted to get to know Amsterdam, not get drawn into someone else's family problems.

'When's your mum coming home?' I asked. 'It must be difficult ... I mean, you must miss her.'

Ethan shrugged. 'I'm used to it. I guess once I'm eighteen she won't bother to come back here much. Amsterdam's good for her to crash between projects, but she can do that anywhere.'

'Oh,' I said. 'Well, as long as you're OK with that, I suppose it makes sense.'

'I'm OK with that. They can all just go away and leave me in peace.' Ethan was half smiling, and I felt as though he was mocking me.

'Thanks for having us to stay. I mean, thanks to your mum ... after all, it's her house ...' I was burbling, I couldn't help it. There was something unnerving about his steady gaze.

'That's fine. She couldn't care less.'

'That's kind of her,' I deadpanned.

'I know,' he deadpanned right back, 'but try and find somewhere of your own as soon as possible, won't you?'

Way to make us feel welcome, Ethan, I thought, taking a big bite of flan, so I didn't have to think of a response.

Mum put down her fork. 'That was delicious,' she said, 'but I'm terribly tired and it feels so late. I'm sure everyone needs to sleep.'

'Yes, I have work to go to in the morning,' said Mieke.

'Which one is it, the cancer kid or the bed-wetter?' asked Ethan.

'The cancer kid,' said Mieke. 'You can come along if you want, make yourself useful for once.'

'Actually, I had plans for Ethan and Kitty for tomorrow,' said Paul. 'Jacqui and I are going to look at some flats, and I thought Ethan could show Kitty around a bit. Take her to see your friend who runs that bike shop on the Overtoom, Ethan.'

Ethan sighed, a long, exaggerated, theatrical exhalation.

'I'll take that as a yes,' said Paul.

'It's fine,' I said. 'I can show myself around.'

'No, really, Ethan has nothing better to do,' said Paul. 'Let me show you your room. Ethan, can you bring up the cases?'

The stairs jutted out of a central pole, and you had to grip it carefully then hoist yourself up on to the floor above when you reached the top. Paul took the stairs quickly; Mum and I followed cautiously. I was curious about how Ethan was going to carry up two heavy bags, but he remained at the table, talking to Mieke. So far Dutch sounded like a load of muttering, throat clearing and some weird English-like distorted words.

'This is the living room,' said Paul. Each wall was covered in bookcases; there was a television and two squashy chairs. Another big window. High ceilings, and a splashy abstract painting in greens and browns and yellows.

'It's gorgeous!' said Mum. 'I can't wait to see it in the daytime.'

I yawned. I couldn't help it.

Paul opened a door. 'And here's the spare room, and there's a bathroom too …' A double bed, covered with an indigo throw. One wall painted blue, the others white. A wicker chair, a silver-framed mirror, a wooden mantelpiece, which held a vase of pink roses and a candle in an amethyst glass. And our suitcases –

our heavy, bulky suitcases – magicked up those spiral stairs by invisible hands.

'How did that happen?' asked Mum, and Paul laughed and opened another door, showing us a second staircase.

'But we didn't see it when we came in,' said Mum. 'I'm sure there was no staircase ... Oh! I get it! It's two houses stuck together.'

'It leads down to the next door along,' agreed Paul. 'Two doors, one house. It's a bit crazy, but you'll get used to it.'

'It's so kind of you, Paul, having us to stay,' said Mum.

'It's wonderful that you're here. It's been tough, trying to build a new life for myself.'

'It was very good of you to move here for Ethan,' said Mum, lowering her voice, even though Ethan was nowhere to be seen.

'It's the least I could do,' said Paul. 'He's had so much disruption in his life. He's not easy, but ... '

Ethan appeared at the bedroom door with some towels.

'Thank you, Ethan!' said Mum, much too enthusiastically. I winced.

He glanced around the room. I remembered what he'd said about doing up the house.

'It's so nice here,' I told him. 'You've done a great job.'

He shrugged again. Somehow Ethan managed to convey hostility with a twitch of the shoulders.

'It's OK. Night.'

'So, you'll take Kitty out tomorrow?' said Paul. 'Get her cycling?'

As we'd walked along the street I'd seen how cycling in Amsterdam worked. No helmets. No lights. People perched on the back of dilapidated bikes. It looked incredibly dangerous.

'I'm not sure,' I said doubtfully.

'Oh, but you must! It's virtually compulsory in Amsterdam.' Ethan smiled. Well, it was more of a smirk, really.

'You're scared of cycling?' he asked, with unmasked contempt.

I wasn't going to admit it.

'No, of course not,' I said. 'I'm not scared of anything.'

Chapter 8

Theo

Amsterdam

Chani met me at the airport. I just about recognised her in her long denim skirt and long-sleeved top. Last time I saw her – the only time I saw her – she was in her wedding dress, whirling in the centre of a ring of friends. Now I couldn't even bring myself to smile at her, because I was still in shock that I was actually here.

Chani was standing next to some guy holding a massive cake box and two balloons, as though he planned to throw a spontaneous birthday party in the middle of the airport. I weaved towards her through the crowd. Some girl bashed into me, but I hardly heard her apology, because suddenly this whole thing felt incredibly real. I suppose, right up to this point, I'd thought my parents would change their minds.

'Theo!' called Chani, with massive fake enthusiasm. I assumed it was fake, anyway, because what pair of newly-weds wants a sixteen-year-old lodger? I wondered why they'd even agreed to take me in. Was Dad paying them? Did they think they were doing a mitzvah? Probably. That's the sort of people they were, actively looking for the chance to do good deeds and follow the commandments, all 613 of them.

Next to us, the tall girl was being handed a balloon. She looked as unenthusiastic as I would, and that made me smile.

'Hey, Chani,' I said.

'It's so good to see you! I'm excited to show you Amsterdam. This is a great idea of your parents'.'

Oh yeah? I wasn't so sure.

Chani drove me down the motorway, chatting the whole time.

'So, our house is in an area called Amstelveen, which is actually a little town in itself. There's a tram right into the centre, it only takes about fifteen, maybe twenty, minutes to get to your college. And it's easy to cycle, right through the Vondelpark. Alex talked to them and you can do all your subjects there. Maths, English, History, French, is that right? You didn't change your mind?'

I shook my head, and then nodded. 'Yes ... no ... I didn't change my mind.'

'You start next week. Of course, you'll need to take some time off for the holidays, but they won't mind that.'

I was not looking forward to the holidays at all. Jewish New Year is nothing like ordinary New Year's Eve. They party; we pray. They drink; we eat. And it's all about praying to live another year, repenting our sins, leading up to Yom Kippur when we do nothing but pray – no meals, no drink – and all you can think about is food. And then there's Succot, when you build little houses in your garden and you're meant to eat your meals there and it always rains, unless it coincides with half term and you can go on holiday to Israel. I just know that Chani and Alex are going to insist that I take part in everything. I'm sure my dad thinks this will make me appreciate my home and family and everything that he thinks Sophie is threatening.

'The first thing we need to do is find you a bike. Do you like cycling? You'll probably prefer it to taking the tram.'

On and on she went. Did I like art? Did I like the seaside? The cinemas where I could see English films. The forest, not far from their house. Museums, shops, Amsterdam's Jewish heritage. It was clear that her instructions were to keep me busy at all times.

At last she pulled into a street full of boxy modern houses. It looked nothing like the Amsterdam I'd seen in films or on television. No gables, canals or bridges. We might have been on a British council estate, except that there was no graffiti and everything looked clean and well looked after, and there was a children's playground and a patch of grass.

'Here we are,' Chani said, pointing out a house identical to all its neighbours, except for the bright-blue door, the white shutters, and some tall yellow flowers in the tiny front garden.

'It's nice,' I said, because she seemed to expect me to say something. 'Nice ... er ... sunflowers.'

'Wait until the spring! Then we'll have beautiful flowers everywhere. The middle bit, the green, is for everyone to share. And then we have a little courtyard at the back.'

'Oh, yeah, uh, nice.'

'I'll show you everything in the morning. Come in, Alex should be home soon.'

It didn't take long to take me round the house, because every room was tiny. Mine was in the attic, up some incredibly steep stairs. 'I hope this is all right for you. It's our laundry room, but I'll keep all the washing behind this screen.'

On one side was a washing machine, a tumble dryer and an airer hung neatly with Alex's underpants. A flimsy screen. And, on the other, a single bed, a little table and a chest of drawers. Everything was IKEA. My dad would be horrified.

'I'll do the washing while you're at college,' Chani explained. 'I hope the table's big enough to work at, if not there's the dining room downstairs. And if you have clothes to hang up, there are the hooks on the door, or you can use our wardrobe.'

I felt a bit claustrophobic already. I'd always had a large room of my own at home, with plenty of space for a proper desk, a sofa, a wardrobe, a computer and a television. I'd never appreciated it before.

'Hey! Theo! Good to see you, mate!' Alex's face appeared at the top of the stairs.

'Hey, Alex.'

He climbed up into the room and gave me a hug. 'Wow, I'm excited to have you here! Someone to watch Arsenal with!'

'Thanks for having me,' I said, trying and failing to match his enthusiasm.

Chani gave him a kiss and said, 'I'll go and get supper started.' Once she'd gone, Alex checked that I liked everything about the room – 'Have you tried the bed? We got a new mattress. Not too firm, I hope?' – then got to the point.

'Look, mate, we're really happy to have you here. I hope it'll give you a chance to get your head together.'

I ground my teeth. 'Thanks, Alex.'

'This teacher, she should be prosecuted for what she did to you.'

'She didn't do anything to me.'

'If you were a girl, and she were a man, the police would be on to her. I think your dad should have reported her to the school, at least.'

'I'm sixteen, Alex. I'm not a victim here. And Dad would never do that. He only cares about what people think.'

'I'm sure that's not true.'

'He's sent me here so I won't be an embarrassment to the family.' Dad's total hypocrisy hit me one more time. He didn't really think there was anything wrong about Sophie and me, otherwise he would have called the police, told my headmaster. He just wanted everything hushed up, and me out of the way.

'He's sent you here so you can spend time in an amazing city, and we get to enjoy your company and you can work out what you want to do with your life without the hassle of dealing with rumours and gossip,' said Alex, 'and also so your mum can concentrate on getting better.'

'I wasn't stopping her getting better!'

'I know. But you must admit that the teacher thing was another worry for her.'

I sighed. I was fed up with talking about Sophie, when no one let me see her and no one understood and everyone assumed that they knew all about it.

'It was just bad luck that she was my teacher,' I said. 'If she'd been someone I'd met, then you would all have had to deal with it. And you will, when I'm eighteen, because I am not giving up. I'll move out and make my own decisions and Dad can't tell me what to do any more.'

Alex was a nice guy, and, despite his puppyish bounce, he actually knew when to stop. So he said, 'Look, kiddo, have a shower, unpack your stuff, and come down for dinner in a bit, OK?'

'Yeah, right.'

'Whatever the reason, it is great to have you here. You know when you're a kid and you get a new toy and you can't wait to show it off? Well, that's how I feel about Amsterdam.'

I could see right away that one of the challenges of my new life was going to be escaping from my cousin's company. Not that I disliked Alex at all. It's just that we'd only really got Arsenal and family in common, and he was way too cheerful to be around when you felt miserable the whole time.

'Did you bring your laptop?' he asked. 'I can give you the Wi-Fi password.'

I tried not to show my surprise. Dad had acted like the Chinese government, censoring any forms of communication that might be used to contact Sophie. He cancelled my phone contract. He took away my computer. He got Simon, his enforcer, to oversee the deletion of my Facebook, Instagram,

Twitter and other social media accounts, so my social life spluttered to a halt.

Naturally I'd defied him by going to the local internet café and setting up a new email account, solely for the purpose of reconnecting with Sophie. But she didn't reply to my emails, and stupidly I hadn't written down her phone number anywhere. She wasn't at school – apparently she was signed off sick with stress – and I was meant to be on study leave. Every time I went in to sit an exam I hoped I'd see her, but she was never there.

I escaped house arrest one day and made my way to Greenwich to her flat, but there was no answer when I buzzed her door. I sat on her doorstep for three hours, but there was no sign of her. And she hadn't replied to any of my letters either.

I hated to think that she was scared to contact me. I was sure she'd find a way eventually. In the meantime, I'd sort of drifted away from my closest friends. Spending time with Sophie at weekends had meant I missed a lot of parties, turned down a lot of invitations, stopped playing Sunday league football. People my own age just seemed immature and shallow. On Results Day I went to school first thing, picked up my envelope, took it home to find out that I'd got the top grades I'd been predicted.

I knew that everyone was talking about me. I didn't want to answer their questions.

'I didn't bring a laptop,' I said, 'but I will definitely need one.'

'No problem.' Alex beamed. 'I've got a spare. It's old, but it's fine. And we must sort you out with a phone.'

Amsterdam, I realised, might not be so bad after all. If only Sophie would get in touch, it could be absolutely perfect.

Chapter 9

Kitty

Amsterdam

I had breakfast with Mum and Paul, listening to them discussing where we might live. Paul showed us where we were on the map, an area called the 'Pijp' which meant 'the pipe' – the word sounded pretty much the same in Dutch and English.

'It's called the pipe because the streets are long and thin,' Paul explained. He showed us the main tram lines, and the Albert Cuyp street market and marked his house with an x.

Then he slid the map over the table to me, along with a key to the house. 'Just in case you need it, although Ethan's promised to show you around today. I've written the address down for you.'

The map of Amsterdam was fascinating, just because there was so much blue on it. Canals everywhere, the sea, and a river running near to the street where Paul had marked an x. Forget getting a bike, maybe Ethan should be sorting me out a boat.

'What time will you be finished looking at flats?' I asked, and

Mum said, 'Shall we meet up back here at about three? Then we can go and get phones sorted out, Kitty, and maybe take a tram into the centre of town.'

'Cool,' I said. Only six hours. I could cope with that. Hopefully Ethan would have forgotten that he was meant to be showing me around, and I could go and explore the street market and beyond. It was daunting, the idea of wandering around a strange city on my own, but also exciting. If I took loads of pictures then my friends would be with me – sort of – via Instagram.

Paul looked at his watch. 'Better go, the estate agent is expecting us at nine-thirty – which, by the way, is called "half ten" in Dutch.'

'Half ten?'

'Yes – half an hour until ten o'clock. I used to turn up late for everything until Ethan explained it to me.'

'Oh, that's difficult,' said Mum. 'We'll have to remember that, Kitty.'

Once they'd gone I had a shower and got dressed – denim shorts and a white T-shirt, a scarlet bandana around my hair, white canvas lace-ups and hoop earrings. I applied my new make-up and took a selfie. I was pleased with the result. I thought I looked like a confident, sophisticated, international photo-journalist. I'd pretend that I'd just arrived in a new city and Ethan was my local guide and translator.

But first I had to negotiate the spiral staircase. It hadn't been a problem at breakfast time, but it was trickier with my bag in my hand. I dangled my legs, swung the bag, and found myself lurching dangerously sideways. I let out a very unsophisticated squeak.

Ethan was standing right underneath me, staring up at my bum. I immediately doubted the wisdom of wearing shorts. 'I'll catch you! Don't panic!' he said, most definitely taking the piss. I swung back to the central pole, found my footing and scrambled down, determined not to be embarrassed but knowing he was laughing at me.

'Just showing off my gymnastics skills,' I said.

Ethan's smile improved his face a lot. Not that there was a lot that needed improving, but he looked less sneery.

'Very impressive,' he said.

'I'll somersault down next time.'

'Go ahead and try now, if you want. I can video it for you to post on Facebook. Maybe it'll go viral.'

'Too much excitement,' I said, hastily. 'I mustn't spoil my Facebook friends. Can't entertain them all day long.'

'So, ready to come and buy a bike?' he asked.

All my newfound poise deserted me, as I contemplated actually cycling in a new city. 'Nah, it's OK, don't bother. I'll just go and do some sightseeing.'

'I told my friend we were coming. He's got a good bike for you.'

So of course I had to agree to it, although by the exasperated look on Ethan's face he was wishing he hadn't bothered.

'Are you OK to balance on the back of my bike?' he asked, gesturing at a battered piece of ironmongery chained to a bike stand outside.

'Um ... not sure ...' I felt sick at the thought of it. It would be so easy to fall off.

'No, you're a bit big, I suppose.'

I gaped at the insult. He didn't seem to notice.

'It's a long walk,' he said. 'I suppose we'd better get the tram. You got a card?'

Paul had presented us with Amsterdam travel cards when we arrived, so I nodded and we set off for the tram stop, just a few blocks away.

Once on the tram, Ethan pulled out his phone and started texting. He totally ignored me. I stared out of the window, but his rudeness was getting to me. It was all very well for him, but I was the newcomer, and he didn't have to rub it in that I had no friends here.

But still, I could look out of the window and enjoy Amsterdam. I admired the sparkling canals, the cookie-cutter gables, the houseboats and their potted gardens. It was all so pretty. If Amsterdam were a girl she'd be taking selfies all the time. And she'd never need to delete or edit any of them.

Ethan touched my hand. 'We get off here.'

I followed him across a cycle lane, three tram lanes and— 'Be careful!' he snapped, as a car whipped round a corner straight towards me. Only his outstretched arm stopped me from stepping right into its path.

'Sorry! It's difficult – wrong side of the road, and all these bikes and trams—'

We reached the safety of the pavement. 'You Brits,' he said. 'So contrary. Have to do everything your own way.'

'Oh, well, sorry. I thought you were British as well?'

'If you'd just change your roads to match the rest of the world, it would be a lot easier. I bet you'd be safer when you go on holiday. And I'm not British. I'm half American, half British, mostly Dutch.'

'Look, I think maybe it's a bit early to be looking at bikes. I need to get used to the traffic first. Why don't you call your friend and cancel?'

'Don't be chicken. It's easy. I learned real quick.'

'Yeah, but you were a kid.'

'Well, you're not so old.'

'Was it difficult, coming here when you were a kid?' I asked, hoping this could turn into a proper conversation.

'I didn't have any friends, and I couldn't speak the language. And I missed Paul a bit, although now I wish he'd just disappear.'

I didn't know what to say. 'But he's here now because of you, isn't he? Because your mum had to go away?'

'I would've been fine on my own. They both knew that. I don't know why he thought he had to come. Mieke would have kept an eye on me.'

'OK,' I said. Clearly a family disagreement, and it's generally better to stay out of those. I once upset Riley by agreeing with his mum that profiteroles weren't a nutritious breakfast. Time to change the subject.

'Do you need to speak Dutch to live here?'

'You do if you're a kid and you're the only English speaker at your school, like I was.'

'OK, but do *I* need to speak Dutch?'

'Probably not. You're going to be in a nice English-speaking bubble, with nice international expat friends, and after a year or so you'll piss off back to England.'

I stopped in the middle of the pavement. 'Look, forget the bike. This is my first day in a new city and your negativity is crushing my excitement. I'm sorry to let your friend down, but I think I'd better just get on and explore Amsterdam by myself.'

Ethan looked stunned, as though no one had ever challenged him on his behaviour before, which was perfectly possible, thinking about Paul's yoga-calm exterior and the absent mother who was apparently fine with abandoning him. Not that I could particularly blame her.

'I'm not being negative! I'm just saying what I think. Actually, I'm very nice to give up my time to get you a bike.'

'You should think about the effect you have on other people.'

'You should take responsibility for your own reactions.'

Huh. We stood there, glaring at each other, and he obviously wasn't going to apologise, so I said, 'Bye, then, see you later,' turned round and started walking up the road, hoping desperately that I'd see a street sign and be able to find it on the map, and work out where I was. In fact, where was the map? I turned a corner, so Ethan couldn't see me, and started searching my bag.

Damn. I must have left it on the kitchen table.

I wasn't going back to find Ethan, and he'd probably

disappeared anyway by now. I'd have to use the GPS on my phone ... but my phone stubbornly refused to show a Dutch map. OK. I'd have to find my way back to the tram stop ... if I could remember where it was ...

'Is this what you're looking for?'

Grrr. Ethan had followed me. And he had my map in his hand.

'Thank you,' I said, with immense dignity, to show him some British manners.

'That's OK,' he replied. No apology for earlier, I noticed, but at least he smiled at me. Despite myself, I smiled back. He was nice-looking after all, although I didn't like his scruffy clothes.

'Look, fighting is boring,' he said. 'Let's get a coffee. You like taking photos, don't you? I know a good place, right here.'

He led me through a passageway, walking too fast for me to register anything except the name *Manege* above the arched entry. He pushed open a door, nodded to a girl behind a desk and said something in Dutch. 'Go ahead Ethan,' she said, and he led me though another door.

'What is this place?' I asked. The surroundings were grand – brass chandeliers and ornate plasterwork – but there was something strange about the smell, which was distinctly farmhouse. Also I could hear muffled shouts, and weird thudding noises.

'Here – look,' said Ethan.

We were at the end of a huge room, with a vaulted ceiling, tiled in white with arched windows surrounding a huge arena. And in the arena—

'Oh! Wow! Ethan!'

The most beautiful, graceful horses I had ever seen, cantering in a ring.

'You got lucky,' he said. 'I thought we'd have to go and see them in their stables. Look.' He pointed out a grey. 'That's Mistral. I think maybe my favourite.'

'Can I take pictures?'

'Sure, but let's go up to the café. You can take them from there.'

We went up some stairs and found ourselves in the nineteenth century. A room full of little white chairs and tables, a grand chandelier and a mirrored bar.

'Wow, pretty,' I said. I liked that the paint was peeling and the edges of the plasterwork looked grubby. It added to the atmosphere, of a place caught in time.

Ethan eyed me. 'Surprise, hey?'

'It's gorgeous. I'd never have guessed from the outside.'

'Welcome to Amsterdam. Quite a lot of surprises hidden behind closed doors. You just have to be brave and take a look. Coffee?'

'Orange juice, please.'

He chatted with the girl behind the bar for a bit, and she gave us our drinks for free. I got the impression that Ethan came here a lot. Meanwhile I was busy taking pictures – not just of the horses, but of the gilt-framed mirrors, the fancy clock in the shape of a prancing stallion, the bottles lined up behind the bar.

Ethan brought our drinks over. 'I work here sometimes.

Mostly what she does, behind the bar, but sometimes they let me help out in the stables.'

'That's brilliant,' I said. 'I love it here.'

'Knew you would.' He looked smug.

'How?'

'Checked your Instagram. It's your sort of place.'

'Oh,' I said. If he were anyone else I'd have accused him of being a stalker, but no one else would have admitted something like that so openly. Particularly when they weren't even on Instagram. Yes, I'd checked.

'I thought you despised social media.'

'I do. But you don't have to stop using it just because I don't like it. I downloaded the app, just to see your pictures.'

'Well, that's incredibly kind of you.' I said, 'kind' meaning 'borderline creepy'. For some reason I was desperate for his verdict on my photography. 'Did you like what you saw?'

'Your eye isn't bad, but you've got a lot to learn,' he said. 'Too much pretty. Not enough real.'

'What do you know about photography?' I said, needled. 'I thought you were into making films that you don't show any-one.'

'It's just my opinion. Ignore me, I don't care.'

So I ignored him and set about cropping and filtering and loading stuff on to my account.

'You ready to go?' said Ethan, checking the time on his phone.

I couldn't put off the bike shop any longer. 'OK. Let's go.'

His friend was a guy called Freek. Yes, Freek, pronounced 'Frayk'. I made him spell it for me. Freek was tall, blond and impossibly gorgeous; he met Ethan with a hug and shook my hand and welcomed me to Amsterdam. 'Here it is,' he said, wheeling out a monster of a bike. It was big and heavy, with old-fashioned handlebars and a wicker basket on the front. I liked the basket a lot. I hated everything else about it.

'It's so heavy,' I complained. 'How am I going to get it up hills?'

'We don't have hills.'

'And I know it's cheap, but it looks really battered.' My eyes went to the shiny new bicycles at the other end of the shop.

'Better that way. It's only the paintwork; the rest of it is sound. If it looks old, it's less likely to get stolen.'

Ethan picked out a huge chain lock, which would add about a stone to the weight of the bike, as far as I could see. 'You'll need this,' he said. 'Lots of bike thieves around.'

'How about a helmet?' I asked.

They laughed.

'You can have one if you want, but no one wears them in Amsterdam,' said Freek. 'People will stare.'

'I'm not getting on a bike without a helmet,' I said firmly.

'OK, have it your own way.' Freek's shop did stock them, so it was obvious that they were just exaggerating. I picked out a bright-blue shiny one, jammed it on my head, did up the strap and immediately felt five times warmer.

They made some adjustments to the saddle height, showed me how to wind the lock around the frame, and I handed over eighty euros from the money Mum had left me with that morning. Then we pushed it out on to the pavement.

'Give it a try!' said Freek.

'I'm not sure … maybe later …' I said. The bike was enormous. I was convinced that I'd fall off the minute I took my feet off the floor.

'Give me your phone,' said Ethan. 'I'll capture the moment for you. Reportage.'

'No,' I said, but he grinned and said, 'Scared?' so I handed it over. My heart was pounding like crazy.

I swung one leg over the bike, perched on the saddle. I was standing on tiptoe. All I had to do was push off … put my feet on the pedals …

Freek and Ethan were laughing as I cycled one shaky revolution of the wheels and came to a halt.

'You'll learn,' said Freek. 'It's just right for you. Take her to the park, Ethan.'

Ethan handed me my phone, and checked his own. 'I've got to go. You going to be OK with this?'

'What do you mean?' My voice turned into an anxious squeak.

'Well, I'll show you where the park is, you can practise there and then cycle back to the flat.'

I was stunned. Wasn't he meant to be showing me Amsterdam? Not abandoning me with a vehicle that I couldn't ride.

'Oh! I, well, yes, I suppose so.' What if I fell off … had to go to hospital … got hopelessly lost … crashed into a tram … got a flat tyre?

Ethan looked at me. 'Where's your map?'

'It's here.' I pulled it out. If he showed me the way home, I could push the bike all the way. It'd probably take me two days, but it'd be safer than actually riding it.

'Look, down that way takes you to the park.' A long green finger on the map: the Vondelpark. At least that's what I called it; Ethan and Freek pronounced it *'Fondle-park'*, which sounded like a wind-up.

'Practise biking there. There are good cafés, too; you can have some lunch. Then come out here, cross the road, through here, around the Ceintuurbaan ... It's really easy.'

He stopped. Looked at my face.

'OK, forget that. Hop on the back. I'll take you home.'

Chapter 10

Kitty

Amsterdam

Mum and I went to look at the most likely flat the next day. She insisted that we cycled, so I fastened my helmet and wobbled after her. The side streets were quiet and fine, but then we had to cross a main road. I was convinced a tram was going to squash me flat. People's heads turned to look at our helmets, just as Freek had said. I was sure they were laughing at us. No one else was wearing one, not even the toddler in a child's seat behind his dad, or the old lady with two shopping bags hanging from her handlebars.

The flat was set back from the main road, a huge modern block in a crescent shape, with shops and cafés on the ground floor. We were seven floors up; luckily there was a lift, and I cheered up right away when Mum opened the door and I stepped into the space.

It couldn't have been more different from the Ruin. No patterns, no colour, no clutter, no smell of damp and blistering paint. Just bright white walls, a wooden floor, two leather sofas, a bookcase and a red shiny sideboard. At one end of the room there was a small kitchen, with a dining table. At the other, doors out to a balcony.

'Wow!' I said.

'Do you like it? Oh, Kitty, your face! I can see you do. Hurray! Come and see your room.'

Two biggish bedrooms, one either side of a sliver of a bathroom. The same white walls, a parquet wooden floor. It was a blank canvas, a clean slate, a bubble of light and space to make my own. Mum warned against putting nails in the walls, but when I protested she said, 'Oh, well, I suppose we can fill up the holes and paint over them when we leave. I suppose our tenants are doing the same right now. Here's the room for Rachel when she comes to stay. It's small, but she won't mind.'

In this clean, bright space, it was as though our past had been wiped away: all the layers of clutter and memories, dusty tattered old art works from primary school, shoes that no one wore, cupboards full of old lunch boxes. It wasn't that we wanted to let go of the past totally; it was more about balancing it out with the present and future.

We went out onto the balcony. You could see for miles over Amsterdam, canals and houses and tiny little cyclists. 'Wow!' I said. 'Just wow!'

'Oh, Kits, I'm so pleased.'

'I love it!'

'So do I!' She hugged me. 'I'm so glad we did this. I feel like a new person.'

'It's been more than ten years since Dad died,' I said, gently, cautiously. Mum talked about Dad a lot, but she never discussed how she felt about losing him. She kept those secrets for Valerie, the bereavement counsellor.

'Ten years goes so quickly, when you're keeping busy and bringing up children by yourself, and thinking about all the practicalities – paying the bills and taking you for check ups and, you know, making decisions and being supportive to you girls.'

'You've done brilliantly,' I told her.

'Thank you, sweetie, but, I don't know, I've just felt I was moving on, but still stuck. I couldn't really leave him behind. Not fully.'

'But now ... you want to leave him behind?'

'Not forget him, obviously, Kitty, but I think I'm ready for a new phase. You're nearly an adult. I'll be on my own soon.'

'And you like Paul?' I dared to ask, and she sighed and said, 'He's lovely, isn't he? And so patient with Ethan, who isn't the easiest kid in the world. But, you know, sometimes it's better to have someone as a friend, not a romance. It's more durable.'

'Yeah, right,' I said, thinking, despite myself, of Ethan. I didn't even like him much, but I'd read enough books to know that sometimes the most obnoxious people were the ones you ended up madly in love with, and compared with some of the bad boys I'd read about, Ethan was positively saintly.

Plus, I was intrigued by him. He'd taken me home the day before, but just delivered me to the front door. Left all alone I'd had a little prowl around, including his attic. After all, hadn't he told me to open closed doors? Didn't he say that he'd be responsible for his own reaction? Not that I expected him to find out that I'd been snooping.

The attic was amazing. Definitely the best room in the house. Ethan had a sleeping area that was clean and tidy – the bed made with fresh, white sheets, his clothes neatly folded and stacked on shelves. The rest of the room was given over to art supplies, equally tidily stacked and sorted. Paints, stacks of old *National Geographics*, glue, scissors. There were boxes and baskets full of stuff – old dolls and toys, chipped china, nuts and screws. There was a sink, a mini-fridge, a kettle and some mugs, all sparkling clean. The room smelled of paint, turps and disinfectant.

He'd tacked up pictures around the room – collages and sketches, mostly, with some over-painted photographs. Ethan's style was surreal and colourful; most of the pictures made me laugh in some way. A portrait of Mieke made her look like an angry parrot, her nose beak-like, her hair a colourful crest. There was a sketch of a girl, a nude girl, better than anything I'd ever produced in GCSE Art. I wondered who the girl was.

If Ethan's room reflected his personality then he was colour-ful – one wall a sharp lime green, another cornflower blue – and creative. I was really quite interested. He just needed a bit of house-training, that was all. I'd read plenty of books in which love had reformed much worse behaviour.

'I think we've done the right thing, coming here,' said Mum. 'I think it's going to change both of us for the better.'

I wondered what she wanted to change about me. I hoped she was right.

Chapter 11

Theo

Amsterdam

The Amsterdam British Tutorial College was in a canal house on the Singel, right up near Centraal Station, very grand on the outside, but inside the rooms had been gutted and fitted with strip lighting and grey carpets. There was a café on one side and a coffee shop on the other. Of course I knew that one was for buying coffee and the other wasn't, but I hadn't realised that it would mean a faint smell of weed wafting up to the classrooms. It was kind of distracting. The only thing you could smell at my old school was bleach, school dinners and teenage boys.

The road behind the canal was a mini red light district. Even in broad daylight there were women sitting in the windows, advertising themselves. They all seemed to be older women, and I wondered if this was a kind of semi-retirement village for prostitutes. I'd had a look at the official red light district and it was very crowded and noisy, nothing like this quiet street, with its flower-filled hanging baskets and lanterns. It gave me the creeps, anyway, just as the real red light district had. I couldn't imagine wanting to buy sex from women sitting in windows. Did that make me abnormal? I just didn't do the whole lad thing.

I'd registered the day before and received a timetable for my four A-levels. This was my first actual lesson, with a teacher who looked like he was only a few years older than us, and who was droning his way through the syllabus, explaining that we'd be reading *Wuthering Heights* and some poetry, some Shakespeare and some modern stuff. He made it all sound completely boring.

Instead of listening, I thought about Sophie. Sophie who was also just twenty-two, completely new to teaching, not really trained but it didn't matter at all because she was just brilliant, a complete natural. She made everything so interesting because of the mad, sideways way she'd look at things. I'd thought of her as a naturally happy, upbeat sort of person, until the day I found her crying in a classroom.

I'd hovered, uncertainly, at the door.

'Miss?'

She'd turned, and I knew I'd made a mistake. I tried to ignore the red nose, the swollen eyes.

'Um, sorry, miss, I've got that homework for you.'

Pathetically, I'd pretended earlier that I'd lost my homework, begged her for more time. It had all been so I could seek her out after school and tell her I'd found it, in the hope that we might have a conversation.

I'd fancied her from the minute she walked into our class-room and explained that, as Mr Morley was going to take the year off to recover from his stroke, she was in charge of our GCSE class. They'd given her the top set, I reckoned, because we were all pretty much at A* standard no matter who taught us. As it turned out, she was about five million times better than Mr Morley, and English lessons turned into jewels in the mud that is a Year 11 timetable. We had a collective crush on her. It was as compulsory as Maths.

'Perhaps you'd like to start.' The teacher's voice broke into my thoughts.

Everyone was looking at me, which is what happens when you start remembering your lost love instead of concentrating on the classroom you're in. I stared at the teacher, and the girl next to me said, 'Don't worry, I'll go first.' Phew.

'I'm Kitty Levy,' she said. 'I'm from Palmers Green, north London. I'm here with my mum; she got promoted at work and sent to Amsterdam. I'm doing English and Geography and Art.'

Kitty Levy? That was a Jewish name and she was from north London and in my English class? I mean, what are the odds? For a paranoid moment I wondered if my parents had planted her there, as a Sophie distraction. But even they couldn't organise something like that.

I glanced at Kitty Levy out of the corner of my eye. She was tall – possibly slightly taller than me – with broad shoulders and long legs. I liked her bouncy hair, her emphatic eyebrows, her wide mouth. She seemed really confident. In a pre-Sophie world I might even have fancied her. Also, she seemed a bit familiar. Maybe we'd already met, at camp or a party.

Kitty's clothes were cool – a baggy green linen dress, a black cardigan, faux-Converses, red lipstick and a *Dennis the Menace* badge. Nothing like Sophie's style, which was simple and unfussy, even out of the classroom. Sophie was short and had tidy, blonde hair. This Kitty girl was her opposite in every way.

The other students were introducing themselves. Damon and Max had been expelled from one of the English-speaking schools in Amsterdam. They thought it was a bit of a laugh; they'd been done for supplying weed to a visiting hockey team from a school in Spain. 'We were just being hospitable,' said Damon, 'we didn't even charge them.'

Finn was Canadian, but he had grown up in Singapore and always attended British schools before moving to the Netherlands five years ago. Lucy was retaking the year after screwing up at her school in Bath. She was scarecrow-thin, with eyes outlined in what looked like black ink. She wore dark clothes, which carried a lingering smell of tobacco smoke. 'My father lives here, so I'm staying with him,' she told us. 'Mum says he can take the blame this time.'

The last girl was called Alice Wightman. She had arty parents who travelled around a lot. 'I thought I'd get some qualifications. You never know when they might come in useful.' She was half Spanish, half African-American; she'd lived in London, Sydney, San Francisco and Edinburgh; she wore baggy shorts and a vest top with the slogan 'Destroy the patriarchy' emblazoned across it; she was one of those girls who doesn't wear a scrap of make-up because she thinks it's politically unsound, but also, in her case, because she didn't need it.

My turn. 'I'm Theo Collins,' I said, 'from Finchley, north London. I'm in Amsterdam because … well … because I'm staying with my cousin for a year or so. I'm studying English, History, Maths and French, with a view to taking English at university.' Oxbridge, I'd thought, but I wasn't sure any more. Nothing seemed very certain in my life.

'Excellent,' said our teacher. 'Glad to meet you all. Now, let me explain how the course will work.' And he droned on and on, and I went back to remembering that first time I talked to Sophie properly, not just as a pupil in a classroom.

'Miss,' I'd said, 'are you all right?' I'd had a cold the week before and my mum had been putting clean handkerchiefs in my pockets, so I was able to pull one out and offer it to her, assuring her, 'It's totally unused.'

'Oh, Theo, thank you,' she'd said, taking it from me, scrubbing at her eyes and blowing her nose. 'I'll give it back to you when it's washed.'

'That's OK, miss.'

'I get terrible hayfever. It makes me look just like I've been crying.'

'My dad had these injections for his allergies. You could try that.' I hadn't believed her, of course: who gets hayfever in November? But I'd liked her for trying to come up with a plausible cover story.

'Maybe I will. So, where is it then?'

'Where's what?'

'Your homework?'

'Oh,' I'd said. 'Here it is.' I'd written an essay on Macbeth, about the relationship between him and his wife, how she totally wore the trousers. Scary stuff.

'Thank you.'

'It's not all that exciting,' I'd told her. 'I wish we could write our own stuff. I'm working on a novel; I'd much rather spend time on that than Macbeth.'

'You're writing a novel?' Her whole face changed. In a sentence I'd gone from blundering schoolboy who'd walked in when she was having an Emotional Moment, to potential child genius.

'Yes ... It's sort of dystopian, mostly, with a touch of sci-fi and a thriller-ish plot. There's a love story, too. But mostly it's, you know, a chance to express myself.'

'That is a lot of genres! How long have you been writing it?'

'Oh, ages. I got about halfway, but then the beginning was quite immature, so I'm reworking it.'

I hadn't talked to anyone about the novel before. I had this crazy vision that one week over Friday night dinner I'd say, 'Oh, by the way, I have some news,' and I'd hand them all a copy of the published book and they'd be excited and happy and proud. And the reviews would be great ('Almost impossible to believe that this nuanced and sensitive work was written by a teenage boy,' *Guardian*) and I'd probably win some prizes, and I'd get interviewed on television. Other boys dreamed of winning the Champions League, and I wouldn't have minded that (assuming I was playing for Arsenal and they didn't stick me in defence), but novel writing seemed a more achievable dream. After all, you just had to get lost in your imagination and write it all down.

The thing that made my book really different – I hoped – was that I'd imagined a class-free, religion- and nationality-free society, where everyone was brought up gender-free. No one was bound by stereotypes or expectations, and people just related to each other as people, not as men and women or gays and straights, or blacks and white, Jews and Christians, or Brits and Americans. I loved the world I'd created. It made me feel a little drunk every time I stepped into it, and imagined all that freedom.

'Maybe you could read some of it?' I'd found myself asking, and she'd nodded and smiled and said, 'I'd like that.' Then she'd tucked my handkerchief inside her sleeve and said, 'Oh, well, back to the real world,' and stood up, and I'd backed out of the classroom, saying, 'Yes, miss' and, 'Thank you, miss,' with a weird churning sensation in my stomach that was mostly happiness and a little bit nervous.

Back to reality, Amsterdam, the smell of weed, the knowledge that Sophie hadn't been in touch with me for six weeks and three days. 'So, if you work hard, attend all the sessions here and do your homework, I anticipate good results,' said the teacher. 'Let's take a short break now and reconvene at eleven-thirty.'

Most people went off to have a smoke or get a snack, but Kitty and I stayed in the classroom. She stood at the window, looking out at the sparkling canal, the dancing, shiny leaves on the trees, the row of houses on the other side, each one so similar, yet utterly different.

I hesitated for a minute or two, then went and joined her. I needed some friends in Amsterdam and I thought she'd be easier to talk to than the others. We had something in common. Time for a bit of Jewish Geography, that unofficial social game where you find out how many people you know in common, without ever actually saying the J word.

'Hey,' I said. 'It's kind of different from London, isn't it?'

'They get this,' she said, gesturing at the view, 'and we get the North Circular. It's a difficult choice—'

'But I'd come down in favour of the North Circular,' I said. 'The spectacular architecture. The landscaping and wildlife.'

'The excitement of watching boy racers late at night.'

'The World of Leather.'

She cracked up at this reference to a particularly unlovely shop on the particularly unlovely road that binds Jewish London together, from Ilford in the east to the notorious Hanger Lane gyratory, where, my dad swears, he has spent a full week of his life stuck in traffic. I made her laugh first. Score one to me.

'There's a pest controller on the North Circular in Bounds Green who has a sign up,"Pest of the Week",' she informed me. 'This week – look.'

She showed me her phone. Someone had sent her a picture of the sign. 'Pest of the Week: Norwegian Rat,' I read.

'Isn't it cool? I like to imagine all the pests, waiting to see who's chosen that week.'

'The disappointment in the cockroach camp when a rat gets the nod. The potential for corruption ...'

'The bitter rivalry between proper British pests and foreign immigrants.'

'It's odd being foreign, isn't it?' I said. 'Here, I mean.'

She nodded. 'I never realised how British I was until I came here.'

I moved on to the really important bit of the conversation. 'So, you're from Palmers Green? I know some people from there. A guy called David Abrahams, goes to my school ...'

She shook her head. 'Never heard of him.' She wasn't playing the game properly. She should have asked which school I went to.

'Then there's Ella Applebaum and Katie Taylor?' I knew them from the youth movement that I belonged to; we saw each other at summer camp every year. I wouldn't, of course, mention the actual name of the group. Too unsubtle.

She shook her head, no; she didn't know Ella or Katie.

'Hmm ... where did you go to school?' I may not have been to the big Jewish schools myself, but I knew loads of people who did.

She named a school I'd never heard of, and said, 'It's the local comprehensive. No one Jewish there, if that's what you're asking me.'

I was a little bit shocked that she had no idea of the conventions around this sort of conversation. But then she continued.

'I don't do the whole north-west London social thing. But my sister's called Rachel Robinson – you might have come across her, she knows everyone.' Rachel had transferred to the biggest Jewish comprehensive for sixth form, she added, and I quickly worked out that she'd have been there at the same time as my brother Simon.

'Robinson? Not Levy?'

'She's got a different dad.'

There was definitely a girl called Rachel Robinson in Simon's Politics class in the sixth-form. I remembered, because Simon really fancied her, but could never do anything about it because he was going out with her friend, Amber.

Simon was the only one of us who'd gone to a Jewish school, because he couldn't pass the entrance exams to our private school, but he'd been richly rewarded for failure, with a social life well stocked with stunning girls. Meanwhile Jonny and I went to the all-boy virtual-monastery.

'Yes! She's friends with my brother!' I exaggerated, delighted to score a near-bullseye at Jewish Geography so far from home. Kitty seemed less impressed.

'Rachel's got loads of friends,' she said. 'She's all about quantity, not quality.'

'So, you're all about quality, are you?' I asked.

'I like to think so.'

'It's an odd coincidence, both of us being new to Amsterdam at the same time,' I said.

'Why, because your brother possibly knows my sister? Yeah, on a scale of oddness that's about three out of ten.'

I really liked her London-flavoured sarcasm. After two weeks of bouncy enthusiasm from Alex and Chani – I'd privately renamed them Chalex – she was a gust of fresh air. And – I had to face it – it was beginning to look as though Sophie was blanking me. I was sure she thought she was doing the right thing, even though she wasn't. Maybe I should be getting to know other girls. Just to test my feelings.

Our classmates were drifting back to their seats, the teacher was shuffling his papers and I decided to go for it. After all, I needed a friend. Just a friend. This was not going to turn into a romance.

'Fancy exploring Amsterdam a bit after this?' I asked. 'We could go and get a coffee.'

She quirked a smile in my direction, but didn't reply before the teacher started talking. I took it as a yes.

Chapter 12

Kitty

Amsterdam

Talk about ironic. The first guy to show an interest in me since I arrived in this brand new world turned out to be a nice Jewish boy from Finchley. And just the sort of guy I'd avoided back in north London, the sort who knew everyone and showed off about it.

On the other hand, his eyelashes were luscious and his cheekbones were chiselled and he had very cute dimples, worthy of a boy band. He'd look good in photos. In fact, if I could casually take a few photos of him, then I could load them on to my Instagram account, which wouldn't look bad at all. Of course Ethan would probably say that Theo was just too conventionally good-looking, but then he'd only be happy if I took pictures of old tramps propped up against rubbish bins.

What's more, Theo was about my height, eye to eye, although I'd tower over him in heels, and actually I was quite enjoying his company as we wandered along the Singel, going down little streets that took our fancy.

'Look at that, oh my God!' I pointed up to a model of a head stuck on to the wall. A black man with popping eyes and a turban. His mouth was wide open and his tongue lolled out, and on his tongue was a pill.

'An ancient anti-drugs campaign?' guessed Theo. 'Or maybe one *for* drugs – a chemist's shop sign, perhaps?'

'It's really offensive,' I said. 'I mean, stunningly so. You'd never see anything like that in Britain.'

'That's weird, because Amsterdam is so, you know, liberal. Welcoming.'

'Is it? I mean, I know about the coffee shops and the prostitutes. That's liberal, I suppose. I didn't know it had a reputation as welcoming.'

'When the Jews were expelled from Spain and Portugal in the fifteenth century, they came here. The Dutch have been taking in refugees ever since,' said Theo. 'My cousins haven't stopped with the history lessons.'

'What are they like, your cousins?'

'Oh, they're nice. Too nice, you know what I mean? Really good people with no irony or sarcasm, they're enthusiastic about everything and they got married two minutes ago so they're incredibly happy all the time.'

'Oh yeah, and you are an embittered old cynic?'

'That's about right.'

'So why are you staying with them?' I asked. 'You didn't really explain in class.'

'I just fancied a change of scene,' he said. 'I got fed up with the same old, you know?'

I don't believe a word of it. Boys like him didn't get bored with north London. They have a thousand friends, all called Jacob. They have a thousand girlfriends, too; they can take their pick from every Ariella and Talia in town. They have an amazing social life, with parties every weekend. Theo was just the sort to be the king of Finchley, the sort that never had any time for me. I'd come across boys like him at family bar mitzvahs and on the rare occasions that I let Rachel drag me to her Jewish youth group. Theo might seem friendly, but that was only because he didn't know anyone else in Amsterdam.

Or maybe my new image was working?

'Yeah, of course you did,' I said. 'I can just imagine how dull you find life in north London, all those parties and going on Tour, and holidays and shopping at Westfield for designer clothes.'

'Do you think I'm a beck?' he said, faux-indignant.

'Not really a total beck.' A total beck would have more designer clothes than him, and be wearing expensive shades instead of screwing his eyes against the sun. 'Just a trainee one.'

'Ouch! I could totally be a beck if I wanted to. I just don't want to, OK? And I did go on Tour, but I didn't really want to.'

'They forced you?' Yeah, very likely, I thought. For people like him, a four-week organised trip to Israel after GCSEs was a rite of passage, just like a bar or bat mitzvah. I couldn't have gone, even if I'd wanted to, because who was going to accept responsibility for a girl with a dodgy heartbeat?

'My parents can be very persuasive.'

'I bet they can,' I said. 'And I'm sure it was hell, hanging out with all your lovely north-west London friends.'

'Look, you don't have to come over all Lizzy Bennet with me, just because you've got the idea that I'm some sort of snob.'

I was almost mortified, but I loved the fact that he'd just referenced Jane Austen. Most of the guys I knew inhabited a cultural world that went from *Top Gear* to *Game of Thrones*, via *Call of Duty* and *Minecraft*.

'OK, fair enough. I promise not to be prejudiced about the fact that you live in the epicentre of the Jewish community.'

'Used to live,' he said. 'Not any more. And there are negatives about that. I mean, everyone knows your business.'

'So why are you here in Amsterdam? How come you're not doing A-levels in London?' I wondered if he'd screwed up his GCSEs.

He didn't answer, which made me all the more suspicious, and instead pointed out a shop that seemed to sell only socks. Amsterdam was like a huge department store, with shops specialising in one thing only. Already, since I'd arrived, I'd seen places exclusively selling dressing gowns, candles and even printing cartridges. My favourite was probably a shop totally devoted to dental care, with a replica fairground wheel in its window, with toothbrushes riding in the cars. But this shop, with a rainbow of socks on display, came close.

'Why would you do that?' he said. 'Start a shop just selling socks? I mean, why socks? Who is that interested in socks?'

'It's no different from a shoe shop, really,' I pointed out, taking a picture of a rack of fluorescent pink-and-green chequered golfing socks. 'It's just one step beyond.'

'I might buy those for my dad's birthday,' he said, and then frowned. 'Or, maybe not. Why don't you buy them for your dad?'

'I don't have a dad,' I said. 'He died.'

Theo blushed, which made me like him a little bit more.

'I'm sorry,' he said. 'Was he ill for a long time?'

'Not really.' I was wary about giving too many details, in case we strayed into the territory of preventative heart checks at Great Ormond Street. 'It was quite unexpected. I was only five. I've totally OK with it.'

'I was ...' Theo pulled a face. 'My mum's ill. I'm a bit obsessed with parents dying at the moment. Not that it's all about me. And no one's saying that Mum's dying. It's just ... you know when you get a feeling, like no one's really telling you the whole truth? They say she's having tests and they just need to get a diagnosis, but I can't help wondering ... Your dad, I just thought ... was he ill? Did you know he was dying?'

'Not at all,' I said. 'It just happened.'

I couldn't help feeling sorry for Theo. He looked as though he'd like to tell someone all about his troubles, which seemed to me to be quite promising, romantically speaking. We reached the end of the street, and turned onto another canal.

'Look, there's a café,' I said. 'Shall we get a drink?'

'OK, yes, great,' he said. 'Look, there's one table free on the terrace.'

The canal was the Prinsengracht, which is where the Anne Frank House is located, probably the most famous place in Amsterdam. I hadn't visited yet because Paul said it was best to wait for a month without too many tourists – November, maybe. But I thought about Anne all the time since I'd arrived in her city. I imagined her, a teenager just like me, cooped up inside, hot and stuffy, talking to the same people day after day, desperate to get out. Never able to do this simple thing that Theo and I were doing, walking and talking and looking at things that we'd never seen before. Just one day like this, with a slight breeze rustling the trees along the canal, would have been an incredible gift for Anne. Thinking about her made me appreciate my life all the more.

Besides, she'd written her diary to me. Well, to 'Dear Kitty', her imaginary friend. It was my duty, I felt, to listen to what she had to say.

'Have you been to the Anne Frank House?' I asked Theo. 'It's somewhere along this canal.'

'Ages ago,' he said. 'My dad comes here a lot on buying trips, and he brought my brothers and me once and took us. It was crowded, I remember, and there were lots of stairs.'

I raised my eyebrows. 'Very profound.'

'It's difficult to get profound about the Shoah,' he said. 'It's too close on the one hand and too far away on the other. And the only way to deal with it is denial. You know, assuming that your family would have been OK, would have found a hiding place or whatever. I mean that's what I do. How about you?'

'I remember finding out about it. Saying to my mum, *there's someone who wants to kill us*. I didn't realise it was in the past; it was terrifying.'

'I always knew about it. I don't remember a time when I didn't know. When I was ten, my parents took us to Jerusalem, to Yad Vashem.'

I must have looked a bit blank, because he explained: 'The Holocaust Memorial Museum. Haven't you been to Israel?'

'Oh, no, Mum thinks it's too full of negative energy.'

He laughed out loud. 'You can't be Jewish and avoid negative energy! That's our legacy!'

'She's a Buddhist. Or a Buddhist-lite, anyway. A Jew-Bu.'

'Are you a Jew-Bu too?'

'Nah. Lighting Chanukah candles with my dad is one of my earliest memories. Not that I'm religious or anything.' I reached into my bag and pulled out my knitting. 'This is what I do when she meditates.'

'That's bright,' he said, blinking at my tangerine beret-in-waiting.

'Yeah, I generally go for zingy colours. They make me feel happy.'

'Are you happy in Amsterdam?'

'I'm actually incredibly happy. It's easier to live for the day here, like being on permanent holiday.'

'But is that a good thing? I don't know that I'd want to be on permanent holiday. I want my life to progress. In fact, there's stuff ... people ... I want to get back to.'

People? Or a person? I wondered if Theo was trying to tell me he had a girlfriend back in London. Funnily enough that made him seem even more attractive.

'In London I had this little group of friends,' I said, 'and everything was very safe and samey. Now, I have to cope on my own. Start again. I feel like anything could happen here.'

'I feel like nothing is going to happen here,' he said.

'Really? That's so sad!' Then I remembered about his mum. 'I'm sorry. You're probably worrying about your mum a lot.'

'Yeah. She's sort of why I'm here in Amsterdam. They said it was so that I can concentrate on my A-levels and not be distracted. It doesn't really work, of course.' He looked towards the canal as he said this, and I felt bad for him. How sad to be away from his family at a time when they should all be together.

'That's awful, I'm sorry.'

'I keep on expecting the next phase, you know? The bit when they tell us she's actually incredibly ill.'

I touched his hand. 'She might not be incredibly ill at all. It could be something very fixable.'

'Yeah, I suppose.'

I decided he needed a pep talk. I'd always prided myself on my ability to inspire others. Who was it who talked Martine into applying for stage school? Who encouraged Riley when he was debating whether to ask Esther out? Me, that's who.

'What I think is that going through tough things means you have to live life to the full,' I told him. 'Take chances and have adventures.' I said this confidently, although up until now the main adventure I'd had was going to Thorpe Park – and even then I wasn't allowed to go on the rollercoasters, just in case it made my heart stop.

'Reach for the stars?'

I slid my sunglasses down to the bridge of my nose. He was smiling at me, and I didn't think he was being sardonic.

'Yes, exactly. Don't settle for second best.'

'Nice thought.'

'Look at Anne Frank. She could have just given up, but she didn't, she wrote her diary, she created something amazing.'

'I bet she'd have preferred just being normal, growing up to be an old lady.'

'Well, sure, obviously, but we don't all get that choice. My dad didn't.'

'How do you deal with that?'

I reached for the ball of wool. 'He left us a house. And loads of books and music, which I read and listen to, and try and work out why he liked them and what he got from them. And he had friends, who are kind and interested in me. He left a lot behind. I just wish I remembered him better.'

'That's sad,' he said.

It was definitely time for a change of subject. I was not sure that tragic semi-orphan was a good image.

'What did you think of the college?'

He wrinkled his nose. 'Not great. The teacher looked younger than us.'

We chatted a bit about school and friends and north London. He was your classic private-school boy, convinced that my school would be full of gang members and knife arches. I quite enjoyed pretending that I was really tough and streetwise, and that Palmers Green was a walk on the wild side. As if.

I finished my lemonade and looked at my phone. There was a text from Mum, reminding me that we were going round to Paul's that evening.

'I hope I've bust some of your prejudices about bog standard comprehensives,' I told him.

'I hope I've bust some of yours about becks from Finchley.'

'Oh, I didn't really think you were a beck. Your clothes don't cut it.'

'You just haven't looked closely enough at the labels,' he said.

'I shouldn't need to,' I said, smiling. I was finding Theo's company surprisingly enjoyable. We had more in common than the North Circular Road. He watched period dramas on television and his favourite authors included John Green and Zadie Smith. I'd hoped for Nicholas Sparks as well, but he said he'd never heard of him. I had to admit that once he'd stopped quizzing me about people I didn't know, he seemed perfectly friendly as well.

'I'd better go,' I said wondering if he liked me as much as I liked him. 'I'm not sure where we are, though; I need to look at my map.' He asked me where I lived, and said he thought I was lucky. 'My cousins aren't even in Amsterdam. It's OK where they live, but a bit, you know, suburban.'

'My bike's back at college,' he said. 'Is yours?'

'No, I got the tram. But I need to go back that way anyway.'

I smiled to myself as we walked back to college. Here we were, look at us, walking side by side through this beautiful city.

Amsterdam was shaping up very well indeed.

Chapter 13

Kitty

Amsterdam

Paul hired a van and took us to IKEA that weekend to buy a load of stuff for the flat. It was almost like being back in London – that is, until we were eating lunch in the café, and a mouse ran across the floor.

Obviously this could have happened in London, but there would be screaming and jumping on tables, someone would call Health and Safety and the whole store would be fumigated. Here, no one seemed that bothered.

'Did you see that?' hissed Mum, over her meatballs. 'Do you think we should tell someone?'

'It's not worth bothering,' said Paul. 'There are mice everywhere in Amsterdam. It's because of all the water. You're lucky you're high up in the flat, it might save you.'

'Do you have mice?' asked Mum, nervously.

'Sadly, yes. Ethan co-exists quite happily with them. I'm doing my best with humane traps, but they come straight back again.'

Mum was appalled, but also laughing. 'You mean that old song about a mouse living in a windmill in Old Amsterdam – it's actually a documentary?'

'Every word is true.'

'You should get a cat!'

'Maybe, one day. Actually, that's a good idea. But it's a lot of commitment, isn't it, owning an animal? You can't just take off for a weekend whenever you feel like it.'

From the way he was looking at Mum, I got the impression that Paul would have quite liked the two of them to take off on a spontaneous weekend there and then. I felt like a big, fat, hairy gooseberry. But Mum just took a sip of water and said, 'Cats are nice. Let's get on. We've got a lot of stuff to get.'

After we'd bought half of IKEA and Paul had loaded it into the van and helped us carry it up to the flat, and he'd screwed together two bookshelves and a dining table, she invited him, Mieke and Ethan to supper the next day.

She did the shopping and cooking, while my job was to clean and lay the table. I felt like a magazine stylist as I set the table with our new cutlery and placemats. I made a little vlog about it, putting gladioli in a vase, transforming the room with candles and cushions. I took pictures and posted them on Instagram. As the comments flooded in – it really helped my follower numbers that Martine's guy was on TV – I felt more popular than I'd ever been in London. I got changed into a cherry-red sundress to match my lipstick and a snowy white cardigan that I'd knitted myself. I took a few selfies and posted the best one on Facebook and Instagram. Like, like, like. My confidence grew with each click.

Our guests arrived promptly at eight. Mieke exclaimed enthusiastically about the flat and she and Mum and Paul took their drinks out on to the balcony. Ethan and I stayed inside. He'd actually put on jeans with no holes in them, and a clean white T-shirt. He smelled nice too, lemony and fresh.

'It's got potential,' he said. 'Pity you haven't done much with it, but it's OK.'

'It's not ours, we can't start painting the walls or changing too much,' I pointed out. 'It's rented.'

'You could paint the walls. You'd just have to paint them back when you move out.'

'I like it like this. It's light and bright.'

'OK, *klopt*.' He shrugged. 'Where's your bedroom?'

I wasn't sure I wanted to show Ethan my bedroom, but I didn't know how to say so. Luckily it was pretty tidy.

'This one.'

His critical eye swept over my knitted patchwork bedcover – the first thing I ever made – my bookcase of romances and my pinboard of pictures of family and friends, of our house in London and the village in Cornwall where we usually go on holiday. I was holding my breath, waiting for his verdict.

'Awesome,' he said.

'Oh, you're so sarcastic. I know the patchwork's a bit rubbish, but I made it myself when I was only eleven.'

'I love it,' he said. 'I'm telling the truth. *Heel gezellig*. Why are you so defensive?'

Huh. I led the way back to the dining table.

'How's it going?' he asked.

'Yeah, OK,' I told him. 'The people at college are nice. Very friendly. You should meet them.'

'Yeah, right, I'd have a lot in common with a load of expats.'

'Nothing wrong with expats. You're not exactly a hundred per cent Dutch yourself.'

'Expats are a pain. All they care about is getting stoned and going to sex shows in the Wallen.'

'What's that?'

'The red light district. Do you know what that is?'

'Of course I do.'

'Going to take some pictures there for your followers?'

'I went there, but it felt too much like, you know, taking pictures of animals in the zoo.'

The girls in the windows horrified me, to be honest. I couldn't imagine how they felt, parading in front of crowds of people in their underwear, then having to sleep with strangers for money. Treating sex as though it was nothing, just something mechanical, seemed so sad. Plus I'd been reading up about how many girls were trafficked into prostitution, and I was all fired up on their behalf.

'They get a better deal in the Netherlands than in most places,' said Ethan.

'But they're selling themselves like it means nothing.'

'Maybe they're not as romantic as you are. Maybe they don't think sex is all about love and flowers and relationships.'

'What do you know about me and relationships?'

'I saw your bookshelf,' he said. 'I know you like to cry over a love story. I bet you even love that film about a prostitute … you know …'

'I don't think I'd like a film about that.' I knew as I said it that I sounded ridiculously prim and about twelve years old.

'Yes, you would. *Pretty Woman*, that's it. Julia Roberts selling herself and finding love.'

'Oh, yeah.' Actually, it was one of my favourite films. I'd never thought about it like that though.

'The schools teach sex education here by taking us to the Wallen,' said Ethan. 'The girls tell us what to do.'

'OK, now you're lying.'

'Are you sure?'

I was glad to see the balcony door open and the others come back in. I frowned at him, and he laughed.

'You have a beautiful new home,' said Mieke, sitting down next to Ethan. 'How are you enjoying college, Kitty? And how are the Dutch lessons going?'

'*Goed so,*' I said, working hard to make that weird *ch* sound for G. I was really enjoying the classes, somewhat to my surprise. My teacher had even lent me a book called *201 Irregular Dutch Verbs*, which was slightly more interesting than it sounded.

Ethan whistled. 'Impressive!'

'It's nice to see you enjoying life in Amsterdam,' said Mieke, sipping her wine.

'I'm getting used to it. I even ate some herring the other day.' Alice had dared me to swallow an entire herring in one gulp – the traditional way, apparently. I'd refused, but did buy some from a stall, and enjoyed chewing my way through it. It reminded me of my grandma, who used to spread chopped herring on black bread. She'd be really cross with me, though, if she knew I was associating her with the smell of marinated raw fish, and the thought of her indignant face made me smile.

'Did you like it?' Mieke smiled.

'I loved it,' I told her. 'And I love walking down the Spiegel-straat and looking at all the antique shops. And I love the Van Gogh Museum. And the Vondelpark.'

'You're just a tourist,' said Ethan. 'I bet you love the Rijksmuseum as well.'

'I haven't been there yet, but I bet I do,' I told him. 'I want to see the dolls' houses.'

'They are beautiful,' said Mieke. 'Always one of my favourite things. I used to take Ethan there when he was a little boy. He liked them too, although he might not admit it now.'

'I still like them,' he said. 'I always wanted one, but we were never in one place long enough.'

'You knew each other when Ethan was little?' I asked.

'I knew Melinda before they even moved to Amsterdam,' she said. 'We worked on a project together with street kids in Colombia. Way back. So, she used to come and visit sometimes. Ethan was a sweet boy then.'

'I'm still a sweet boy now,' he told her, and she grimaced and said, 'When you want to be.'

Mum called us over to the table and served up salad and spaghetti and more wine, and they talked about Mum's job and Paul's creative writing workshops, my college, and Ethan's mum and her relief work in Afghanistan. Mum and Paul seemed to be getting on very well. Maybe I'd got it all wrong about Paul and Mieke. It occurred to me that I'd never actually seen them touch each other.

'It's such a lovely evening,' said Mum when we'd finished. 'How about a little stroll, down to the Museumplein?'

'You go,' said Mieke. 'I must be getting back – busy day tomorrow. Thank you for a lovely evening.'

'Let's walk you to your bike,' said Paul. So we all went down to the square, and saw Mieke off as she cycled down the Ferdinand Bolstraat.

'So,' said Mum. 'Who's up for a walk?'

'Maybe Kitty and I will stay here, get a drink,' said Ethan, jerking his head at one of the cafés in the square. 'You go, have a good time.'

They didn't even try and persuade us to come along.

'A drink?' said Ethan. 'Or shall we go back to your flat and finish the wine?'

'Let's stay here,' I said, leading the way to one of the terraces. I actually preferred it in the flat, because a lot of people were smoking, but there was a slightly mysterious quality to Ethan that made me feel it could be safer to stay in a crowd.

OK, I fancied him. But if Ethan had been an animal, he'd have been something wild and untamed, like a wolf. Theo was more of a Labrador. Also, Theo's eyelashes were longer. I definitely felt safer with Theo. But that didn't mean I was totally not interested in Ethan either.

Despite the smoke, there was a nice social buzz about the

square, which I liked a lot. Mum and I quite often came down to have a drink here so we could watch people. It was all very different from Palmers Green and the autumn heatwave made us feel as though we were on holiday.

'So,' said Ethan, once we'd found a table and ordered coffee for him and mint tea for me. 'How long do you reckon, then?'

'How long? What do you mean?'

'Before we become brother and sister.'

'Oh, no, I don't think ... Mum hasn't said anything ...' I was cringing with embarrassment.

'Don't worry about Mieke, nothing's going on there, although I think she hoped something would develop. The ladies like Paul, although I can't see why.'

'He seems very nice,' I said.

Ethan shrugged. 'Yeah, he's nice. If that's what you like. Nice.'

'What's wrong with nice?'

'It's kind of ... *saai* ... Boring. That's why Melinda left him.'

'Melinda? Oh, your mum.'

'Yeah. Takes a lot to hold her interest, and Paul didn't do it.'

'Oh. Isn't that kind of harsh?'

'Nothing worse than boring,' he said, eyes gazing off into the distance. Clearly he thought that I was just as dull as Paul. There was an awkward silence, and then he yawned, slowly and deliberately.

I blushed and struggled to think of something to say. 'So ... have you made any films recently?'

He laughed at me. 'You're so easy to wind up. Don't worry, I don't find you boring at all. You don't need to make polite conversation.'

'Well, stop it. If it's easy, it can't be any fun.' I was pretending to be cross, but inside I was thrilled. He didn't think I was boring! That was almost a compliment.

'It's more fun,' he said, taking out a cigarette and lighting it without asking me if I minded. 'What? Oh, you don't like me smoking? Are you worried about my lungs?'

'No, I'm worried about mine,' I said, annoyed. Ethan was not like a wolf at all. He was a stupid, buzzing wasp.

He held the cigarette away from me. 'I'll be good, I promise. So, you don't think we will be a family then?'

'No,' I said, although Mum had seemed really happy tonight, laughing at Paul's jokes throughout dinner and taking his pronouncements about creativity and the power of language incredibly seriously.

'Shame,' he said, 'because there's something really sexy about incest, isn't there? If they got together, we could have quite an interesting time.'

His left hand was dangerously close to my saucer as I put down my cup in a hurry. I'd almost spilled mint tea down my front. He put his hand over mine. I should have been completely creeped out, but instead I felt an unwelcome shiver of pure desire.

I removed my hand. 'It wouldn't be incest at all,' I pointed out, 'because you aren't my real brother.'

His eyes crinkled with laughter. 'Oh, so that's all right then?'

'No, it is not!' I was sure I was blushing again.

Luckily for me, his phone rang.

'I need to take it, sorry.'

There was nothing for me to do while he talked, so I got out my phone and looked at my Instagram account. People loved my selfie from earlier. They were asking where I'd bought the dress, so I added a comment telling them about the Albert Cuyp street market and promising to do a tour of it on the vlog.

'Yeah … yeah … I know, but … look, I never promised … I know. Yeah, well, stop being so paranoid.' Ethan ran his hand through his hair. He wasn't wearing it tied back today, and it fell to his shoulders.

'I know you do. No … No. Don't be like that. OK. Look, you don't have to … OK … OK. You know I do. Yes, well, I don't do promises. No. I can't. Of course I do. OK.'

I couldn't help myself; I was listening. It sounded like he'd pissed off his girlfriend but I couldn't make out her words.

'OK. Have it your own way. Forget it. You know me well enough … OK. Well, I'm not sorry. OK. OK. Oh, Jesus, don't cry …'

Ethan stubbed out his cigarette, violently mashing it into the ashtray, and stood up, walking a few metres away so I couldn't hear his conversation any more. His face was exasperated more than upset, almost bored by his girlfriend's anguish. I thought about how he'd been coming on to me, and bit my lip. He was clearly bad news, and yet I'd been slightly tempted there.

Ethan flopped down in his chair again. 'Phew. What a pain.'

I tried to sound casual. 'Everything OK?'

'Some people. Jesus. You flirt with them, maybe a bit more,

and then they think you're the love of their life and they get upset when they see you with a girl. Talk about a mad stalker.'

I went cold. 'You mean … she's here? Your girlfriend? But she's got nothing to worry about … I mean, she could join us …'

He looked amused. 'I can't stand people who are jealous,' he said, 'especially when it's all in their imagination. Of course, you can always give them something to worry about. Kitty – can I kiss you?'

'What?' I said, but not quickly enough. Ethan's arm went round my shoulders, his face came towards mine, and his lips planted themselves on mine, tasting of smoke and coffee, and feeling so soft and kissable that for a moment I forgot to be furious. Only for a moment though.

'How dare you!' I said, as he pulled away.

'I enjoyed that, we can do it again sometime if you want.' He looked up. 'Here comes trouble.'

And a tall, handsome guy started walking towards us from the other side of the square.

Chapter 14

Kitty

Amsterdam

'You complete rat,' I said to Ethan, after he'd finally got rid of his boyfriend.

'It's not my fault! I didn't do anything wrong!'

'You kissed me!'

'What's wrong with that? It was nice, wasn't it?'

'You only did it to make that guy ... Tim ... to make him jealous.'

'Yeah, well, he was making an idiot of himself. Stalking me and phoning all the time ... You did me a big favour. I think he's got the message now.'

My mouth was wide open. 'Perhaps you could ask next time you want to use me as a ... a decoy for your exes.'

'I will, I promise,' he said.

'You just told Tim you never make promises.' I thought of Tim's pleading face, and how he had retreated, almost in tears.

He was only about a year or so older than me. I wondered if this was the first time he'd been in love.

'Promises to lovers.' Ethan smirked. 'Not to friends. I keep my promises to friends. And you're my friend, aren't you?'

I could still taste him. Normally I hate the faintest whiff of smoke. How annoying to find myself wanting to forgive him.

'Poor Tim,' I said.

'Poor Tim nothing. We met; we had a great week. A really great week. And that was enough. I told him I didn't want to get involved. And now, months later, he's hassling me. Remind me to get a new number.'

'Remind yourself. I'm still angry with you. You'll have to do a lot better than that if you want us to be friends.'

'Oh, Kitty, Kitty. I already showed you one of my favourite places in Amsterdam.'

'You can show me a few more,' I said, and then realised that I was virtually begging him to spend more time with me, so I added, 'or text me a list or something.'

'I'll show you a good time,' he said, all banter and smiles.

'I should tell Tim he's had a lucky escape,' I retorted. 'Anyway, why didn't you tell me that you're gay?'

Ethan looked surprised. 'You think I'm gay? After I kissed you? I must be losing my touch.'

'Yes, but ... Tim ... ' And then I got it. 'Oh. You're bi.'

'Aren't you?'

'Not so far,' I said, to mask my almost complete lack of experience with either gender.

'I think most people are,' he said, 'given the opportunity. Oh, look, here come the parents.'

Mum and Paul sat down before we could continue our discussion, which was a very good thing because I had no idea what to say next. Ethan winked at me, and I decided that he was not someone to be taken seriously. And definitely not someone to kiss, ever again.

After he and Paul left, Mum and I went back up to the flat and sat out on the balcony, looking out over the twinkling lights of the city.

'I'm glad you and Ethan are getting on,' she said. 'Paul finds him very difficult.'

'Yeah, well, I can see why,' I said.

'Really? Paul says he's sulky and won't talk to him. He's probably missing his mum a lot, and worrying about her – she does seem to thrive on danger. I think Ethan's quite vulnerable.'

I spluttered into my glass.

'What makes you think that, Mum? You hardly know him.'

'Oh, just a vibe I get from him,' she said. 'He seems unhappy. Restless. Nervy. I feel sorry for him, being dragged from country to country.'

'I wish you'd stop being all psychic and start basing your judgements on observations!'

'Well, what do you make of him? You've just spent an hour talking.'

'He's very pleased with himself,' I said. 'So, what about you and Paul?'

'Oh, nothing's going to happen,' she said. 'We're just good friends.'

Then she took a shower and I could hear her singing. My mum never sings in the shower. Amsterdam Mum was younger, somehow. More carefree. Happier. I wasn't sure how much that was to do with Paul, and how much it was about Amsterdam.

Rachel and I had pre-arranged a Skype chat, so I confided in her about the new Happy Mum.

'That's brilliant,' she pronounced. 'Mum totally needs to move on. She shouldn't spend any more time looking backwards.'

'I know, but ...'

'You've got to get used to it. Come on, Kitty, she can't always protect you.'

'What do you mean, protect me?'

'She's been telling herself for years that you couldn't take the stress of adjusting to having a stepfather. I know, totally unfair. It's because she felt all the guilt when she broke up with my dad and got together with yours.'

'Oh, that's crazy, Ray.'

'Yeah, well, it is Mum we're talking about. So, Paul, is he nice?'

'He's definitely nice,' I said, 'but it's difficult to get past the nice, if you see what I mean. He's all nice. He smiles a lot. He's one of those calm, yoga people.'

'Like Mum pretends to be?'

'Like Mum is most of the time.'

'Oh, OK. And what's his son like?'

I closed my eyes and remembered Ethan's kiss. How surprisingly good it felt. How I instinctively wanted more.

'What's that soppy grin on your face?' demanded Rachel. I vowed to disable the camera for future Skype chats.

'He's very annoying. I think he's actually socially inept. And also he's bisexual.'

'Bisexual's very in at uni,' said Rachel. 'Everyone's trying it.'

'Even you?'

'No, I'm way too conventional. I'm concentrating on my studies at the moment anyway. So, you like this Ethan?'

'No! Not that way! I mean, sort of, but just as a friend, except he's really, really annoying, like I said.'

'I get it.' Rachel was laughing at me. 'How's college? Made any friends?'

'I've made loads of friends at college. Loads. Actually, one of them has a brother who was at school with you. From Finchley. His name's Theo Collins. I think the brother is Simon.'

'Really? Simon Collins? You mean, sweet, gorgeous Simon who used to go out with Amber? Simon's brother is in Amsterdam?'

'Yeah.'

'Oh my God! So that's what they did with him!'

'What do you mean?'

'Well. I don't know if I should tell you.'

'Oh go on! Rachel!'

Rachel pursed her lips. 'Oh, OK then. But it might not be

actually true. Amber told me that her friend knows a friend of Simon's cousin, and she said that the little brother had an affair with his teacher.'

I was stunned. 'Really? Theo?'

'Well, I don't think there's another little brother. There's an older one who got religion and went off to yeshiva in Jerusalem.'

'So what actually happened? How old was this teacher?'

'I don't know any details. Amber said that Simon's family were really upset about it, and trying to hush it all up. Apparently the teacher was very young – a trainee, I think – and not some hideous old paedophile hag. That's what Amber said anyway. But she's a bit of a flaky source, Kits. Why don't you ask him?'

'Are you *mad*?' My head was whirling. I'd thought Theo was just a Nice Jewish Boy from North West London, the sort who have everything easy and think they're walking on the wild side if they eat a prawn sandwich. But now I could picture him at the centre of a doomed love affair, desperately in love with someone he could never be with, having to fight his overbearing parents to keep the flames of his passion alive. Of course it didn't matter that she was his teacher. He must feel so misunderstood and devastated, to be sent into exile for daring to love someone forbidden to him.

'Are you OK?' demanded Rachel. 'You look a bit peaky.'

'I'm totally shocked!' I told her. 'Poor Theo!'

'I can't wait to tell Amber that he's at your college. What a coincidence!'

I love coincidences. They almost always mean that something

is Meant to Be. What if I'm the one destined to help Theo cope with the trauma of losing the woman he loves? Maybe that's why I'm here in Amsterdam.

'Don't tell Amber,' I beg. 'Please, Rachel. It's not fair to him.'

'Oh, c'mon Kitty ...'

'If he finds out I've been gossiping about him, I'll be mortified!'

'You like him, don't you?' Rachel put on her 'I'm your big sister and I know everything' face.

'He's a nice guy.'

'And nice-looking, if he's anything like Simon. Ah, lovely Simon. He's working in his dad's furniture business now. I might message him, see how he is. You don't mind me mentioning the coincidence to him?'

I wasn't interested in Simon, unromantically selling chairs and tables.

'Poor Theo,' I said again. 'It is over, this relationship, isn't it?'

'Don't you get involved with him, Kits; he'll be on the rebound.'

'I'm not!'

After talking to Rachel, I sat and knitted for an hour to calm down and think things through sensibly. It didn't really work because I dropped loads of stitches.

I couldn't see Theo as someone vulnerable enough to be groomed by a predator. So he must have really loved this teacher. He must be suffering now, missing her and either wanting to be with her or resigning himself to live alone ... forever ...

It was exactly like my favourite books. My heart warmed to Theo. He needed a friend, an understanding, sensitive good listener. Who just happened to be a beautiful (ish) independent, stylish woman looking for love in a brand new city. Slowly he could rebuild the wreckage of his broken (if it was broken) heart with her patient help.

As for Ethan, with his dangerous kisses and stalker boyfriends; he could keep them to himself.

Chapter 15

Theo

Amsterdam

It was raining that weekend and Alex's football match was cancelled, so he decided to take me on a personal tour of Jewish Amsterdam. I wasn't wildly looking forward to it. Genocide and guilt wasn't my idea of a good time.

We bypassed Anne Frank's house, partly because I'd already seen it with my dad, all those years ago, and partly because of the queues. Instead, we headed east, to the old Jewish neighbourhood.

'It's all very well, the Anne Frank Huis, but for me it misses the point,' said Alex.

'How can you say that? It's like ... she's like a symbol of the Holocaust. *The* symbol. People all over the world know about Anne Frank.' I felt protective of Anne because she, like me, was a writer, and she, like me, was a teenager. I'd have gone crazy cooped up in a little apartment with my family for years on end.

Also, she didn't get a happy ending. She had the worst

ending possible. All that hope and optimism and talent, and it ended up in betrayal and horror and death.

'It's a wonderful memorial, that's true. You should definitely go there. But, you know, it's so popular because it reduces the Shoah to one girl and her family. It's manageable, it gives you someone to identify with. But it takes the focus away from the vastness of it, the number of people affected. We Jews aren't about individuals. We're about communities.'

He pointed out the Jewish Museum, built out of two synagogues, and the historic Spanish and Portuguese Synagogue across the square, where they still held services by candlelight. Then we walked down to an old theatre, the Schouwsberg. 'This,' he said, 'is what Amsterdam lost.'

The theatre had been the meeting point for Jews when they were transported from Amsterdam. Some children were saved, smuggled to a nursery across the road by brave resistance members. Most of them were taken away to concentration camps.

The building was full of photographs. Family groups. Bar mitzvah boys. Kids camping. A boy on skates who looked just like my friend, Jacob. People like Kitty, Chalex, Mum, Dad, my grandparents, my brothers. People like me. Except my mind had always stubbornly refused to believe that I would have been one of them. Somehow clever me, brilliant Theo, would have outwitted the Nazis. It's a fantasy based on superpowers and magic and fear.

Downstairs there was a wall engraved with names, and what looked like a poem. Alex translated for me: '*These are the family names of fathers and mothers, aunts and uncles, nephews and nieces, grandfathers and grandmothers. 104,000 people. 104,000 Jews living in Amsterdam and the Netherlands were deported and murdered.'*

I scanned the names, trying to imagine all those people, all those families. Alex was right; it was a much harder concept to grasp than the story of one girl. 104,000 people. That, Alex told me, is about half the number of Jews in the UK. I tried to imagine the crowds of people squashed into this building. Some of them had handed over their children to resistance workers, who smuggled them into hiding.

My imagination failed. I could only think about the skating boy, the one who looked like my friend Jacob. What happened to him? Did he survive the war?

Afterwards, we walked back to the Jewish Museum, where there was a kosher café. We ordered falafel, pita bread and hummus.

'So,' Alex said, tearing a pita in two. 'How are you coping? Is it getting easier?'

'What do you mean?'

'Being in Amsterdam. Not seeing her. Is it easier?'

'Is that why you brought me here? To confront me with the Shoah, make me feel guilty about Sophie?'

'No, obviously not.'

'What do you mean, obviously? Aren't you going to hit me with the "you're doing Hitler's work for him" argument?'

Alex chewed on his pita, took a gulp of water. 'How old-fashioned do you think I am? My own sister-in-law converted to Judaism. Don't try and call me racist.'

'I didn't mean that ...' I'd totally forgotten about the girl his brother fell in love with. It took her years to convert Orthodox. The rabbinical court turned her down four times.

'Yes, you did. You thought I'd make some crude comparison between genocide and having a relationship with a non-Jewish woman.'

'OK, yes, I did. I'm sorry.'

'Look, Theo, you had a relationship with a teacher. She's clearly not the most stable of people.'

Why did no one understand about love? 'Yeah, well, who is?'

'She's got a lot to learn.'

'I can't live my life according to what Mum and Dad want. It's too restrictive. And nor can she.'

'Yeah, maybe. But it's also what the law says.'

'I don't care about the law!'

'I don't agree with everything your parents do or say,' he said. 'I do understand how difficult this is for you.'

'When I'm eighteen, I'm going to run my own life.' I said this as definitely as possible, just in case he was feeding stuff back to Mum and Dad.

'Just give yourself some breathing space,' he said. 'Don't rush into any decisions. Things will become clearer.'

'Look, just because you and Chani are the perfect couple ... it's not as easy for other people ...'

'Why do you think I came to Amsterdam in the first place?'

'You got a job in IT with a Dutch bank.'

'I wanted to lie around in the Vondelpark, smoking dope and

chatting up blondes, somewhere I wouldn't be spotted by five people from shul.'

I almost laughed at the idea of earnest Alex kicking back in the park.

'I did it for a while. Then one Shabbat I went to shul and I saw Chani. And that was it for me.'

'Very romantic,' I said, gloomily. I bet this story was why Mum and Dad had sent me here. *If it worked for Alex, it'll work for Theo.*

'Yes, actually, it was. Very. I'm not saying that will happen for you, Theo. I'm just saying keep an open mind. Don't waste time on a girl, a woman, who doesn't know right from wrong. Look, Rosh Hashanah is coming up. Why not try and make it a real new start?'

He was annoying, but equally I could see that he really cared about me.

'It's not that easy,' I said.

'Isn't it? You seem to have made lots of new friends.'

'Yeah, people are nice.' I wasn't going to mention Kitty, although we were getting on really well. She was both reassuringly familiar and a bit different – more edgy and streetwise – than the Jewish girls I knew in London. Part of me wished I'd met her before I ever met Sophie, but how could I think like that when I was still totally and completely in love?

I was in love with someone who wasn't communicating with me, though. I was running out of excuses for her silence.

Alex and I finished our lunch and went and looked around the house where Rembrandt used to live. Both of us got kind of overexcited about his cabinet of curiosities, which included a stuffed armadillo, swords, spears, Greek statues and a Roman helmet. I would have liked Rembrandt a lot, I reckoned. He'd be like one of those guys who always has a new gadget to show off.

I got back to the little house in Amstelveen feeling more hopeful than before. Chatting to Alex had made me wonder how well I knew myself. Could I forget Sophie? Just the thought of her made my heart ache. But was that real love, or was it my stubborn need to be right, not to let my parents, my school, society generally, tell me what to do and who to love?

But when I went to bed that might, I lay in the dark listening to the whirr of Chalex's washing machine. I remembered the peachy smell of Sophie's hair. I remembered the soft touch of her skin. I relived our kisses, every single one burned into my brain in high-definition detail.

How could I ever forget her?

Chapter 16

Kitty

Amsterdam

Ethan called me a few days later.

'Hey, *susje*. Are you free tomorrow afternoon?' I knew *susje* meant sister, a sort of baby form of the real word for sister. The Dutch seemed to add *–je* onto the end of almost every word. Usually I thought it was quite cute. But not when it was Ethan teasing me.

'I've got college,' I said, mentally checking my timetable. 'But it's only Dutch.'

'Only Dutch? What's more important than Dutch? But you don't need to go to class. I can teach you *Nederlands*. Want to come to the Concertgebouw with me? They have free concerts at lunchtime.'

'Oh. I don't know. What are they playing?' My mind was in a whirl. Was this a date? Did Ethan even do dates? Would he try and kiss me again? Or was this a way of making up for his crass behaviour the other day? I knew he wouldn't apologise. After two weeks at work Mum had warned me that Dutch people don't ever say sorry, it's just not in their DNA.

'It's Beethoven,' Ethan explained, adding patronisingly, 'Entry-level classical music, anyone would like it.'

'I've got a very wide-ranging taste in music, thank you very much. Beethoven's a bit vanilla for me.'

'OK, so you don't want to come along?'

Argh. What to do? I decided that Mum needed me to be friends with Ethan so she could build a romance with Paul. I would, completely unselfishly, in the interests of middle-aged love, accept his invitation, and make sure no more kissing occurred (between Ethan and me, obviously, not Mum and Paul).

'No, I love Beethoven. Of course I'll come.'

'Good,' he said, and rang off without telling me where or when or anything. Honestly, he needed lessons in social inter-action. I had to text him to find out the details.

The next day I left college early and cycled to the concert hall, which was a big, grand, stripy building. We queued up together and heard the concert, which was actually a rehearsal for the performance that evening, so you had to forget hearing the whole piece perfectly done and instead concentrate on what the conductor did (apart from waving his arms around) – how he made the sound better and pulled the musicians together into one big harmonious noise. I found it more inter-esting than an actual concert, although I felt sorry for the musicians, being corrected in public.

Afterwards, we went and had lunch at Ethan's favourite café

in the park, one with a huge terrace overlooking a playground. We ate pancakes – 'You have to live the stereotype at least once,' he said – and drank apple juice (me) and milk (him). I started giggling when I saw his glass.

'What?' he said.

'It's just … in England, no one drinks milk like that. Only little kids.'

'I know. Tell me about it. You forget I spent my childhood shuttling between London and Amsterdam, not to mention the occasional war zone. Kids don't take well to people with different tastes.'

'Your mum took you to war zones?'

'Not usually while the wars were going on. But afterwards, sure. Melinda believes in children knowing the facts of life. Well, this child anyway.'

'That's … ' I struggled to find a word that wasn't judgemental, 'different. I mean, most parents would try and protect their kids from going to places like that.'

'Melinda would say that most parents don't get that choice. The parents caught up in the war zones, that is. The ones with the kids who wet themselves from fear and draw pictures of men hacking limbs off their neighbours.'

I winced. He added, 'To be fair, most of the aid workers thought Melinda was batshit-crazy to bring me along. Paul wasn't too keen either, but he hadn't got any say back then.'

'Why not?'

'Custody stuff. Melinda called the shots. She had to decide how much it suited her to have Paul involved. Once she gave up on turning me into a saint like her, she let him take up the slack.'

'Do you think she was wrong to take you along to places like that?'

He shrugged. 'I'm a disappointment to her. She thought she'd inspire me to save the world, instead she got someone who likes to keep house.'

I smiled, and he said, 'What? Just because I don't put pictures all over Instagram doesn't mean I'm not house proud.'

'Paul said you'd done a lot of work on your house.'

'In a parallel universe, I'd be an architect. But I'd have to go to school for that and classrooms are not for me. So I stick to painting walls and putting up shelves.'

'Maybe one day,' I said. 'You don't need to do everything right away.'

'Tell that to my mom and dad. They're all "Why don't you apply to art school?" and "Why don't you volunteer to help orphans in Africa?" They never leave me alone. I guess I'm just weird, wanting to live my life without actually working towards anything. Just being. I suppose you've got it all planned out, your future career?'

I wished I could go and volunteer at an African orphanage. It was just the sort of bold and adventurous thing that I'd never been able to consider. But I wasn't going to tell Ethan that.

'I have no idea,' I said, 'and I kind of like it that way. One day at a time, that's my motto.'

He smiled properly then, and I realised how unusual it was

for Ethan's face to smooth out with no frown marks or tension, for his eyes to crinkle and those tense shoulders drop.

'You're OK,' he told me. 'I'm quite happy to have you as a little sister.'

I was almost taken in by his charm, but he followed it up with, 'But you'd better go easy on the pancakes, or you'll be my big sister. What? It was a joke! Haven't you English people got a sense of humour?'

'Huh,' I said. 'And I am *not* your sister.'

'It's going to happen though. Paul's been splashing on the aftershave. And you can see they like eachother a lot.'

'Mum says they're just friends.'

'Jesus, it must be complicated, living with your mum.'

'Why?'

'Never saying what she feels. I mean, if you like someone, you just go for it, no?'

I eyed him nervously. Was he going to pounce again?

'It's just normal British behaviour to tread cautiously.'

'It's kind of dishonest.'

'My mum is not dishonest! She just wants what's best for everyone.'

'Yeah, right. She wants to get with Paul.'

'I don't even know if that's true. I mean, I don't think she knows.'

'Well, she followed him all the way to Amsterdam.'

'We happened to come and live in Amsterdam because she had a new job,' I said.

'Or maybe she applied for a transfer because it was in

Amsterdam and Paul was here, hey? That's what Melinda thinks.'

'No way,' I said, although I had wondered this myself. I was annoyed at the idea of Ethan discussing Mum and me with his mother. 'My mum's an independent person, and she's got a good career. She doesn't plan her life round a man. And your mum can't possibly judge, as she doesn't know anything about it. She should keep her nose out and concentrate on helping people in Afghanistan.'

'You are much more direct than your mom,' he said, approvingly. 'Amsterdam is obviously good for you. Only a few weeks and you're insulting my mom.'

I couldn't help laughing. 'Amsterdam is good for me, although I'm sorry if you think I'm rude.'

'Oh, be rude. It's fine. I prefer it to pretend politeness.'

'I suppose I'd better go back to college,' I said, although it was such a perfect day – blue skies and sunshine, a slight breeze rustling the trees – that I didn't want to move.

'Have you ever tried rollerblading? There's a place where you can hire the gear.'

'I've never rollerbladed, but I can ice skate.'

'Same principle, I suppose. Shall we give it a go?'

'I'll only fall over.' I'd seen the Vondelpark rollerbladers before, performing incredible tricks, slaloming round rows of obstacles. They were the coolest guys in the park, which was saying a lot as the park was full of people doing interesting stuff – capoeira, buskers, jugglers; someone had even strung a rope between two trees and practised walking across it. At the weekends, people put up bunting and gazebos and had parties. Given that the weather was changeable – I'd never seen so many rainbows – I admired the optimistic Dutch attitude.

'Oh, come on, Kitty, give it a go. Life's not worth living if you don't take a few risks.'

We cycled to the skate-hire place – yet another little café, tucked into a far corner of the park – and I insisted on knee and elbow guards as well as my cycle helmet.

'You're so pessimistic,' grumbled Ethan. 'If you have the idea of an accident in your head, you're much more likely to fall.'

'That is such rubbish.' I strapped the boots on, tightened the knee guards and promptly fell over. Ethan hauled me up.

'OK, hang on to me. Don't worry, I'm not going to let you fall.'

His way of making sure of this was to hold my right hand with his, while putting his left arm round my waist. We looked like a couple out of a picture I'd spotted the other day in the Rijksmuseum, Avercamp's *Winter Landscape*. Theo and I had decided to take the museum bit by bit, and I'd fallen in love with this wintry scene, full of people enjoying the ice.

I wondered if I could create a modernised version for my Art course, with rollerbladers instead of skaters. Anyway, I slipped and slid along, all too conscious of his closeness.

'That's good … you're getting it. Just pretend you're on the ice.'

It should have been easier than ice skating, but it wasn't. The pavement was rougher, for a start, and the stopper was on the heel of the boot, not the toe. I stumbled a few times, and each time Ethan caught me. Gradually, I relaxed, found myself gliding more confidently. I didn't mind the bicycles alongside me. I quite liked the feeling of support that came from Ethan's arms, but I made myself let go of his hand. 'Let me try on my own,' I said.

We managed a circuit of the park, and then another. Soon we were soaring past the skate-hire place for the third time and my confidence was growing; I was faster, stronger, braver ... I was flying ...

Until a cyclist called my name. Startled, I lost my rhythm, arms windmilling wildly. I lurched sideways into Ethan, bringing us both sprawling to the ground.

'I'm sorry!'

Hang on. I knew that voice. It had to be Theo.

'I just saw you – I didn't think—'

Ethan was scowling, rubbing his wrist.

'Who's the idiot?' he asked me.

'Ethan! That's so ...' I grimaced apologetically to Theo. 'I'm sorry. He's always like this.'

'No, it was my fault, I shouldn't have distracted you.'

'This is Theo,' I said to Ethan. 'He's from my college.'

'Oh, yeah, British. I might have known. Always apologising.'

'Oh Ethan, stop insulting the British,' I told him. 'After all you're actually British yourself.'

'Half a passport,' he retorted.

'Half a passport and you lived there a long time.'

'Are you OK?' Theo asked him. 'I didn't mean to make you fall over. It was quite funny though.'

Ethan straightened up and contemplated Theo's face, which managed to look concerned and amused at the same time. Was there a touch of curiosity as well? I'd quite possibly avoided ever mentioning Ethan to him.

'For that you can buy us a drink.'

'Oh, sure, no problem.'

I sighed. 'Theo, this is Ethan. Ethan is a friend of mine ... sort of,' I said.

'She's my nearly-sister,' said Ethan.

'No, I am not. Not even nearly.'

We went back to the skate-hire place, and Theo bought us Cokes.

'So, what do you mean, nearly-sister?' he asked, once we'd handed back the skates.

'Kitty's mum came to Amsterdam in hot pursuit of my dad,' said Ethan. I flicked a piece of ice at him.

'That is totally not true. Take it back or I'll ... I'll have my revenge.'

'Ow, I'm scared.'

'His dad and my mum were friends in London,' I explained to Theo. 'So naturally we looked Paul up when we came to Amsterdam. Any romance is in Ethan's wild imagination.'

'I can see the future,' he said. 'And anyway, why wouldn't your mum like my dad? He's almost as handsome as I am. Not as pretty as you,' he nodded to Theo, 'but not bad.'

Was Ethan actually *flirting* with Theo? Or was he like this with everyone? He was impossible, anyway.

'This weather is great. It can't last for long,' said Theo, clearly uncomfortable.

Ethan let out a laugh. 'And now, talking about the weather. Oh, so British.'

'Of course we talk about the weather. It's interesting,' said Theo, recovering well. 'I was thinking we should have a picnic here sometime. Maybe next weekend? Before it gets cold.'

'You'd be better off at the Bos,' said Ethan. 'It's bigger, and there are some good places for picnics.'

'What's the Bos?' I asked.

'It's a forest. A little way south of here.'

'It's near where I live,' said Theo. 'I've cycled there a bit. You're right, it'd be a good place for a picnic.'

'Where do you live?' asked Ethan, and Theo told him his address. 'You're right under the flight path there. Do the planes bother you?'

'My cousins tell me I'm going to get used to it.'

'Are you staying with them a long time?'

'I don't know. Maybe two years, if I do my A-levels here. But I suppose I might go back to London after the exams in June. It all depends.'

'On what?' asked Ethan.

'I don't even know,' said Theo. I was sure I was not imagining the sudden sadness that crossed his face. I knew he must be thinking of his lost love, so far away.

'So, what about this picnic?' I asked. I was already picturing it in my mind, framed and filtered for my followers. Plaid blankets and straw hampers and little tea lights …

'Let's do it,' said Ethan. I gaped with mock amazement.

'What?' he asked.

'Well, it's just I didn't think you'd want to come. My friends are all annoying British and American people.'

'That's why you need me there, to add some authenticity.' He stood up. 'I'd better go.' He dropped a light kiss on my sweaty curls. 'See you, sis.' He nodded to Theo. 'Nice to meet you, Theo.' He pronounced it '*Tay-o*', which must be the Dutch way.

Once he'd cycled off, I felt the need to explain Ethan to Theo. 'He's OK really. He just comes over as rude and obnoxious and a bit weird.'

'He seemed friendly. He likes you, I think.' I couldn't tell from Theo's tone of voice whether this bothered him or not.

'Nah. He's just a tease. There's absolutely nothing going on. I have no interest in him at all, and I shouldn't think he'd be interested in me.' I realised I was protesting far too much, and made myself stop babbling.

'He looks like the sort of person who wouldn't let himself be pushed around.' Theo's voice was wistful and now I could guess why. It must be awful to be sent away by your family.

Should I ask him now, about his lost love, his grand passion? Ethan would have said I was being too repressed and too polite and too British and I should just spit it out. Looking at Theo's sad brown eyes, his luscious eyelashes, I felt desperate to know his secrets, to share in some small way, the anguish he must be feeling. If the rumours were true, that is. What if it was all rubbish and he thought I'd gone mad?

I opened my mouth and then closed it again. It was impossible. How could I say anything without sounding like a stalker?

So instead, I said, 'It looks like we were destined to meet up today. Do you want another drink?'

Chapter 17

Kitty

Amsterdam

I'd got into a routine over the first few weeks of term of meeting Theo for a walk, if we both had a class at the end of the college day, but that Thursday was different. Alice, Jane and Lucy had organised a trip to the cinema, and invited a whole group of people to come along. We girls walked along the Singel to meet the others at the cinema.

'So, how are you adjusting to Amsterdam?' Jane asked me. 'You're a complete virgin, aren't you?'

'I ... um ...'

'I mean, when it comes to living abroad. This is your first time?'

'Oh, right, sure. Yes, that's right. I've only ever lived in London.'

'I've lived in Tokyo, Frankfurt, Boston, San Francisco, Madrid ... and now here,' said Jane, ticking the cities off on her fingers.

'I've mostly been based with Mum in Wiltshire, but then I've stayed with Dad all over the place,' said Lucy. 'Moscow was my least favourite. The Cayman Islands was the best. Amsterdam's OK. This is his second time here, so I know it quite well.'

'I lived in London for a while,' said Alice. 'Knightsbridge. Do you know it?'

'Yeah, sure, but normal Londoners don't live there. It's too expensive.'

'It was OK,' she said. 'The school was hideous. So traditional. They made us wear hats. Did you wear a hat to school?'

'Er ... no.'

'We had to learn Latin. Did you learn Latin?'

'Um ... no.'

'You can't be picky about friends when you're an expat,' said Jane. 'Honestly, we don't have time. You get in there, meet people and bam! They're your friends. It's like speed-dating.'

'Er, OK.' I wasn't sure if this was a good thing. On the other hand, insta-friends were better than no friends. But I did miss Martine and Esther and Riley a lot. Social media was a life-saver.

'You take what you've got, go from nought to sixty in an afternoon and you never make enemies.'

'How come?'

'Because you never know who'll move where. There was a girl I was at school with in Tokyo; she was OK, nothing special, and when I moved to Madrid five years later, there she was, and totally the queen of the school. Luckily we'd always got on, so I was in there with the populars right from day one.'

Jane was one of those girls whose head was slightly too big

for her body. Her long limbs looked snappable. She was nearly as tall as me, but she had an elegant poise that I envied. Her red hair was swept back into a perfect ponytail, and her make-up was so perfectly natural that I could have spent ages looking at all the clever ways she'd created her face. She was studying Maths, Spanish, Economics and German.

'So, you're taking Dutch classes?' she asked me.

'*Ja*,' I said, '*en jouw?*'

'Seems like a waste of time,' she said. 'All the big companies in the Netherlands use English as a business language anyway. I'm trying to improve my Mandarin.'

'Yes, but … living here, I mean, it's useful to know the language, isn't it?'

'I suppose so,' said Jane, 'but I'm aiming to be at an Ivy League college in two years, so it's a bit irrelevant.'

'I'm really getting into it,' I said. 'I like how you learn about Dutch culture as well. The teacher was explaining to us how many phrases are about water, because of Holland being below sea level and all the land reclamation and dykes and stuff.'

'Just wait till she gets on to Sinterklaas and his black slave, Zwarte Piet,' said Alice, kicking a stone into the canal. 'Then you won't think Dutch culture is so interesting.'

'I don't think I've heard of that,' I said.

'Right, you and me are having coffee tomorrow. I'm going to recruit you for my protest.'

'Sure,' I said, anxious to please my new friend.

'So, what about the guys, what do we think?' said Lucy. 'You've already nabbed Finn, haven't you, Jane?'

'Mmm,' said Jane, 'I couldn't possibly comment. We're at an interesting stage.'

'And didn't we see you going off with Theo the other day, Kitty? Fast work, girl.'

'Oh no,' I said, 'it's just because we're both from north London. Turns out we were virtually neighbours.'

'Oh yeah ... we believe you ...' They were laughing, and suddenly it was just like being at home with Esther and Riley and Martine. I laughed back and said, 'We'll see!' And then we reached the flower market and spent ages finding the silliest fridge magnet; we were torn between one of a mouse with a gigantic cheese, and one depicting a sex shop in a canal house. The cinema was just across the road, and the boys – Theo, Finn, Damon and Max – were waiting for us there. I noticed how Jane effortlessly manoeuvred herself next to Finn, who was beanpole-tall, wore geeky glasses and spoke with a *Gone With the Wind*-type accent.

'Finn does modelling in his spare time,' Alice whispered in my right ear. 'He's got lots of cash for a student.'

'Oh, right,' I said, looking again at Finn and noticing startling blue eyes behind the thick, black frames of the glasses. 'Wow. OK.'

It wasn't until the film was over and we'd shared a falafel that I spoke to Theo.

'Hey,' he said. 'You've not got your bike?'

'No, I walked this morning. It's OK. I can get a tram straight home.'

'My bike's tied up at college,' he said. 'I suppose I'd better go back and get it. Do you fancy a walk first? Everyone says the weather's going to break soon, seems like a shame not to make the most of it.'

The cinema had been hot, and the evening air was like a delicious cool drink. Finn and Jane were walking away, his arm round her shoulders, hers round his waist. My fingers twitched for my camera: they would have made the perfect romantic portrait.

'OK,' I said, 'you're right. Let's go for a drink.'

We walked past office blocks, and then turned off down a canal.

'It beats the North Finchley Vue,' he said, pausing by a bridge to admire the way two canals intersected. As the North Finchley Vue is a cinema set in a car park, just off the North Circular, this was not much of a competition.

I admired the way the light reflected on the ripples of the water. The houses leaned crookedly on each other, like old friends. And the glimpses of people's homes inside the houses, each room stylish and tasteful, a frame for a beautiful life. The kind of life we could have had if Dad hadn't died when he did.

The setting was so ridiculously romantic that it was making my head spin. Did Theo feel the same way? I wondered if it made him miss the teacher he loved, made his heart ache that they couldn't be together in such a gorgeous setting?

Or maybe it wasn't like that at all. Maybe she was predatory and threatening, and he'd made the choice to come here to get over their toxic affair. Maybe he was hiding out in Amsterdam, desperate to escape from her clutches? There were so many possibilities. Theo was like the romantic hero of a book ... I just wasn't sure which book. I had to find out!

'It's perfect,' I said, taking a picture.

'It is,' Theo agreed. 'Almost too pretty. It's very pleased with itself.'

'I love it,' I said, 'and I love the atmosphere. If Amsterdam were a guy, he'd be so laid back and chilled and happy. Not like London guy, who'd be a depressive, neurotic, awkward mess. Amsterdam guy would be the type to give you flowers.'

'Amsterdam isn't all like this. The Red Light district is about ten minutes walk from here and it's possibly the least romantic place in the world,' said Theo. 'Your Amsterdam guy has a sleazy side.'

'Don't most guys?' I countered. 'He'd just be honest and upfront about it.'

'London's not all bad,' Theo said. 'Look at the Thames. The view from Waterloo Bridge is grander than anything they have here.'

'Amsterdam doesn't need grand. It has cute and charming instead.'

'I suppose it comes down to what you want in a guy,' he said, deadpan.

'Or a city. I just took it for granted that they were all messy and difficult to navigate.'

'Are you talking about cities now, or guys?'

'Both.' He was almost definitely flirting, so I thought I would too. Which meant he was at least trying to forget the teacher. Well, I would help him heal his broken heart, if I possibly could.

'London's built on clay, which is a bit firmer than sand,' he said. 'I can't believe they built Amsterdam on sand. I mean, why do that?'

'Clay dries out and then it makes your house have cracks,' I said, because this is exactly what happened to our house last year. 'They didn't have any choice. Almost the whole of the Netherlands is under sea level.'

'Yes, it's a crazy nation altogether. Metaphorically speaking, your Amsterdam guy might look all chilled and non-neurotic, but his foundations are shifting.'

'Oh,' I said, 'well, lucky I don't have an Amsterdam guy.'

'Mmm,' he agreed. 'Lucky, that.'

And then he kissed me.

My knees buckled with the shock of it, but I didn't let it show. I kissed him back, trying to convey gentle passion through the medium of two mouths meeting, sending psychic waves of sympathy and understanding in his direction. Surely he would understand that I was the perfect girl to banish his mysterious older woman from his memory?

At last, he pulled away. He blinked a few times, as though he'd surprised himself.

'I . . . um, Kitty . . . '

I smiled, sweet as the caramel centre of a *stroopwafel* – my favourite Dutch food so far.

'Don't spoil it,' I said.

'It's just . . . I didn't mean . . . '

'It doesn't have to be a big deal,' I said. 'We don't need to analyse it. It can mean whatever it needs to mean. Just an unexpected thing that happened in a beautiful place, on a perfect evening.'

I sounded just like someone in a foreign film. There should be subtitles around my ankles. You couldn't say something like that in Palmers Green, because the other person would say, 'Eh? What you on about? Spit it out, Kits, do you fancy me or what?'

But I totally got away with it in Amsterdam. Theo blinked and said, 'Oh. Right.' And then he leaned forward and gave me a very sweet, very gentle kiss on the lips, which made me tingle all over.

I knew Amsterdam well enough by now to realise that my tram stop was just yards away.

'I think I'll go now,' I said, hoping I sounded carefree and experienced. 'See you tomorrow.' And I walked off into the night, careful not to look back even once.

Chapter 18

Theo

Amsterdam

Sophie

I don't know what to do. You never write
or email or call or anything, even though
I've tried to contact you, really tried. I
feel ninety per cent sure you must have at
least my address in Amsterdam, even if
you're avoiding the internet. I can't
understand why you wouldn't write to me.

The only possibility is that you have written
and my cousins have been told to look out for
your letters and hide them from me. Maybe
you could contact me at college? I think I
gave you that address already, but I'll put it
at the end of this letter just in case.

Sophie, being apart from you is killing
me. I feel empty inside, because if I think

about how much I miss you it's actually physically painful, like I've got some creature clawing out my guts. Sorry, that's a bit Game of Thrones, but you understand. I know you do. You understand everything about me.

I suppose I should be sensible and face facts, but I can't. Even if I try and make friends here, I'm only passing the time. I have empty, superficial conversations, banal chitchat with shallow teenagers, because I have to. No one can fill your place. I'm yearning for you. I never understood that word before, but I do now. I can't write my book, I can't do anything worthwhile. All I can think about is you.

I'm getting desperate, Sophie. If I don't hear from you I'm going to have to defy my parents and upset everyone and run away back to London. Don't be surprised if I turn up on your doorstep.

Your ever-loving Theo.

It was a terrible letter. It pleaded, threatened, moaned, whinged and – frankly – lied. It didn't even mention Kitty, even though I'd accidentally kissed her. I felt incredibly guilty about that kiss. How could I be unfaithful to Sophie? How could I mislead Kitty? Luckily Kitty seemed really cool about the whole thing.

'Call me old-fashioned,' she'd said the next day, after an evening drinking Coke and eating chips, our legs dangling over the edge of a canal, 'but I really have a strong belief in taking things slowly. Savouring the moment, know what I mean?'

'Mmm … yes …'

'It's always worked best for me before.'

'Um, yeah, me too.' I'd kept my eyes fixed on a cat, deftly jumping from houseboat to canalside. Kitty was so cool and confident. She clearly had a lot of experience with boys. She might even be seeing that Dutch guy with the long hair from the park, she'd never really explained what their relationship was. He was really striking-looking, one of those classic faces that you see in old carvings of angels. I felt secretly chuffed that Kitty was interested in me, if he was on the scene as well.

'Some guys are too impatient,' Kitty had said, smiling to herself.

'Not me, don't worry.'

'That's so sweet of you, Theo.'

'No problem.'

I didn't feel very experienced, although I'd never have admitted it. Before Sophie I'd been out with a grand total of two girls: Ariella, who I'd known since we were three, and Sasha, from camp. Ariella and I dated for a few months when we were fourteen; we met at my cousin's batty. She was great to go around with, and to kiss, but we mutually decided it was too weird to go any further, partly because we were only fourteen, but mostly because her sister was married to my cousin, so we felt like family.

Sasha and I got together at camp, in the summer of Year 10. Actually that was only a year and a bit ago, but it felt like forever. Sasha was what Kitty would call a beck – not just Kitty: Sasha would call herself a beck – because she mostly talked about designer clothes and expensive holidays. Although I enjoyed making out with her, I couldn't take the conversation. Her idea of culture was watching *Friends*. I finished with her the week after camp ended. That was round about the time that Mum got ill and started having tests. A few months later and I was obsessing over Sophie.

I read my letter through, put it into an envelope and posted it on the way to college. After class we were going out clubbing. Damon and Max had offered to show us Amsterdam nightlife. I assumed I'd crash at someone's place for the night and I'd told Chalex not to expect me back.

Kitty and I went for a walk after college, as usual, and then we cycled back to her flat to get changed and dump our bags. She pointed out Ethan's house on the way ('The weirdest house, Theo; it's got two front doors'). Her mum was in when we got to their flat, and we had one of those awkward friendly-mum conversations when they're trying to suss out if you're a good thing for their kid. It turned out that she came from Finchley originally, and Kitty had told her that I liked writing and suggested that I came along to some creative writing workshop at an English bookstore. She seemed nice, which made me miss my mum yet again

We met up with the guys at an Indonesian restaurant. We ordered a rice table, which involves lots of small dishes, beansprouts, chicken in a spicy peanut sauce, little silvery fish and toasted coconut, and two sorts of rice. I felt vaguely rebellious, as though I was paying my parents back for exiling me by eating non-kosher meat. Then I realised that eating satay chicken was a pretty pathetic rebellion, considering how they'd treated me, so I put a spoonful of prawns on my plate. Prawns being loads more non-kosher than the chicken. I couldn't bring myself to eat them though. They sat there, contaminating the other food, like a pile of large maggots.

'You're not eating much,' said Kitty.

'Who are you, my mother?' I said, teasing her.

'Oh, ha ha.' Kitty had no problems with non-kosher food, I noticed, as she took a spoonful from all the meat dishes, without even asking which ones were pork. I couldn't do it though. If prawns looked like huge insects to me, then the idea of eating pork was like eating a baby. I'd been brainwashed too young.

'Maybe Richard Dawkins was right,' I told Kitty.

'I've heard of him ... he's a scientist, isn't he?'

'Yeah. He says that exposing children to religious indoctrination is like child abuse.'

'What's that about child abuse?' said Jane from the other side of the table.

'There's this guy, and he says that you should bring children up without any religion or anything like that. Just neutral. Then they can make up their own minds.'

'Why single out religion?' said Alice. 'There's all sorts of political crap that's even worse. What about racists? They should have their children taken away from them.'

'You could say that it's abuse to bring up kids if you're different from them at all,' said Jane. 'So, my parents are always playing jazz at home, because they love it. But I hate it. Is it abuse to inflict it on me? They claim it's educational.'

'My point – and why I'm talking about it – is that I've been so indoctrinated that I can't even contemplate eating a prawn,' I said. 'But is that abuse?'

'No, that's mad,' said Damon. 'I swear they didn't even have prawns in the Bible. Anyway, what's food got to do with religion?'

I couldn't explain how it felt to grow up with a religion that involved everything you ate, the people you mixed with, even the way you did the washing-up and where you stored your plates and cutlery. They all came from a different world, even Kitty.

'Just try it,' said Alice. Her eyes challenged me. 'Break the tradition. Make your own decisions.'

I speared a fat, pink maggot and held it to my lips. I put it in my mouth for a nanosecond, then pulled the fork away, prawn intact. 'Um. I think I might be allergic. It's sort of tingling.'

Everyone burst out laughing, but Kitty rubbed my arm sympathetically. 'It's OK. I never grew up with any of that stuff, and I always kind of envied you boys who knew everything.'

'Knew everything?'

'I'd sit up in the ladies' gallery at synagogue with my grandma, three times a year, and look down, and you'd all seem so competent. Knowing when to get up and sit down, and do that bowing thing, and reading all those Hebrew words. I didn't know much at all. I never even had a bat mitzvah.'

'It's not very useful, knowing how to pray,' I said.

'Yeah, but at least you've got it.' She helped herself to a spoonful of unidentified dead animal. 'I'm just destined to be an outsider, wherever I am. You belong.'

'That's what's nice about being an expat. We're all outsiders together,' said Jane.

After we'd eaten we wandered around looking for a club, but the one that Finn knew refused to let Alice and Lucy in, as they didn't look old enough, and the one Damon suggested was too touristy, according to Finn. So we played pool for a few hours at a bar in Leidseplein, and then went back to Finn's house. He lived in Amsterdam New South, a big expat area. We walked through the Vondelpark to get there, then past the Amsterdam Hilton hotel, famous as the location for John Lennon and Yoko Ono's Bed-In, back in the sixties.

'They lay in bed naked and lectured the press about world peace,' explained Alice. 'My parents, when they were scouting Amsterdam as a place to live, had a weekend in the Bed-In suite. I mean, what a waste of money. Since Dad's dotcom got sold they've been splashing the cash like there's no tomorrow.'

'That's nice for you though,' said Lucy. 'They're not mean, are they, about your allowance and things?'

Alice sighed. 'I just ask myself, what would John Lennon say about people paying so much to sleep in a room where he was trying to say something profound about life? Why not give the money to poor people in developing countries?'

'Well, John and Yoko didn't have to have their Bed-In at the Hilton, did they? They could have Bedded-In at a B&B somewhere,' Kitty pointed out.

'Bit thoughtless, really,' said Finn. 'OK, here we are.'

He had the whole top floor of the apartment to himself – bedroom, bathroom, spare room – and his parents were out at some reception at the American Embassy in The Hague. 'They're staying overnight,' said Finn, 'so we've got the place to ourselves. Make yourselves comfortable.' He put on some music, handed out beers. 'Let's dance.'

The girls kicked off their shoes and danced. Alice with intense energy, Kitty with a floaty grace that surprised me. Lucy turned circles and waved her arms around. Jane and Finn wrapped themselves into each other and slow-danced through every song that Max and Damon put on.

Damon passed me a joint. 'Here you go,' he said. 'This is my favourite brand.'

'You some sort of connoisseur?' I took a cautious drag. I'd had weed a few times in London, but generally avoided it. I'd watched one of my best friends, Noah, develop a habit that affected his performance at school so badly that he'd screwed his GCSEs up completely, and was now retaking at some cramming college, surrounded by a load of other potheads. Just a little bit was enough for me, just enough to stop me worrying about the whole Kitty/Sophie thing, to blunt those sharp pains of love.

Kitty flopped down at my side. I offered her the joint.

'Nah, that's OK,' she said.

I'm not sure why I pushed her on it. 'Oh, go on,' I said. Maybe I was still feeling embarrassed that she'd eat prawns and I wouldn't.

'I don't do weed,' she said.

'You mean you've never even tried it?'

She fanned herself with her hand. 'That's not so unusual.'

'Don't you want to try? Just this once?'

She always seemed so in control, so mature and experienced, so cool and perfect. Kitty was a mystery to me, really, and I wondered what she'd be like if her edges were blurred by a little chemical reaction.

She pushed her hair behind her ears and looked me straight in the eye. 'I shouldn't really.'

'We all do things we shouldn't.' I remembered her friend in the Vondelpark, the one who seemed so intense. 'What about your friend, Ethan? I bet he does a lot of things he shouldn't.'

'Who cares about Ethan?' she said, but she took the joint from me and inhaled. 'Just this once,' she said.

'You like?'

She coughed a bit.

'Not much. Come and dance.'

So we danced to Dutch dubstep, and even through the fog of weed, I admired Kitty's style. I was enjoying myself.

But then I remembered an evening – *the* evening – at Sophie's flat in Greenwich. Feeling warm and happy, because we'd shared a bottle of wine. Dancing to music that was nothing like this: Sophie loved her power ballads. Kissing her properly for the first time. And more. Much more. Going so far we couldn't go back. Knowing that I was truly in love; it wasn't just some friendship, it wasn't a schoolboy crush.

My life would be so much easier if I could transfer that love to Kitty. But love isn't simple. Not for me, anyway.

Kitty lurched into me. 'Steady.' I grabbed her arm. 'You OK?'

'Theo ...' Her eyes were scared. 'I need fresh air. Theo!'

'OK,' I said. I tapped Damon on the shoulder. 'We're going,' I told him.

I supported Kitty downstairs and opened the door. It slammed shut behind us. The cool night air sobered me right away. Not Kitty, though. She couldn't stand up. She was on her hands and knees on the pavement.

'Theo ... I'm not ... Theo, help me.'

'Come on, Kitty, get up – you'll be OK.' Maybe she was having an asthma attack? 'Have you got an inhaler?'

'I can't ... Theo, help me! Help me!'

I had no idea what to do. I thumped on the front door, buzzed the bell, but no answer. They probably couldn't hear over the music. I pulled out my phone, called 999, but it disconnected. Then I remembered that wasn't the emergency number in the Netherlands.

A car pulled up, a woman got out, and spoke to me in Dutch. I gawped at her. 'English ... She's not well ...'

'Put her in my car, I'll run you to hospital,' the woman said. 'It's quicker than calling an ambulance. It's not far.'

She could have been anyone, but I trusted her and between us we picked up Kitty and put her into the car. I squeezed in next to her. Kitty leaned against me, gulping and wheezing, trying to talk but making no sense.

'It's an allergic reaction? Or she took something?'

'Just weed,' I said, 'as far as I know.'

Luckily, the roads were empty. She drew up outside the entrance to A&E. 'Here you go. Good luck!'

I half carried Kitty into the hospital. There was a nurse at a desk, and we staggered towards her. 'Help, please,' I pleaded.

'I can't breathe,' gasped Kitty. And then she fainted.

Chapter 19

Kitty

Amsterdam

Oh, the embarrassment.

The hospital was great, gave me lots of tests and called Mum. By the time she arrived, they'd pretty much worked out that it wasn't my heart and it wasn't an asthma attack (not surprising as I don't actually have asthma). I'd had a panic attack. Brought on by one tiny, tiny puff of weed.

Of course I didn't tell Mum that. I said that the room had been hot and stuffy and I thought I'd felt my heart pounding and that made me scared and worried, and I supposed that's why I panicked. I didn't say that I'd panicked because as soon as I inhaled I thought about all the reasons it was bad for me. I didn't say that I was convinced my heart was about to stop.

'You must ring that nice boy, Theo, and thank him for looking after you,' said Mum once she'd got me home. 'I paid for him to take a taxi home. He was lovely, so caring.'

'He's OK,' I said, knitting furiously.

'He's gorgeous too,' said Mum, totally inappropriately.

'Stop it!'

'You must call and tell him that you're feeling better.'

'You didn't tell him about my heart check-ups, did you?'

Mum looked surprised. 'I don't think so – I was so worried about you. But why wouldn't I?'

'I just don't want people knowing. It's so nice, not being the girl who could drop dead any minute.'

Mum blinked a few times, and I worried I'd said the wrong thing, but then she said, 'I can see that. A new image for a new city? I've noticed your lipstick and clothes.'

'It's my Amsterdam look,' I said.

'It's lovely. Just as long as Amsterdam Kitty is still the sweet, kind person she always was.'

'Yeah, yeah, that's enough.'

'I hope he'll come along to one of Paul's workshops,' she said.

Inevitably, when I'd invited Theo to get ready for our abortive clubbing mission Mum had subjected him to an interrogation about everything from his exact address in Finchley ('I grew up just around the corner') to his A level subjects and plans for the future.

'Why would he want to go to one of Paul's workshops?'

'Because he might enjoy it. He told me he likes writing and Paul's an excellent creative writing tutor. Also, you would enjoy the next one he's doing, Kitty, it's all about love stories. Why don't you ask Theo?'

'Oh, for God's sake, Mum.'

'What? Come on, Kitty, he might enjoy it. Give me his number and I'll call him and invite him myself.'

'You have no boundaries!' I protested.

'He seemed quite keen,' she insisted.

So I called Theo and reassured him that I was fine and grudg-ingly invited him to Paul's workshop. He was surprisingly enthusiastic. Two evenings later we showed up at an English-language bookshop in the Jordaan.

We got there five minutes early, but there were already twenty people gathered in an upstairs room, most of them middle-aged women. I cringed inwardly – how embarrassing that we were the youngest people there – but didn't say any-thing to Theo because that would make it worse. Instead I took a quick picture of the room, and then had the brilliant idea of making a vlog about the whole thing, so I got him to hold my phone while I filmed a very short introduction.

'If you can sit down, please?' Paul was looking at Theo and me, because most of the women were already poised over their notebooks, so we found seats in the back row and I looked for a good filming angle. I hardly noticed when someone slid into the seat on Theo's other side. But then an unmistakable voice said, 'Hey, Theo. Hey, *susje*.' I couldn't believe it. Ethan?

'What are you doing here?' I whispered across Theo.

'What's the problem? I thought I'd take an interest in what my dad does. It's a chance to keep an eye on his plans to give me a sister.'

'Two sisters,' I said, thinking of Rachel. 'Not that I think it's going to happen or anything.'

Mum was looking very pretty, I thought, in a flowery dress

and dangly green earrings. Paul had whisked her into a corner for a bit of pre-workshop feedback on her latest chapter.

'He told me you were coming. I thought you'd be pleased to see me. All this effort to make friends ... ' he sighed, totally for effect, 'and you're so hostile.' He caught Theo's eye and winked.

'I'm not hostile!' I said.

'Oh, I think you are. Don't you agree, Theo?'

Paul clapped his hands and everyone went quiet, while he introduced the workshop.

'Several of you have asked me to talk about writing love stories,' he said, 'as that's a theme that comes up in so many books, from traditional happy-ever-after fairy tales, through Mills & Boon-type romance, to more classic literary examinations of love, such as Tolstoy's *Anna Karenina* or Charlotte Bronte's *Jane Eyre*.'

A woman raised her hand. 'What about chick-lit?' she asked. 'Don't you think it's sexist the way that so many books about love and romance get dismissed as fluffy, silly, girly reads?'

'That's marketing,' said Paul. 'Let the publishers worry about that. Remember, the cover is just there for selling purposes. The story you choose to tell is your own. And for a love story to work, no matter what the cover, you have to have protagonists who are fully realised and whose love, whether it ends happily or tragically, is hard-won.'

My mum put her hand up. 'How about love at first sight?' she asked. Ethan looked at me and smirked.

Paul was in full flow. 'Even books that feature love at first sight – and there are a surprising number – generally feature couples who find their path is far from smooth. Love stories are about adversity and difficulties in the path of true love.'

One of the women started explaining the plot of her novel in enormous, boring detail. Ethan whispered across Theo, 'It's all shit, don't you think? Like every story has to be the same.'

'That's not really what he's saying,' said Theo. 'It's more, how do you get people interested in your story if it's all straightforward?'

Ethan shrugged. 'He should start by asking what the hell love is in the first place, because I'm not sure that he knows.'

'If you don't mind being quiet in the back row,' said Paul, 'we can proceed. Thank you, Ethan.' I guessed he'd caught Ethan's last words, because his smile had disappeared.

Paul talked a bit longer but my mind was wandering. Theo and I could potentially be a perfect love story, and every kiss we shared made me more certain that we were heading that way. But what about his secret affair? Was it over? Was the teacher the obstacle we had to overcome, or was I just a pathetic afterthought in their grand passionate love story, just another complication to be swept aside so that they could be together? I had to talk to Theo about it. But why hadn't he confided in me?

'So, divide into pairs and we'll do our writing exercise,' said Paul. He did a quick head count. 'Tell you what, you at the back can work as a threesome.'

Theo and Ethan both snorted out loud at this. From the look that Paul gave them, I guessed that future workshops would have a minimum age requirement.

'I'm going to come round with two bags. I want you each to take one name from either bag, and then discuss with your partner the issues facing the people you've chosen, assuming they were the protagonists in a love story. Make a list of the obstacles they would have to defeat, both external and internal – that is, the problems encountered in their interactions with others, and the way their personalities could bring them together or tear them apart.'

By the time he reached us, there were only a few names left in the bags. I pulled a name from one; Theo picked the other. We unfolded them. 'Queen Victoria,' I read. 'Heathcliff,' read Theo.

'Oh, that is ridiculous,' I said. 'But at least we're doing *Wuthering Heights* for A-level.'

'Well, they were sort of around at the same time. It could've been Katniss and ... Batman,' said Theo.

'I think they'd be great together,' said Ethan, 'but then Batman goes with anyone, doesn't he? He's just so adaptable.'

'We're meant to be making a list,' I said. 'Number one, she is royal and he isn't.'

'Number two,' said Theo, 'he's a headcase and she isn't.'

'We don't know that,' said Ethan. 'She might have had a wild side. She might have been wilder than him. You don't know a thing about anyone until you sleep with them.'

'That is such rubbish,' I said.

'Oh, really? You've got the experience to tell?'

'I think you can know someone perfectly well just from talking to them. And I know you're just winding me up on purpose, because that's what you do.'

'But why do I do it, Doctor Kitty?'

'You just like the attention,' I said.

'Queen Victoria might have been attracted to Heathcliff – to the way he's so different from anyone else she knows,' said Theo. 'If you grow up with everyone being nice to you, and protecting you, then someone who says what he thinks and is all pure emotion … that could be amazing.'

'He shouldn't be in a relationship with anyone,' I pointed out, 'until he's got his anger issues worked out. Alice and I were talking about it the other day. She reckons he's a classic abuser.'

'Is Heathcliff the one from that film?' said Ethan. 'Out on the moors, shouting, *Cathy, Cathy?*'

'That's the one.'

'Well, I agree with Theo then. She'd totally go for him. She's in a world of fakes and prettiness, and he's a big lump of raw sex.'

'He hangs little dogs,' I protested. 'I can't even understand what Cathy sees in him, let alone Queen Victoria. I mean, Prince Albert never did anything like that and she was totally devoted to him.'

'But that's what Paul was saying: that's the difference between love and a love story,' said Theo. 'Love can be all neat and proper and suitable and sort of boring. That's Victoria and Albert. But a love *story* needs to have conflict. That's Victoria and Heathcliff. Or Beauty and the Beast.'

'You're good at this,' said Ethan.

'Theo's writing a book,' I told him.

'Is it a love story?'

'Sort of,' said Theo, 'but it's about a world where the conflict has been stripped away. You literally can't tell what the conflict or the obstacles might be, not until ages after you've met the person you think you love.'

'Sounds interesting.'

'It is, but it's … I don't know … I'm having problems with my plot.'

'We all lose the plot sometimes,' I said, trying to be funny. But they didn't laugh. Instead, Ethan said, 'I'll read it for you, if you want,' and Theo said, 'Maybe. I haven't shown it to many people,' and I wished I'd thought of offering to read it because Theo looked really pleased. I'd spent too long trying to avoid reading Mum's attempts, it never even occurred to me. Oh well.

Paul told us to switch over to write dialogue. 'Perhaps a first meeting,' Paul said. 'We'll hear some afterwards.'

Instead of writing dialogue, I got Ethan to film Theo and me improvising Queen Victoria's first meeting with Heathcliff (Queen Victoria: 'Pray, who are you, rough, dark stranger?' Heathcliff: 'Shut tha mouth!'). Then we had some juice and biscuits, and listened to one woman's version of an encounter between Spider-Man and Jane Eyre, and another's attempt at a first date between Mr Darcy and Phoebe from *Friends*.

'That was great!' said Mum when everyone else had left.

'It put me off my stride having Ethan sitting there,' said Paul. 'You've never shown the slightest interest in creative writing before. And you three were being very noisy when everyone was trying to write.'

Ethan's smile was his most pleased-with-himself.

'I enjoyed it,' he said.

Chapter 20

Kitty

Amsterdam

Mum and I had started having breakfast out on the balcony, making the most of the warm weather. 'It'll be strange when it starts getting colder,' she said. 'It feels as though we're on holiday at the moment, doesn't it? When it's cold and grey and raining all the time, then we'll find out what it's really like, this living-abroad adventure.'

'Not before tomorrow!' I said. 'We're having a picnic.'

'Oh, that's nice, Kitty. Actually, Paul and I were thinking of doing a day trip. He wants to show me Delft ... it's very pretty, apparently ... I was going to ask if you wanted to come with us.'

'Look, Mum, it's OK. You don't have to include me in your dates with Paul. It's fine to go by yourself. Unless you need a chaperone?'

She looked flustered. 'No – it's not a date – it's just that Paul has been so kind, and wants to show us more of the Nether-lands—'

'I bet he does.'

'Oh shush.'

'You know, if you want, I can always stay over at my friend Lucy's house. If you want privacy.'

She paused just a second too long.

'Because it can't be easy at Paul's house, can it? Not with Ethan lurking around being weird.'

'He's such a worry to Paul,' she said. 'So moody all the time. And he never confides in him at all. Paul doesn't know his friends or what he's up to, or anything. He turns eighteen in March. Paul doesn't know what will happen then, if Ethan will even want him to stay on.'

'So Ethan gets to make the decision? He can kick out his dad?'

'It's his mother's house and she's left Paul responsible for everything. Obviously Paul can still go on living in the house, but it's going to be difficult if Ethan's hostile. Paul says it feels like this is his last chance to make a connection.'

My dad's last chance to make a connection came when we sat on that sofa and watched that football match. I didn't feel all that sympathetic. 'Well, he needn't worry about Ethan tomorrow because he'll be having a picnic with me and my friends,' I said.

'Really, Ethan's joining you? That's lovely!' said Mum. 'I was so pleased when he turned up for the workshop. And Theo is such a nice boy.'

'Yeah, right, don't put me off, OK Mum?'

*

Sunday was another golden, glorious morning, and I was up early, chopping fruit and making sandwiches. I adored picnics in theory. As done by YouTubers and in magazines they were casual and glamorous at the same time. As done by my family, they were always plagued by melted chocolate, angry wasps and no one remembering wet wipes. This time was going to be different. A picnic fit for Instagram.

We met at the entrance to the Amsterdamse Bos. Twelve or so of us from the tutorial college, plus Ethan and some friends of his, a scrawny guy with spiky hair called Bart, and a girl with hair so short that she looked like a boy – a very beautiful boy, though, with huge blue eyes and one of those naturally pouty mouths. 'This is Rosa,' said Ethan, and I wondered if she was his girlfriend or Bart was his boyfriend, or both or neither, or some sort of weird combination of the above. I never knew with Ethan.

I made the introductions; Ethan nodded at Theo. We waited ten minutes to see if anyone else was going to turn up. Then Ethan led the way on the cycle paths that threaded through the forest. It was all so flat and easy, and everyone looked so cool on their retro bikes. I felt completely happy, watching Theo cycle in front of me.

'Here,' said Ethan, eventually. 'Nice enough for you?' A meadow by a lake, with no one around. Butterflies fluttered around the wild flowers and there was no sign of any wasps. It was perfect. 'Wow, Ethan,' I said. 'Thanks! This is gorgeous.'

We spread blankets on the ground and unpacked the food. Sandwiches and fruit, some cheese, crisps, a whole pack of coleslaw, beer, cranberry juice. Bart had a ginger cake in his backpack, and Rosa offered a pack of *krentenbollen*, which turned out to be currant buns. Even Ethan had a contribution, a bottle of white wine, which he put in the lake to cool down.

'That was nice of you,' I told him. I was sitting on a gingham tablecloth. He was lying in the grass next to me.

'It's my dad's.'

'Oh, well, that was nice of him.'

He grinned at me. 'He doesn't know. I think he bought it for tonight. They've gone to Delft.'

'I know. Mum was looking forward to it. Because it's so historical.'

'Very pretty place. Very romantic. Do you think it's going to happen?'

'I don't have a clue.'

'I sort of hope it does.'

'Er, why?'

'Because you're not staying for good, are you? She'll take him back to London. Then I don't have to bother with him.'

'We're not planning to go back soon,' I told him. 'We didn't make a decision on how long we're going to be in Amsterdam. Mum loves her new job and I'm happy as well, when people are being nice to me.'

'I'm always nice to you, Kitty, *susje*.'

Rosa came and sat with us, putting a proprietorial hand on Ethan's shoulder. 'You OK, *schaatje*?'

'*Ja, hoor*,' he answered, moving his shoulder away. I smiled to myself. It wasn't so much that I wanted Ethan for myself, but I didn't think he was the sort of person to let a girl label him as taken.

Finn, Jane, Alice and some others had started a game of football. The others were eating, talking, sleeping or just lying in the grass, checking their phones. The sweet aroma of weed mingled with the fresh forest air. Ethan scrambled to his feet and stalked off, without a word.

'He can't stand the smell,' said Rosa.

For a moment I thought she meant me: that I smelled. In a land of people who spoke their mind, I'd stumbled across the rudest girl in Amsterdam.

'I beg your pardon?'

She giggled. 'That is a very formal phrase, isn't it? Like something out of a history book. I love English. Real English English, you know, not American. I read all the Harry Potters, looking for British ways of saying things. *I beg your pardon.* That's awesome.'

'Oh. Um. Ethan?'

'He hates the smell of weed. It reminds him of his mom.'

'Oh ... OK.' This didn't fit with the picture of Ethan's mother that I'd built up, a kind of superwoman who flew into disaster areas and made everyone's lives better.

'She's away too much,' said Rosa. 'When she comes back she's here to relax, forgot all the bad stuff she's seen. She's stoned a lot. He says he doesn't care, but I've known Ethan a long time, and he never tells the truth.'

'He gives me a hard time for not telling the truth about my feelings!'

'Yeah, he attacks others so no one can attack him. He's all kinds of screwed up. I pity anyone who falls in love with him.'

'Maybe you should look for him?' I suggested, but she shook her head and said, no, it was better to leave Ethan alone when he was in a mood, and she was going to have a little sleep, 'because I was up all night with some smoking-hot guy from the university.'

That suited me fine. I shuffled backwards a bit so I was right next to Theo.

'Hey,' I said. 'How's it going?'

Theo gave me a sleepy smile. 'OK. And you?'

'Yeah. Good.'

'Where's your friend Ethan gone?'

'Just a walk, I think.' I lowered my voice. 'Rosa was saying he doesn't like the smell of pot. It reminds him of his mum.'

'What's wrong with his mum?'

'She's gone off and left him. Work. She does disaster relief sort of stuff. She's out in Afghanistan.'

'Yeah, I bet he misses her.' Theo grimaced and I remembered about his mum.

'How is your mum doing?'

'OK, I think. They don't really tell me. I mean they say not to worry, but it's all so vague.'

'Won't you go home for New Year?' I was feeling a bit odd about being away from London at this time of year. I wasn't sure if it would make me miss Grandma more, or help me to stop feeling sad about her.

'Nope,' said Theo. 'I'm not even welcome back for the holidays.'

I saw a chance. 'Why aren't you welcome? I mean, I thought it was just because your mum needed peace and quiet. Is there another reason?'

He looked at me. Just for a moment, I thought he'd tell me everything.

Then he put his arm round me, drew me in, so we were lying body to body, close enough to feel each other's heartbeats. He ran his finger down my face, over my bare shoulder. 'It's complicated,' he said. And then he kissed me for the second time.

Chapter 21

Theo

Amsterdam

I was living for the day. It was the only way, I'd decided, to stop hurting over Sophie abandoning me, to stop worrying about Mum. Every time I phoned home, I asked if the useless doctors had worked out what was wrong with her, and every time there were no answers. I was exhausted from feeling hurt and anxious.

But that day was one of those comfortably hot, sunny autumn days that feel all the sweeter because you know winter's about to come. I was with a group of friends, and just months before I'd felt that I'd never have friends again. The food was good; I'd had some wine. My head was muzzy, even though I was avoiding weed because I felt bad about the other day. Everything was in soft focus; Kitty looked completely gorgeous in a yellow top and denim shorts.

I didn't feel anxious. I wasn't obsessing about Sophie. I was completely focused on the moment, and what a good moment it was. I hardly noticed that Kitty had asked me something that – thinking back – suggested that she actually knew about Sophie. I just thought how nice she was, how easy it was to spend time with her. And this was the right thing to do on this particular day and her lips were sweet, and her body was soft against mine, and one kiss wasn't enough at all.

We must've kissed for about five minutes, and then I happened to look up and see Ethan in the distance, walking back around the lake towards us. So I nudged Kitty and she spotted him too, and she sat up, just leaving her hand brushing against my arm. Which was enough to keep that nicely excited feeling going. I rolled over on to my front and buried my head in my arms and tried to quiet the voice in my head that went, *Oh, shit, what am I doing?* over and over again.

Then the football game ended and Ethan and Kitty went to get ice creams from a nearby kiosk. By the time they got back I'd entangled myself in a conversation with Damon and Max about *Call of Duty*. I ate my ice cream, tongue probing the chocolate edges, and I decided that a YOLO relationship with Kitty was totally worth going for. Everyone would be happy, including my parents. Including me. Sophie was never going to get in touch. I needed to start moving on.

We left the forest about four p.m., when it started to get chilly. It was clear to me that Kitty was hanging around, waiting for the two of us to be left alone.

I could have just gone home, and I did have homework to do.

But I said to her, 'Shall we get something to eat?' And she said, 'You can come back to my flat, if you want. Mum won't be back until late, and I could make us some pasta.'

So we went to hers, and she opened a bottle of wine and put on some weird country and western music; she made pasta with lemon, and then we somehow ended up in her room, on her bed, kissing again. My head was muddled with wine and lust, and I was totally living for the day. But I knew I ought to explain to her about Sophie. What had happened, and why I thought it was over.

'Mmm ... Kitty ...' I said, between kisses.

'Theo?'

'I'm not sure ... I'm a bit complicated ... it's ... we have to talk ...'

'Oh, that's OK,' she said. 'You only live once, hey?'

'Yeah, but ...'

'Seize the moment,' she said.

'Yeah, it's just ...'

'Shall we just do this and see what happens?'

Do what exactly? I thought, lazily, hazily but then we heard her mum's key in the door and we sprang apart.

I managed five minutes or so of polite conversation with Kitty's mum and Ethan's dad about the workshop and the picnic.

'What are you doing for New Year?' asked Kitty's mum. 'We're going to something called the gay shul. It's a progressive community; Paul assures me it's for everyone, not just gay people. You could come with us, if you'd like?'

'We're having lunch at my house afterwards,' said Paul. 'You'd be very welcome.'

I explained about Chalex. 'They're expecting me to go to shul with them. They're modern Orthodox, so it's all very traditional. And then there's a big family lunch at Chani's parents' house. I think she said they were expecting twenty-four people.' I couldn't imagine going to some Dutch progressive service. The only time I'd ever been to a Liberal synagogue in London, for a distant cousin's barmy, it felt like going to a church, what with sitting together as a family, loads of English in the service and an actual organ and choir.

Paul wrote his address down on a scrap of paper. 'Just in case it's all too much with a big Dutch family. It's very near here – right by the Amstel River.'

'Thanks,' I said, stuffing the paper in my pocket. 'That's really nice of you.'

It took fifteen minutes to cycle home. 'Hey, Theo,' said Chani when I came in. 'Did you have a good time? I'll make some tea. By the way, did you see there's a letter for you? It's been sitting there since yesterday.'

One of my mum's letters, I thought, stuffing it in my pocket so I could open it in private upstairs. Every week she wrote to me, strangely stilted letters that didn't mention Sophie, didn't mention her illness, but did tell me about my father and my brothers and grandparents, about how much she loved me, about how they would come and visit soon. But the letters never gave a date.

But it wasn't from Mum. The envelope was brown, the address

written in block capitals. The postmark was central London. It looked like something official, some forgotten exam results, maybe, or a letter from the school demanding a textbook back.

So my expectations were low when I tore it open. It took a moment to comprehend that the letter inside was handwritten, that I recognised that writing, that this was the moment I'd prayed for, hoped for, longed for.

Sophie had written to me.

Dear Theo,

I know I shouldn't be writing this. But I am coming to Amsterdam on October 4. Can you meet me? Don't worry about trying to reply to this, just know that I will be at the Hotel American in Leidseplein at 11 a.m. I'll see you in the foyer – if you want to see me. But I understand if you don't. If that's the case, then take my love and best wishes and build a great future for yourself.

Sophie

I must have read it twenty times. I would see her again. I could touch her, talk to her. Our love was real. It had to be; she was coming all the way here to see me.

My heart was racing. Maybe we could run away together, get on a train, cross Europe. Maybe she'd come and stay here. Maybe … maybe …

Obviously she'd been getting all my letters. I'd email her the next day to tell her that I would be at the hotel, of course I would, and she wasn't to move until I got there, just in case something happened, like my bike got a puncture.

Tuesday mornings weren't great for me: I had English and French. But I'd just have to miss class. It wasn't as though I was learning much anyway.

And then it hit me. This wasn't just any Tuesday. It was Rosh Hashanah, Jewish New Year, a day when I had no choice at all about where I was going to be.

Chapter 22

Theo

Amsterdam

I didn't go to college the next day. My hangover felt as though my forehead had been surgically tightened around my throbbing brain.

I couldn't get past what had happened last night. I'd been about to be totally unfaithful to Sophie – while hiding the truth from Kitty – and then I'd got her letter. A Sign. Or was it? Did I really love Sophie, given how happy I'd felt with Kitty? Was I just totally shallow and unworthy of either of them? I couldn't bear thinking about it, so I made myself useful by peeling potatoes and apples for Chani, cycling to the supermarket to buy juice and milk, laying the table for dinner. We weren't seeing her family that evening, but she'd invited three other couples, and two of them had toddlers.

My parents rang mid-afternoon to wish me a happy and healthy New Year. I'd been giving Dad the full-on sulk treatment, but I was too frazzled to keep it up. So I wished him a good Yom Tov, and had the intense irritation of him telling me that clearly Alex and Chani were proving to be a good influence, and he was very happy I was staying there. Huh. And then he said, 'Pray for your mother, this year, won't you?' and I got an enormous lump in my throat and growled, 'You don't have to tell me what to do.'

Then Mum came on the phone and was all, 'Hello, darling, how are you? Oh, I miss you so much; I'm desperate to see you, I can't believe it's been six weeks.' I breathed in and out and said, 'Well, it was your idea to send me here,' and, 'I thought you were going to come and see me,' and, 'you know, I'm missing a lot of people as well. Like all my friends.' I went on like this until she started crying and Dad grabbed back the phone and said, 'If you can't even be nice to your mother, maybe it's better that you don't speak to her.'

'Oh, great, Dad, that's a nice thought for the New Year.' I was feeling horrible already, and now I felt even worse, because I'd made Mum cry.

'Let me talk to him,' I heard, and the next thing my brother Jonny was on the line.

'Hey, Theo.'

'I didn't even know you were home,' I said. That's all I could manage. Inside, I was going, Jonny's *home*? He's in London and I don't get to see him? They must actually *hate* me.

'Look, Theo, why don't you come and stay with me in Israel? I'm sure you'd enjoy it more than Amsterdam, and get more out of it.'

The last thing I needed was Yonatan shipping me out to Jerusalem and taking an interest in my spiritual well-being.

'Nah, thanks, Jonny. If Mum and Dad can't bear the idea of having me live with them then I'm doing just fine here.'

'Any time you change your mind, I'm here for you, kid. It'll be OK.'

I couldn't actually get angry with Jonny. He'd been my hero for too long. But I felt sick with anger against my parents, and so jealous of Simon, boring, normal, stupid Simon, who got to stay at home and get on with his life and see Jonny, that I could hardly force out the words.

'Yeah, thanks. You know, Amsterdam is OK. It's just worrying about Mum, really. I'm sorry I made her cry. I was just feeling upset.'

'I know,' he said. 'I understand it's difficult. And it is harder when you're away. Theo, if there's anything I've done or said to hurt or upset you in the last year then I apologise.'

I was kind of touched, until I remembered that this is what people say the week of New Year, running up to Yom Kippur, the Day of Atonement itself, so it wasn't an especially personal thing for me.

'That's OK, Jonny. I apologise too.'

Then my dad took the phone and apologised for upsetting me over the last year as well, which he'd never have thought of if Jonny hadn't done it first.

'Dad, I can't believe you! You upset me, like, five minutes ago! You won't even let me come home for Rosh Hashanah!'

'You're meant to accept my apology. And it wouldn't hurt to ask for our forgiveness.'

'Get lost!' I said, and slammed down the phone.

Chani didn't even pretend that she hadn't been listening.

'It is a shame to fight with your father just before Yom Tov,' she said. 'I know it must be so difficult for you, not to be with them.'

'Actually it's not so hard. I can live my own life here, without them breathing down my neck the whole time.'

Chani was putting bowls of potato salad into a box. 'I'm going to take these round to my mother's,' she said.

'Chani, I might duck out of all the family meals. It might feel a bit emotional, you know, not being with my folks.'

'They'll all be so disappointed! They're looking forward to meeting you.'

'I got an invitation from some English people in Amsterdam. I might have lunch with them ... sorry ...'

Chani looked disappointed, but was too nice to point out that I was being rude. 'You see how you feel,' she said. 'You know we love having you here, Theo. You are very welcome.'

She went off in her car and I went to lie on my bed and think about Sophie ... about seeing Sophie the next day ... about what she might say ... what might happen.

My phone buzzed. A text from Kitty.

Hey, are you OK? Missing you today x

Am OK. Just helping cousins get ready for RH

Oh yeah. See you maybe?

Maybe. Not sure. Family pressure.

No worries. Mum + Paul a bit full on.

Will Ethan be there?

Dunno. Maybe.

Don't worry if I don't make it.

I won't. Happy New Year

And you.

I don't know why I asked about Ethan. I found him a bit dis-concerting. He seemed a bit intense, underneath all that banter. Plus he'd asked to read my book, so I'd emailed him a copy and now I was desperate to hear what he thought of it, but he hadn't mentioned it at the picnic, in fact he'd hardly said a word to anyone. What if he hated it? What if he thought it was rubbish?

I wished I could be a character in my own book. Growing up free from other people's expectations and opinions. Sending an avatar out into the world, so that no one knew what you really looked like, even what sex you were. Interacting without telling anyone your history, your gender, your worldview. Finding out about that person and then meeting them. Letting the important stuff matter.

Who would I be with in that world? Sophie or Kitty?

I didn't know. Maybe seeing Sophie again would help me find an answer.

Chapter 23

Theo

Amsterdam

In the end, my escape was easy.

The shofar was blown, with all the usual huffing and puffing, squeaks and spittle, and finally that eerie crying wail that is meant to sound like a mother crying for a dead child. I don't know who had the idea of using a ram's horn as a musical instrument, but the sound it makes takes me back in time to the days when I used to sit with my Papa Sam in shul, and he'd give me sweets and lift me up to stand on the seat so I could see where the noise was coming from.

As the ark was shut and everyone sat down, I moved towards the door (I was standing at the back; the place was full and I'd given up my seat for an old man), slipped out into the lobby, nodded at the people standing there, wished them a happy New Year – *'Chag sameach … L'shana tova'* – and stepped past the security guard and on to the street. Most people were still arriving. It's a long haul, the New Year service, and they did things slowly in Amsterdam. I didn't think the service would finish until one-thirty at the earliest, all depending on how much their rabbi liked the sound of his own voice.

No one could blame me for missing a sermon that was all in Dutch, could they? I'd already mentioned to Alex that I had a bit of a headache. They'd assume that I'd gone for a walk to clear my head, and then gone to my English-speaking friends for lunch. It would be fine.

I felt bad about deceiving them, but had no choice. I had to see Sophie, and if we ended up running off together then everyone would have more to be upset about than a missed lunch.

I was still carrying my prayer shawl, which was annoying. I removed my kippa from my head and stuck it in my pocket. I folded up the tallis and tucked it under my arm. I needed a bag; maybe I could pick one up on the way.

A tram arrived a minute after I reached the stop, and ten minutes later I was getting off at Leidseplein. You don't see many people in suits in this bit of Amsterdam, and I felt like a freak. Freakishly nervous, too, my armpits were sweating and I just hoped my face wasn't as moist and pink as I suspected.

The American Hotel was right in front of me. I hesitated then pushed open the door. Would she even be there? I was ten minutes late.

I have no idea what the lobby of the American Hotel looks like; all I saw was Sophie. Her heart-shaped face, her toffee-coloured hair. The cautious smile on her lips. She was wearing some kind of raincoat – leafy green – and it suited her; it made her blue eyes swimming-pool-bright. Despite the smile, there were frown lines creasing her forehead, and when I started towards her, she didn't rush to kiss me, so I faltered, uncertain.

'Sophie! I can't believe you're here!'

She was looking me up and down. 'You're so smart in your suit. Are you working, or ... ?'

'No, just a family thing,' I said, wishing I'd had time to acquire a bag to hide the tallis. I'd folded it as small as possible, but it wouldn't fit in my pocket.

'Let's go and sit in the bar and talk,' she said.

'Can I kiss you?' I asked, and was immediately struck by how pathetic I sounded, how awkward and teenaged and wrong. Someone of Sophie's age wouldn't need to ask, they'd just know. And when she took my arm and just lightly brushed her lips against my cheek, I knew what was coming.

My heart didn't sink. It actually exploded. I felt stabbing pains inside my chest, and my mouth went dry and I had to keep myself standing up because my knees were trembling. But simultaneously I believed that I could turn things around. I'd listened to too many love songs to give up easily, and the surge of hope was like a shot of adrenalin. *Our love is too strong to die*, I thought, and I truly believed it.

The bar was full of red furniture, so much so that it hurt my eyes – red furniture and black-and-white pictures of celebrities. Sophie and I found a quiet corner and sat down, and I tried to think of something to say that wasn't, *You're dumping me, aren't you?*

'You're dumping me, aren't you? That's why you're here.'

Sophie did that thing that she does, twiddling a strand of hair around her finger. I'd watched her do that in class. I'd watched her do that in cafés, at the cinema, in her flat. Was this the last time?

'Theo, I really don't want to hurt you. And I'm not dumping you. That's not ... people my age don't do that.'

Who was she kidding? When I'd first met her, she was heartbroken because her boyfriend had gone off with her best friend.

'You don't love me any more?' I was determined to take this like a man. So I made my voice as flat and unconcerned as possible.

She sighed. 'This has turned into a big mess. I should never have let it happen; I've tried to let you down gently.'

'So, what are you saying?'

'It was wrong, Theo. I failed to maintain proper professional boundaries. It was my fault.'

'You didn't *let* it happen, it just happened. We found each other.' A hideous note of pleading had crept into my voice.

A waiter swooped on us, asking in English what we wanted. Sophie ordered a black coffee. I asked for still water, '*Een Spa blauw, alstublieft.*'

Sophie was impressed, as I'd hoped she would be. 'You've learned Dutch already?'

'Not really. Just enough for cafés.'

'I couldn't believe it when I heard they'd sent you away. Taken you out of school. It seemed so harsh. I'm not working there any more, I resigned. I don't know if anyone told you.'

'Yeah, I heard.'

'I resigned. I'm doing supply teaching in ... somewhere else. I thought I'd better tell you. You need to forget about me, Theo. Get on with your life.'

'I'll be eighteen in just over a year. Then I can do what I want, my parents don't get a say. I can come and be with you.'

Sophie looked down at her hands.

'Theo, I had to make a choice. I'm six years older than you. I should never have crossed that boundary and become your friend.'

'We're more than friends!'

My voice must have been getting louder, because people were looking. Sophie's voice dropped to a whisper. She looked less adult and sure of herself; she was stirring her coffee, even though she hadn't put any sugar in it.

'This is so bad for you, Theo.'

'You didn't hurt me!'

'It's so obviously wrong!'

I was exasperated. 'It never felt wrong. You know that. You're just saying this because of rules and laws that have nothing to do with us.'

'You're really young, Theo. You'll find someone else.'

'You're as bad as my parents!'

'Don't get angry, Theo, please ...'

'Don't patronise me, then.'

'You're not making this easy.'

'Why did you think it'd be easy?'

Somehow we'd finished our drinks. Sophie signalled to the waiter and signed for them. I strained to see which room she was staying in, but wasn't quick enough to read the figures upside down. And anyway, what would I do with that knowledge?

'Come for a walk with me,' I said. 'You don't know Amsterdam, do you? It's a nice day. We can go to the park.'

'There's no point, Theo.'

'I don't know why you bothered to come and see me. You could've put all this in your letter. Or are you just here anyway? You thought you'd spare an hour of your mini-break to split up with the deluded schoolboy who's got a crush on you?'

'I'll come for a walk. But only a short one. And I'm not changing my mind.'

'OK. Right. Good.'

The only problem with going for a walk was that I had to retrieve the tallis, which I'd stashed under my red swivel chair. I was hyper-aware of it, stuck under my arm, and knew that Sophie must have noticed it but hadn't said anything. It felt worse because Sophie didn't mention it. I was embarrassed about being Jewish, which is not a great feeling.

The entrance to the park was just by the hotel, but involved crossing two bike lanes, two tram lanes and a road, so I had a completely legitimate reason to take her hand and guide her, especially as she kept looking the wrong way. And she didn't take her hand away when we got into the park and started strolling along the path.

Once we got past the rollerbladers, the Film Museum and the café with a children's playground attached, the park was quiet and calm. Joggers passed us, and cyclists, but we were able to talk. Sophie seemed more relaxed. And she still hadn't let go of my hand. Side by side, I was a head taller than her. It equalled us out a bit.

'How are the A-levels going? You are still doing A-levels, aren't you? I'd hate to think I'd screwed that up for you.'

'They're going OK,' I said.

'You did so well in your GCSEs! You've got a wonderful future ahead of you, Theo.'

I'd been waiting for her to acknowledge my results. Top grades in eleven subjects. I only slipped up in Spanish, and as I got an A for that, no one was that bothered. (Simon, by the way, only got two As. And he downright failed Geography. Just saying.)

'I did OK,' I said, trying not to show her how pleased I was that she'd read my email telling her about my results.

'I always wanted to be a teacher,' said Sophie. 'I told you that, didn't I? I never even thought of doing anything else. I worked for it all my life, and I think I'm good at it. I don't know what I'd do if I couldn't teach. I should never have risked it all – I was crazy – but you, with results like that, you could do anything. I can't stand in the way of your future, Theo. I'd never forgive myself.'

I couldn't believe she'd somehow used my results against me when it was clear that all she cared about was her teaching career. But I couldn't get angry. I was too desperate to stop her throwing everything away.

'If we wait until I'm eighteen ... I'll have left home ... No one says a teacher can't go out with a university student—'

'Theo, I have to be the responsible one now. God knows, I should have been much more responsible before.'

'But it's done! And once I'm eighteen, none of it will matter!'

'Your family would never … and anyway, Theo, I can't … I don't want to hurt you, I really don't …'

The Sophie of my memories was all smiles and curves, honey curls and soft skin. Of course, I remembered that one night in her flat in Greenwich. It played again and again in my head, like a video clip. Was I too clumsy, too eager, too inept? I hadn't thought so, but maybe she had just been kind.

Sophie was different now. She was all points and angles, her mouth stretched tight in a long, grim line. She'd lost weight, I suppose, and grown the highlights out of her hair. I'd never felt the age gap before, but suddenly it felt like twenty years.

She didn't love me. I knew it. A part of me died, right there and then in the park.

Chapter 24

Theo

Amsterdam

I knew it was over but I kept on arguing. What else could I do?

'We just need to spend time together.'

'I was lonely, Theo, and my self-esteem was low, and I took advantage of you. I'm so, so sorry.'

'Don't be.'

'I've been talking to a counsellor, and I can see now that your admiration, your devotion ... it was what I needed because I was so low about Charlie leaving me for Evie. But I'm over that now. I can see that he wasn't worth having and that she wasn't a real friend.'

I ground my teeth in frustration. 'I told you all that! You don't need a counsellor!'

'She's helping me to get my head together, Theo, honestly. You're only sixteen. You've got your whole life ahead of you.'

'Look, we can just write, stay in touch. We don't even need to see each other. Not until I'm eighteen.'

'Theo, I'm strong enough now to end this friendship. I

know it's better for you, and I'm pretty sure it's better for me.'

'Let me come back to the hotel—'

'I'm checking out. My plane is at five p.m. This is it, Theo, I'm sorry.'

'Sophie—' I said, but she reached down and picked up my tallis, which I'd dropped on the ground. I hadn't even realised.

'What's this?' she said.

'Oh, it's nothing.' I tucked it under my arm again.

'It's one of those things, isn't it? Those Jewish things . . .'

A little voice in my head – my mother's voice – was asking me if I really thought I could be happy with someone who didn't know that it was Rosh Hashanah. Who didn't recognise a tallis for what it was. In normal circumstances I'd have dismissed that voice, by pointing out that it's easy to learn things like that. I'd have said that cultural differences aren't really relevant in a multicultural world, that these things are superficial and easily learned.

But right then, I just wished she knew what day it was and what a prayer shawl was called in my world.

We were nearly back at the rollerbladers, and she gestured towards the Leidseplein entrance and said, 'I go this way, don't I? Let me do this, Theo, my darling. I'm sorry if I screwed you up, but you'll survive. I promise.'

Then she strode off, fast, before I could catch her hand, a small figure in her green coat, weaving through the crowds.

I wondered whether to follow her, but I was tired and hungry and discouraged and sad. Just sad. She wasn't going to change her mind.

A tiny, tiny part of my brain – not my heart – was relieved to see her go, which made me even sadder.

I turned round, and almost cannoned into a rollerblader. 'Oi!' he said. And then, 'Theo? Are you all right?'

'Ethan?'

'Are you stalking me? That's the second time you've nearly killed me in this park,' he said.

'It's a coincidence,' I said, stupidly, and he said, 'Hey, is there something the matter? You look sort of ill.'

'I'm ... no ...'

'Did something happen? You want to talk?'

I seemed to have lost the ability to form coherent sentences. 'I ... no ...'

Ethan gestured towards a bike rack and I followed him, watching in silence as he changed into trainers and slung the skates into his saddlebags. 'Come on. You want to get a drink? OK, no, bad idea ... You got your bike here? No ... OK, jump on the back of mine. It's fine. Hold onto my shirt, I know you Brits aren't used to balancing.'

I felt a bit stupid grabbing onto his T shirt, but as soon as he gathered speed on the bike I was grateful because there is no way I could have balanced by myself. The trees were blurry, my mind was curiously numb and blank and I was as near to tears as I'd ever been. I tried to feel angry, but I couldn't do it. I couldn't hate Sophie. I still loved her too much.

'Hey,' said Ethan, 'we're here. Well done, Kitty was screaming all the way when I gave her a ride.'

He locked his bike to the rack and opened a door. Nothing

but stairs, all the way to the top. By the time we got to the attic I was out of breath.

Ethan pointed towards a chair. 'You don't have to talk to me, if you don't want. Just sit here –' He moved a pile of old magazines off a sagging armchair, 'and I'll do my stuff and if you want anything, just tell me.' He gestured towards a mini-fridge. 'Coke? Sprite? Beer? I'm going to get a shower. Take what you want and I'll be back soon.'

I sat and breathed, and sipped my Coke, and tried to adjust to a world with no Sophie in it. No hope of Sophie. No future with Sophie. And I thought about how happy my family would be when they heard the news, and that made me want to vomit.

And then I remembered how only a day ago I'd thought I was fine with Sophie fading out of my life, and my head throbbed with the unfairness of it all.

Ethan left me alone for about half an hour, and when he came back he'd changed his clothes and his long hair was wet, which made him look younger somehow. He grinned at me – 'Feeling better? Take your time, everything's OK' – and sat at his laptop, headphones on. Somehow his presence was comforting – calming, even – and I liked this orderly room of his, far, far away from London and home.

'Kitty's here,' he said after a while, taking off the headphones. 'She's downstairs, having lunch with Paul and her mom, and I think a few of Paul's new friends. You want me to go and get her? Or you could go down and join them if you want.'

I dimly remembered being invited to that lunch. But I

couldn't face Kitty. I couldn't even remember properly what she looked like.

'No, thanks,' I said.

'I can leave you on your own if you want?'

'No, thanks,' I said again, and my stupid eyes filled up with tears, and my mouth started trembling and I had to do a lot of blinking to make myself OK again.

Ethan didn't say anything, but he found a clean towel and tossed it over to me. 'You might want that. It's a bit dusty up here.'

'Thanks,' I said, and he tactfully looked away as I mopped my eyes.

'They went to the synagogue for New Year. You've been too, yeah?'

I slowly worked out that Paul was taking Kitty and her mum to this weird gay shul, and Paul was Ethan's dad, so therefore … 'You're not … ?'

'My dad is. Doesn't count, hey?'

'Not usually,' I said. Only Liberal Jews included the children of Jewish fathers and non-Jewish mothers as Jewish. Liberal Jews and Hitler.

Ethan seemed to be able to read my mind. 'It would've counted in the war, huh? I've thought about that a bit. Trust me to get the negatives and nothing else.'

'Oh, we all get plenty of negatives.'

'The reason you're so … is it to do with that woman I saw you with?'

'You did?'

'Earlier. You walked right past me. It's a small place, Amsterdam. If you've got secrets, don't go to the Vondelpark.'

'It's like living in a village.'

'Yeah, that's what they say. You always meet someone you know in the Vondelpark. I mean, look at you and me. This is the second time we've bumped into each other.'

We seemed to have moved off the subject of Sophie, which was good, and I didn't want to go back there. So I said, 'I like your pictures.'

'I make art because I'm useless with words. I can't spell in two languages. I kind of gave up with school after a bit. I can't cope with classrooms. All that information being thrown at me – it stops me thinking.'

'School doesn't suit everyone.' I'd heard this at home about Simon enough times.

'Yeah, well, it doesn't suit me.' His attention switched to his laptop. 'Crap. I have to take this Skype call. Hey, Melinda.'

I should have left, I suppose. I didn't. I sat and listened to his end of the conversation. He'd put his headphones on, so I couldn't hear this Melinda, whoever she was.

'Yeah. Yeah, that's bad. He's OK. Yes, I am. Totally. No, I'm not. Leave it out, OK? I'm not interested. No, it's not because it's Africa. No, I'm not going to South America. No. No. No, I'm not saying that. Just saying, that's all. No, I'm not more important than anything. Why would I think that? Just leave it, OK? Christmas? Really? Oh, OK. You know I don't care either way, OK? So don't feel guilty. Everything's cool. Yeah, looking good. I might paint the kitchen next. Yes, OK. Love you too.'

He switched off the laptop, removed the headphones and threw them down on the desk. 'Parents, huh? Always bossing you around.' His smile was forced.

'Yeah, tell me about it.'

'She even tries to run my life when she's in Afghanistan.'

'What's she doing there?'

'She's a saint. She's the person who makes everything better.' His laugh was clearly fake. I didn't know what to say.

'She prefers looking after lots of people with real needs than staying home with me. Being my mom is just boring. Too many First-World problems.'

'She can't find you boring,' I said.

He looked at me. 'That's a nice thing to say.'

I was embarrassed. 'I mean, she's your mum. She must love you.'

'Oh, well, of course. To know me is to love me. Anyway, never mind that. You were going to tell me about the woman in the park.'

'I was?'

'Definitely.'

'Sophie ...' I swallowed. 'She was my teacher. But we were friends, and then we fell in love. We did, really. But then my parents found out, and it was all spoiled.'

'How was it spoiled? Look, you don't have to tell me anything, but if you think it would help to talk, go ahead.'

Ethan was curiously easy to talk to. He didn't say anything, just sat and drew, while I babbled on and on, and told him the story of Sophie and me.

Chapter 25

Theo

London

It started with Sophie – Miss Thwaites, I called her then – reading my novel. She printed it out, I remember. I'd never seen it as a big, heavy lump of paper, and it made my heart beat quicker because it felt so much more real than words on a screen. A week later she asked me to come to the English room at lunchtime.

She'd put it in a carrier bag, and she'd written stuff on it in blue biro, and it was exciting to know that she'd bothered to read it, let alone have thoughts about it, have ideas about my characters, who felt as real to me as anyone at school, and considerably more real than nebs like Jack Pollard or Jonah Shapiro, who thought he ought to be better than me at tennis but wasn't.

I think her plan was to have a quick chat about the book, give me encouragement, show enthusiasm, and then hand me back the brick of printed paper so I could work through her scrawls on my own. But that day there was a meeting going on in the English room. It was awkward. So she said, 'Look, are you free after school? I could meet you for a coffee, tell you what I think. There's so much good stuff there!'

'Oh,' I said, taken aback. I wasn't displeased, but all the coffee places I knew would be packed out with kids after school, which could be awkward.

'Great,' she said. 'Wait for me in the car park after last period and we'll find somewhere quiet. I've got a red Ford Ka.'

Scrunching into her tiny car felt weird enough, but seeing that it wasn't exactly tidy – empty plastic bottles on the floor, a crumpled crisp packet on the back seat – was extraordinarily intimate, somehow. It was as though she was saying, 'I'm not a teacher really. I'm no different from you. I'm a normal human being.'

A normal female human being.

In my avatar world, I wouldn't have known that she had hair like golden syrup. I wouldn't have seen that her dress was only just covering her knee. I wouldn't have noticed the slightly northern accent, the pink lip-gloss, the lingering smell of peaches and lemon.

But I would have fallen for her without all that. Because at the coffee place she found – in Crouch End, nowhere near my school – she told me everything she liked about my book. How much she loved the characters. How intrigued she was by the ideas. And how she had books I should read, films I should see ...

'There's a film by Spike Jonze; it was nominated for an Oscar.

It's about a man who falls in love with his computer operating system. It's very good.'

'I've never seen it,' I said.

'I can lend it to you.'

That's how it started. I saw one film, read a book. We had coffee again to discuss them. I wrote more chapters, she read them, she loved them. 'Call me Sophie,' she said, one Thursday after school. 'It feels silly, all this miss business, when we're not even in school.'

'Oh, all right, miss ... er, Sophie.'

'I've been enjoying these coffees,' she said. 'This is my first real job out of college, you know. It's strange, having to be so formal with everyone all the time.'

I gulped down my coffee. 'You mean with the pupils?'

'And the teachers.' She wrinkled her nose. 'They're all a bit stuck-up, you know. Between you and me.'

I loved that. My crush had reached monumental proportions by that stage.

'Yeah, I wouldn't argue with that.'

'London's quite a lonely place,' she said. 'Everyone's so busy with their own lives, and it's tiring getting around town. I suppose I ought to be meeting people, doing things after school, but I find I'm just going back to my own flat, marking books, planning lessons, and, well ... that's it.'

'That's it?'

'I'd like to be going to the theatre ... the cinema ...'

'Maybe I could come with you sometime?'

So that was it. She was lonely. I was besotted. Once we

started meeting up at the weekends, queuing for half-price theatre tickets, things took a subtle shift. I wasn't wearing school uniform, for a start. I dared to risk more personal questions.

'Have you ever been in love?' I asked her one cold, wet night, walking along the Thames after seeing *Citizen Kane* ('A classic film! Everyone should see it!') at the BFI. My parents thought I was at a party. I'd been at a lot of fake parties recently.

'I thought I was in love,' she said, 'but I was a fool.'

'What do you mean?'

'I moved down to London because of a guy. Charlie. Very confident, very full of himself. He's a trainee barrister.'

Her voice was bitter and I knew I'd asked the wrong thing, and I wasn't sure what to say to make things right. So I put my arm round her. I hoped she'd find it comforting.

That was the moment when she could have stopped it.

But she carried on talking.

'He promised me everything. He said we'd be together, for ever. But it was all nonsense. He was sleeping with my best friend.'

'Oh God, Sophie, that's terrible.'

She was crying. 'I haven't told anyone about it. Not even my family. You're the first person ... the only person ... I don't know why I'm telling you this ...'

Any minute now she was going to realise how inappropriate this was. Any minute now she'd remember that we weren't really friends, that I was just a kid from her GCSE class. Not even a sixth-former. I'd be back in school uniform on Monday, one of the masses, putting up my hand to get her attention in class.

But now I had her attention.

I wrapped both arms around her, held her close. 'He didn't deserve you,' I told her. 'He didn't know what he had.'

'I shouldn't ...' she started, but she didn't finish the sentence and I didn't let go.

That's when I kissed her. I knew and she knew that we were crossing a line. But it felt too good to stop.

Chapter 26

Theo

Amsterdam

'So you fell in love,' said Ethan. 'I hope it was worth the pain you're feeling now.'

'It was brilliant, until people started interfering.'

'People are stupid,' he said. 'But you don't need to tie yourself to anyone right now. You don't need to be in a couple for ever and ever. Play the field a bit.'

'You don't understand.'

He shrugged. 'No, probably not. I can't imagine trusting anyone enough to fall in love.'

'You've never fallen in love?'

'Nope,' he said. 'I never found the right person. And maybe I didn't want to.'

I felt completely embarrassed. Obviously, Ethan was like the guys at school who saw girls as a chance for a get-with. Falling in love was old-fashioned and unmanly and weird.

'Yeah, well, it just sort of happened,' I said.

'It's beautiful. Don't be ashamed.'

I must have raised an eyebrow or something, because he added, 'I'm not making fun of you. It is beautiful, to fall in love. You must have a lot of love within you, to be able to do that. Not like me, so *voorzichtig* … careful? With caution?'

'Oh. Um. Thanks.'

That's what your book is about really, isn't it? I only started reading it, so I don't know what happens, but I get that it's about cutting out all the shit that's around relationships, just being with the right person.'

'That's what I want it to be about. It's just hard to make the story what I want it to be.' That was partly because I didn't even know what I wanted it to be, but also ever since I'd fallen in love with Sophie I'd been trying to make the book about her and me. But the characters in my book weren't anything like us.

'I try and live my life like the people in your book. In your world. Free and unprejudiced. But I only make trouble for myself. Maybe I need an avatar, hey?'

He seemed to be deadly serious. His grey eyes stared right into mine.

'I sometimes think it would be easier,' I said. 'But it'd be boring, wouldn't it? And you'd miss out on so much.'

'There's a danger of just falling into a computer and never getting out,' he agreed. 'That's why I like stuff like skating and cooking and riding, when I get a chance. And working on the house. I like the smell of the paint, and picking the colours, and making everything look different.'

I looked at my watch. Soon, Alex would be going back to the synagogue for the evening prayers.

'I'd better go. Thanks, Ethan.'

'You don't have to thank me. I was happy to help out.'

You rescued me was what I wanted to say, but I couldn't think of a way of putting it that didn't sound stupid. 'You really helped,' was what I came up with.

'No problem,' he said. His eyes went back to his computer. I got up to go.

'We could have a drink sometime if you wanted,' he said, casually, eyes still glued to the screen.

'OK. That'd be good.'

Ethan got up from his computer, came over to me. 'Theo, how much do you know about me?' he asked. 'What did Kitty tell you?'

'Um, nothing much,' I said, searching my memory. 'Just that her mum's friendly with your dad. And you've grown up here.'

'Oh, right. OK. Look, you take care of yourself.'

He gave me a half-hug, patted me on the back and opened the door. 'If you go out this way they won't see you.'

I'd actually forgotten that Kitty was in the same building.

'Thanks again,' I said.

'You feeling better now?'

I was feeling better. In the space of an afternoon, Sophie seemed to have been wiped from my mind. I was tired and headachy and sort of sad, but it wasn't half as bad as it had been. I felt reasonably confident that my heart hadn't actually been broken.

In fact, I felt better than I had for ages. Talking to Ethan had done something strange to me. Whenever I thought of Sophie, I saw his face instead.

Chapter 27

Kitty

Amsterdam

Two hours of lunch was enough for me. Of course, Theo didn't turn up, fair enough really. I knew he had to go to his cousin's family for a big, traditional meal.

But Ethan could have eaten with us, surely? I was certain he was just sitting up there in his attic room, laughing at the thought of spending time with us. Mocking the whole idea of Mum and Paul actually falling in love and wanting to be together, creating some new sort of family. A few times, as I ate cold chicken and potato salad and made polite conversation with Paul about my English A-level, I thought about marching upstairs to Ethan's room and dragging him downstairs.

In fact, if it had been possible to march up the stupid spiral staircase, that's probably what I would have done. But I was wearing a skirt (Mum insisted that, for shul, I wore something Grandma would have approved of, even though Grandma died two years ago) and ankle boots. I was not dressed for gymnastically challenging architecture. And I was not in the mood for Ethan's barbed banter.

He was right, though. There was no question about it. Mum and Paul were falling – had fallen – in love. You could see it in the way their eyes locked onto each other's. You could see it in their identical smiles. They held hands as they walked along. They listened to what the other person had to say as though every word was sparkling with originality and wisdom. They talked about the future as 'we' and 'us' without the slightest hesitation.

I'd never really thought of actually having a stepfather, or of our all-female family turning into something different. I imagined living with Paul all the time, of him being there for every meal, of having to include Ethan and Paul in family stuff, birthdays, Chanukah …

I didn't like it at all. My head hurt.

So, after we'd drunk lemon tea and eaten honey cake, I said I was going for a walk to clear my head, and I'd rather go on my own, thank you very much.

I wandered up and down the waterside for a bit, and then slowly made my way back to Paul's house. I wasn't sure why I was feeling so melancholy. Maybe it was remembering Rosh Hashanah in the past, when Grandma was still alive, and Rachel hadn't gone off to university. I'd liked the gay shul's atmosphere, the way everyone felt part of the service, which was part English, part Dutch and part Hebrew, with lots of singing and not so much muttering; but it was very different from sitting with Grandma looking down on the men praying below and giving points to the ladies' hats around us.

Maybe there were just too many new and different things this year. Or perhaps it was seeing Mum and Paul together and wishing that Theo and I could be like that. I wished I could be sure that his kisses – those gorgeous kisses – actually meant something. He couldn't still be in love with this teacher, could he? Did she even exist? Had Rachel just got everything wrong?

I was fed up with the YOLO approach. I wanted to live for more than a day at a time. And I wanted Theo to feel the same way.

When I saw someone tall and dark walking towards me, I didn't realise at first that it was him. First, I thought, *Who's that good-looking guy in a suit?* Then it registered that he'd come all this way to see me.

I almost skipped down the road to meet him. 'Wow! You made it! But you're so late!'

He blinked at me, adorably confused.

'I'm late – yeah, I suppose I am. I couldn't get away before. And actually, I need to get back.'

'But you'll come in? There's really nice honey cake. Ethan baked it, apparently.'

'Ethan?'

'Yeah, you remember. He came on our picnic. This is his house.'

'No ... I mean, I do remember. I just didn't ... put it all together ...'

I looked at him. He seemed really out of it.

'Are you OK?'

He answered me with a kiss. A real, passionate, five-minute kiss, a New Year kiss, sweet as honey, refreshing as an apple, a kiss full of promise and potential. He held on to me as though he never wanted to let go. And I wondered if Rosh Hashanah had helped him decide anything about his future. Who he really loved, and who to leave behind.

'I'm OK,' he said at last. 'More than OK. I'm actually more OK than I've been for months.'

I took his hand. 'That's so good to hear.'

'This morning ... in shul ... I felt so homesick. I missed my family, but, more than that, I missed everything about Yom Tov at home. Even the boring stuff. But now, I don't know, I'm just pleased to be here. Now. Here, in Amsterdam. I feel like I can change things and everything will be all right.'

'You can leave the past behind,' I prompted him.

He gazed into my eyes. I felt a bit wobbly. Those eyelashes!

'You are amazing, Kitty. Sometimes I feel like you can actually read my mind.'

Argh! Could I ever explain that I knew about the rumours? Obviously not right at that minute.

'Thanks,' I said. 'You're not so bad yourself.'

He looked at his watch. I noticed that he was carrying his prayer shawl with him, which meant he'd either come from the synagogue or was going back again.

'I'd better go,' he said. 'They'll be expecting me for supper.'

'But you only just got here!'

He looked uncomfortable. 'I know. It took longer than I'd thought ... '

I got it. He must have had lunch at his cousin's and then walked all the way here, just to see me for a few minutes.

'Don't worry, I understand,' I said, and I kissed him again. Then I stood and watched as he walked away down the river's edge.

I'd kidded myself before that I was just having fun, just playing around. Now I knew. I was in love.

Chapter 28

Theo

Amsterdam

My dad called me on my mobile on Friday afternoon. I was braced for bad news about Mum, or at least a telling-off about dodging lunch with Chani's family.

'You're coming home.'

'You *what*?'

'I've bought you a ticket. You're coming back on Sunday.'

'What are you talking about? I thought I was in exile.'

'Your mother's very upset that you weren't with us for New Year. It wasn't the same without you. She wants you home for Yom Kippur.'

'Whoa,' I said, running a hand through my hair. 'What do you mean? Am I coming back for good?'

'We'll talk,' said my dad, as if he were negotiating the delivery of a consignment of top-end dining tables. 'We'll see how things stand. Maybe, if you make us some promises.'

'Dad, actually I'm quite happy here. It's going very well. So forget your promises, I'm staying in Amsterdam.'

'I'm emailing Alex your ticket,' said Dad, gruff as a bear, 'and I expect to see you at Luton Airport on Sunday. We'll have a few days together before Yom Kippur.'

'But I've got stuff ... stuff here ...' I said, feebly, and Dad said, 'We're all missing you, Theo. This isn't easy for us either.'

'Well, sending me away was your idea.' I couldn't resist pointing it out.

Silence. Then, 'None of this was my idea, Theo.'

Chalex, it turned out, knew all about this plan. They seemed relieved. I'd behaved perfectly on the second day of Rosh Hashanah, but that hadn't stopped Chani's mother from making some pointed remarks about having missed me the day before, and how she hoped I'd had a good time with my English friends.

Maybe Alex had called my dad and demanded that I go home for Yom Kippur? Because what other family keeps their son away for the festival – New Year – and recalls him for the fast day, when we don't eat or drink for twenty-five hours, and it's all very solemn and serious and about repentance and atonement?

My family were mad, I concluded. Kitty agreed, although more tactfully. 'Your mum must have underestimated how much she'd miss you,' she suggested, as we strolled along the Singel, hand in hand, on the way to our afternoon English class. 'Anyway, lucky you, getting a weekend in London. You'll be able to see all your friends.'

'Yeah, well, I'd rather be here with you.' I squeezed her hand, and she beamed at me.

Kitty was the perfect girlfriend. Seriously. It was like she was auditioning for a role. She agreed with almost everything I said, but she was up for banter too. She was fun and funny and we had a lot in common. She was warm and sympathetic and she never gave the impression that she took us very seriously. Perfect.

In every way possible, Kitty was my best option. And I liked her, I really did. I fancied her too. Living for the day had never seemed so attractive. There was absolutely no need to think about Sophie or anyone else, because somehow I had found the right person. It was spookily meant-to-be.

Surely if I just kept doing what we were doing, I'd fall in love with her? Wasn't that how love worked? I didn't want to do anything to upset the potential that was Kitty. My life was complicated enough without messing it up any more.

She called me when I was at the airport. 'Have fun – if that's possible over Yom Kippur. Will you bring me back some salt and vinegar crisps?'

'Yeah, sure, and a tin of rice pudding if you want.' We had a running joke about the things we missed the most. Occasionally we went to a funny little shop called the British General Stores to buy British snacks, but mostly we just moaned about it.

'I hope it won't be too difficult, you know, spending all that time with your family.'

'Well, at least I'll see my mates,' I said, and then it hit me properly. I was going to have to go to shul. See – and be seen by – hundreds of people who had been gossiping about me. I'd be stared at, whispered about, questioned by Jack Pollard and his crowd. I wasn't sure I could do this at all.

On the plane I listened to music, read *Wuthering Heights* (Kitty was spot-on: no one in their right mind would want a relationship with Heathcliff) and tried to stop worrying about going home. Instead I remembered plane rides with Mum, when I was just a tiny kid. 'Get ready for the bump,' she'd tell me, when the plane was coming in to land. That was typical Mum, trying to protect me from stuff that hadn't even happened yet.

I sleepwalked through passport control, found my case, headed for the European Union exit.

I was looking for Dad, the giant, angry patriarch who wanted to control my life. And then I saw him, and I was shocked.

My dad wasn't a giant at all. He was just a pale, old man with a lined forehead, and he looked as lost and scared as I felt.

Chapter 29

Kitty

Amsterdam

The day after Theo left for London, I got up and headed for the bathroom. Mum was in there – although she usually showers earlier than I do. I banged on the door and said, 'Are you going to be much longer?' and a man's voice boomed, 'Five minutes!'

I got the shock of my life.

Later on, when I came out of my bedroom, Paul and Mum were sitting in the living room drinking coffee, looking a little bit embarrassed but very happy at the same time.

'Err … hi,' I said. 'I'm going to college.'

'Won't you have some orange juice, darling?' said Mum, totally styling it out. 'It's freshly squeezed.'

'Um. No. I'll be late for Dutch.' It was a lie, but a useful one.

College felt a bit flat without Theo, so I was actually quite pleased when Ethan rang me just as my last class ended.

'Hey, Kitty. Are you free?'

I wasn't sure. I was still annoyed that he hadn't bothered to show up for lunch on Rosh Hashanah. On the other hand, I was missing Theo, and it'd be good to take my mind off him for an evening. And maybe Ethan and I should talk about Mum and Paul now it was clear that they were a couple.

'Yeah, I suppose so.'

'I'm at a friend's ... Can you make it to the Prinsengracht?'

Fifteen minutes later, I was standing on a bridge wondering where Ethan was. I was sure I'd got the right spot.

'Hey!'

Where was his voice coming from? I turned round – no sign of him. Oh, hang on. Ethan was calling me from a boat just under the bridge.

'Hey, you.'

'Want to come aboard?'

It was a small boat and he was with his friends from the picnic, Rosa and Bart.

'Um, yeah, I suppose.' I walked down to the canal's edge. It was quite a jump to get down to the boat, and I was a bit dubious.

They laughed at me.

'Come on, Kitty, you can do it.'

'Um, maybe not,' I said.

Ethan stood up, offered me his hand. 'It's OK. Just take one step ... OK ... there you go.'

I gasped with relief and grabbed his arm, tighter than I meant to. We jostled each other, as I dropped into the boat, and I felt his arm steady me. 'Careful,' he said. 'There you go.' Grateful not to have tipped the boat over into the canal, I sat down next to him. 'Whose boat is it?' I asked.

'It's my brother's,' said Bart. 'He lets me borrow it sometimes. Ethan thought you'd like a tour.'

'Oh, well, I don't want you to go to any trouble ...' This was great! What a fabulous idea!

'Relax,' said Ethan. 'Enjoy.'

So I sat back and watched the canal houses, and the bridges, the boats where people had made their homes and the little container gardens on steps and balconies. The others talked in Dutch and I let their words float by, not even trying to understand.

After a bit, Ethan moved to sit next to me. 'You like this?'

He meant the boat ride, I assumed. 'I love it. I love Amsterdam.'

He seemed genuinely pleased.

'You reckon you'll stay?'

'Maybe. If my Dutch gets good enough.'

'*Ik kan Nederlands spreken om je.*'

'Well, I know you can. Show-off.'

'To you! I can speak Nederlands to you! I'll teach you.'

'When I've learned a bit more. Otherwise we'll have a very boring conversation. *Ik heet Kitty. Ik komt aus London.*'

'Is your mum learning?'

'She's thinking about it.'

'So's Paul. I think they might take lessons together.'

'Yup,' I said. 'They're doing a lot of things together.'

'I know,' he said. 'What do you think of that?'

I tried not to let my real feelings show on my face. 'Well, if they're happy, that's got to be good.'

'You don't want my dad moving in? I don't blame you.'

I was torn. On the one hand, Ethan was being incredibly mean about his own father, who actually seemed to be a very nice person. On the other, he was completely accurately describing my feelings.

'I really like Paul a lot. It's just ... I don't think they should move too fast. In fact, I don't think anyone should move too fast. You have to take these things slowly.'

Ethan laughed at me. 'All those books in your bedroom, all those love stories. Is that what happens in them? People take things slow?'

'Er, not always. But there's a difference between books and real life.'

'One day you will meet someone and fall in love and you won't want to take things slow at all, I promise you. You'll think about nothing except when you can see them and how you can be with them, and you won't worry about anything.'

'Oh yeah, you're the big expert, are you?' I said, and then realised that actually, yes, Ethan probably did know a lot more about these things than I did.

'If only,' he said. 'But you are right. It is much more sensible to take everything slow and make sure that you are with the right person, and never take any risks.'

'Well, I'm not saying that exactly.'

'I've never had a sister before,' he said. 'Paul's last wife, she had two sons.'

'Oh yeah ... I think I remember that.'

'You know them? Oliver and Sammy?'

'I heard about them.' When Paul's marriage was breaking down, he felt terrible about those boys. They were a bit younger than me, and he'd been in their life for four or five years and was gutted to leave them. 'It's so unfair,' I remember Mum telling me. 'Stepfathers have no rights at all.'

'I miss them.'

I hoped he wasn't blaming Mum for Paul's marriage breaking down. She'd insisted to Rachel and me that she had nothing to do with it, she'd never get involved with a married man, she was only a shoulder to cry on. But now, seeing them together, I wondered how Paul's wife had felt about their friendship.

'Paul said I could keep in touch with them, but it's difficult.'

'That's why you need to be on social media!' I said. 'I bet they're on Facebook.'

'Yeah, yeah, Facebook whatever. You'd better be careful or you'll end up sitting at a computer all day, living your life online. Like Theo's book.'

'What about Theo's book?'

'That's what it's about.'

'It's about social media?' I felt a bit guilty that Ethan had read it and I hadn't.

'Sort of. It's sci fi.'

'I ought to read it. Maybe I'll ask Theo if I can.'

'So, you and Theo ... what's going on?'

'He's in London,' I said.

'That's not what I meant.'

'Now you're acting like my big brother,' I protested.

'No, just your friend.'

I hadn't encountered this Ethan before. What had happened to the banter? He seemed dead serious.

'We're kind of seeing each other,' I said. 'But, you know, nothing serious.' No way was I going to tell Ethan how much I liked Theo. He'd probably try and mess things up by kissing me, just to be mischievous.

'You're not in love?'

'You're so nosy!'

'Just asking.'

'We're friends,' I told him. 'It's nothing major.' *Yet*, I added, silently.

'He's a guy with some secrets, I think.' He ruffled my hair. 'No good for you. You want to find a nice Dutch boy. Someone straightforward like Bart, there. He'd be good for you.'

Bart and Rosa were deep in conversation, so luckily didn't hear this. Bart was tall but scrawny, with pimples and painfully short hair. Not my type at all, although obviously I'd never judge someone purely on their looks. But anyway, I was not looking for anyone else.

'I'm in no hurry to fall in love,' I lied. 'I'm just having a good time with Theo.'

'Are they in love, do you think? Paul and Jacqui?'

'She likes him . . .' I said, reluctant to say anything specific.

'He likes her, but that means nothing.'

'Nothing?'

'Well, look at his track record. Bad at commitment. Two wives already. I wouldn't trust him if I were her.'

'She's very independent. She's been on her own for ten years.'

'I think he likes her a lot. But he's a closed book, you know, he's always the same on the surface. He keeps his feelings to himself. I don't know him very well.'

I'd been looking at the passing houses, but now I turned to Ethan. 'You sound like you care. I thought you didn't need anyone.'

He smiled. 'You found me out.'

I felt quite smug. 'My mum's very sensible,' I told him. 'She won't get involved if it's not right. And your dad does seem to be a very nice person. Maybe it just hasn't worked out for him before?'

'Maybe. So, you and Theo, it's definitely nothing serious?'

Oh blimey, what was all this? Did Ethan have a crush on me? How was that going to work out? I had to admit that much as I loved Theo, I still felt a prickle of excitement at the prospect of getting closer to Ethan.

'Nothing serious,' I said.

'That's good.'

'That's good?'

'Well, it leaves you free to explore other opportunities.' He was teasing again and I could feel myself blushing.

'I don't want to get too involved with anyone,' I said.

'Oh, surely you could make an exception for someone special,' he drawled, raising an eyebrow.

'No way!' I splashed him, and he splashed me back, Bart and Rosa joined in, and it was all jokes. I took a load of pictures. My Instagram likes were going to go through the roof.

But later on, when we'd left the boat tied up and were walking down the Prinsengracht again, I grabbed Ethan's arm.

'If you think there's a problem with Paul, you've got to tell me, OK? I don't want my mum getting hurt.'

'Sure thing,' he said. 'And I can easily arrange you a date with Bart. Just think it over. I want you to be happy, *susje*.'

'Oh, behave!' I laughed. And somehow the idea of having a new sort of family, with a stepdad and a stepbrother, didn't seem so horrible after all.

Chapter 30

Theo

London

A few days back in London and Amsterdam felt like a dream. I was back in my old bedroom, getting mildly irritated by Simon, eating British food and watching British television (most of it American, but none of it available on Chalex's rubbish TV).

I felt as though I'd gone back in time, because Jonny was there. Jonny who never teased me or wound me up or made me feel small. My main ambition as a kid was to be like Jonny. It was a shock when he swapped our world – Finchley, university, friends and family – for Jerusalem and studying Torah and praying a lot. My role model disappeared, and I wasn't sure what he'd found missing from the path that I was all set to follow.

He came into my bedroom that first evening home and collapsed onto a beanbag.

'So, kiddo, how's it going?'

'You know how it's going. I've been sent away to Amsterdam.'

Jonny's face was completely different now that he was all beard. But his kind brown eyes hadn't changed.

'You can come and stay with me if you want. One of my flat-mates is going back to Argentina soon. I'm sure you could move in.'

I was touched, but horrified at the idea of living with a load of people even more religious than Chalex. Also, although Israel was great as a holiday destination, there was something about the culture that always made me feel incredibly British. Maybe it was the way that no one knew how to queue. And then there was Kitty, and Ethan and all the other friends I'd made.

'It's OK. I'm sort of settled now. I don't like it that they sent me away, but actually I'm quite happy.'

'Really?'

'Yeah, honestly. But thanks for the offer.'

'We should talk more,' he said. 'I feel like I've let you down. All this going on with Mum as well.'

'Yonny?'

Simon was at the door. I glared at him, but he ignored me.

'Yonny, Mum wants you.'

Jonny unfolded himself from the beanbag. He and Simon exchanged glances as Jonny left the room, but I couldn't work out what they meant. I felt excluded: the baby, the little brother. It was a familiar feeling, though, so I didn't let it bother me.

I turned on my phone, and Amsterdam became real again. Texts from Kitty, Alice, Lucy and Ethan.

How's your mum? That was Kitty. *Missing you. Give my love to the North Circular.* Alice sent me updates on her protest plans. Lucy invited me to a party she was organising. And Ethan texted asking if I fancied a drink sometime.

I'm in London, I replied. *Let's do it when I get back.*

I found myself thinking about Ethan a lot, which was strange because I hardly knew him. I found myself wanting to talk to him. I dreamed about the journey we'd taken through Amsterdam, how I'd held on to his shirt as the bike bumped over tram tracks. It worried me, the way I thought about him. It felt a bit … well … gay. I didn't have anything against gay people, obviously, but I certainly wasn't one of them. I'd never liked boys that way. It was probably just that Ethan had been there for me when I needed a friend.

I was even thinking about him as I walked to synagogue with my dad and my brothers. Wondering if Ethan minded being excluded from being Jewish, even though it was half his genetic inheritance. He probably didn't care much, because let's face it, being Jewish is a bit of a pain, even if you're lucky enough to live in one of those rare times when people aren't actually trying to kill you for it. It's especially a pain when you're part of a big, close-knit, gossipy community.

'You all right?' asked Simon, and I glowered at him.

'None of this is my fault,' he protested.

'Look, it's not you that everyone's staring at, OK? We haven't even got there yet.'

'They're staring at Jonny and his big, bushy beard,' said Simon. 'Aren't they, Yonatan?'

Jonny put his hand on my shoulder. 'Don't worry, Theo. It'll be OK. If they gossip, it's their problem. They ought to know better.'

'There's nothing to gossip about,' I said.

'Just concentrate on Mum. She's what matters right now.'

All Mum wanted to do was talk about my life in Amsterdam. She lay on the sofa, her clothes hanging loose on her stick-like limbs. She insisted that she was feeling better, but she seemed to have no energy. Why couldn't the stupid doctors work out what was wrong with her?

She wanted me to describe the house in great detail, tell her all about Chani's family, the neighbourhood, the college, my friends. In the end, I cracked and told her about Kitty. Big mistake.

'A Jewish girl, from north London, in Amsterdam, at the same time as you? That's extraordinary, Theo.' She was so happy, and I immediately felt guilty for not loving Kitty enough.

'Not really.'

'And you've made friends? Is she a nice girl?'

'I suppose so. I mean, yes. I like her.'

'You like her, that's wonderful.'

'We're sixteen, Mum, we're not about to get engaged.'

'No, but ... Well, it's nice when you have something in common, isn't it?'

'It's just a coincidence.'

'What's her name?'

I told her.

'Where does she live in London? Why is she in Amsterdam? Where did she go to school?'

Honestly, being Jewish in London is a bit like being a member of the upper classes in the nineteenth century. You just have to say your name is Collins and you come from Finchley and some old man will go, 'Oh, yes, the furniture importers. I knew your grandfather when he was still called Solly Collinsky and he was selling handkerchiefs in Petticoat Lane.'

Anyway, Mum was pleased that I'd made friends with Kitty, and that was a good thing, I suppose, although it didn't really help with the trauma of arriving at shul and seeing loads of people I knew.

'Here we are,' said Dad. 'Theo, I'm expecting you to stay with me. No running off with your friends.'

'There won't be a seat for me.'

'There will,' he said. 'I had a word with Melvin Goldfine. He does the seat allocation. He knows who's here, who's away, who's gone to his daughter's in Tel Aviv ... '

'Oh, right.'

'I'm proud to have all my boys with me. You've got nothing to be ashamed of, Theo.'

I was saved from answering this by a massive slap on my back. 'Theo! Mate! We thought you'd died!'

Jake. Noah. Jacob. Zachary. I'd known these guys forever. Jake and I were in the same class at every school we went to, I knew the others from football, shul, camp, Israel. I felt suddenly ashamed that I hadn't tried to contact them to explain what was going on. What did our lifelong friendship mean, if I could let it drop so easily?

'I'll see you inside,' said Dad, looking at his watch. 'Ten minutes, OK?'

The guys looked embarrassed. 'He's let you out on day release?' said Jake. 'Why haven't you been in touch? Jeez, Theo, we were worried about you.'

'You can tell us the whole story,' said Noah. 'We're not going to tell anyone.'

'That little shrimp, Jack Pollard, he started the rumour, didn't he? We saw to him.' Jacob liked to position himself as a tough guy, although I knew that with him being a soft, middle-class, north London Jewish boy, 'seeing to' Jack meant a few vague threats and possibly a Chinese burn.

'But was it true? You got off with a teacher?' Zachary had always been pretty tactless, and, judging by the way the others frowned at him, he'd broken an agreement not to interrogate me about Sophie.

I shrugged. 'Look, stuff happened. My parents shipped me off to my cousins' in Amsterdam. I'm OK. I kind of went off social contact for a bit.'

'But you're back now? Are you coming back to school? She's left ... Miss Thwaites ...' Jake looked away, embarrassed. He'd know exactly what was being said about Sophie and me at school. I only had to ask.

Maybe that's why I hadn't been in touch.

'Nah,' I said. 'I'm taking A-levels in Amsterdam at a tutorial college. It's pretty cool out there.'

'I bet ... drugs ... girls ...' Jacob loved to think of himself as a hard-living rebel. We knew he was all talk and no trousers.

'Yeah, I've got my own personal brothel ...' I winked at him. Unfortunately the rabbi was walking past at that point, and may have overheard. He frowned in our direction.

'I'd better go inside,' I said, aware that people were looking at us.

'There's a youth service upstairs,' said Jake. 'I'm meant to be leading it. You want to come?'

'My dad's expecting me to sit with him,' I said. 'Maybe I can escape from him a bit later.'

Jacob, Noah and Zachary had all disappeared – possibly to join their dads or friends. Jake touched my arm. 'How's your mum doing? I'm sorry she's been so ill.'

'She's OK. It'd help if they found out what was wrong with her.'

Jake looked confused. 'I thought – maybe I got it wrong, but I thought she had ... never mind ...'

I went all cold inside. 'What? She had what?'

Jake blinked, which is what he does when he's put on the spot.

'I thought someone said she had something. I can't remember who or what.'

'I think I'd know, wouldn't I? If my own mother ... She's seen loads of doctors. No one knows what's wrong. She says she's getting better though. She says she's going to come and see me in Amsterdam.'

Jake smiled. 'That's good anyway. I'd better go and run this service. Take care, mate. Maybe we can come and see you in Amsterdam too. Are you going to go back on Facebook?'

'Yeah, but if you get a friend request from me, don't tell my dad or anyone who might tell him, OK?'

'Got it. See you.'

The service was well underway in the main hall. I located Dad, and Jonny handed me an open prayer book. We hadn't even got as far as the end of the morning service – although that didn't mean much anyway, because on Yom Kippur the prayers go on and on, with no break for lunch. Morning service. Reading of the Law. Memorial Service. Additional Service. Afternoon Service. And on and on and on until the Concluding Service.

I couldn't focus at all. Hebrew prayers whirred around me, a buzz, a rattle. I watched Jonny instead, the concentration on his face. The way he knew every single word. How did he fall in love with this religious way of life? What if it turned out to be just a phase?

Time for the rabbi's sermon. *We are all connected*, he said; *we ask for forgiveness for all of our sins. The individual is important, the community more so. It is more than the sum of all of its parts. Together we are strong. Alone, we are vulnerable.*

I hung my head, sure he was talking about me. I'd been sent away from the community. It felt like a punishment, although I could also see that it was liberating. I remembered Alex telling me about the philosopher Spinoza, excommunicated by the Jewish community of Amsterdam for heresy. I couldn't even compare myself with him though. He was shunned for his beliefs. I'd been sent away for falling in love.

He moved on. And now I was sure he was talking about me.

'*Lashen hora,*' he said, 'is the downside of a close community. Bad talk, gossip. So easy to do harm, so hard to take back. As we contemplate our actions of the last year and plan to do better from now on, it is easy to overlook *lashen hora*. But with all the new technology, new means of spreading information, how much easier is it for us to pass on stories about others that might do irreparable harm. Let me remind you of the words of the Chofetz Chaim ...'

I couldn't listen. How could he do this to me? I knew he was trying to do a good thing, but still. My face felt hot and clammy, and my shirt collar too tight. I stared at my trainers and thought about Amsterdam. Not Kitty or Ethan or Sophie. Just the way the houses reflected in the water, and the feeling of absolute freedom that I got cycling through the Vondelpark. And eventually he stopped talking and the memorial prayer started. Normally I'd have left the room because both my parents are alive. But this time me and my brothers stayed put, almost as though my mum had already died.

More praying. Silent praying, standing up. Praying out loud, sitting down. Singing. Chanting. Silence again.

A massive long list of sins we had committed. *We*, the book says, not *I*. All of us, guilty of everything.

The sin we have sinned by being stiff-necked. The sin we have sinned by omission. Lying. Disrespecting parents.

And I filled up with resentment that this list was being

lumped in along with murder and theft and whatever, that I had
to face all these things that I might have done every year, and
feel bad about them. I felt faint and dizzy, too hot, too thirsty.
I've always fasted well, never had a problem with it. But this
year, well, this year it meant something. Sin and judgement,
punishment and illness were part of my life.

I glanced over at my dad. He was reading the list of sins with
great concentration, eyes nearly closed, shockelling backwards
and forwards. A tear escaped from one eye and trickled down
his face. My dad was crying. Jonny, next to him, was lost in
prayer, his fist thumping his chest. Simon had his arm gently
round Dad's shoulder. He wasn't looking at his book at all.

I looked up at the ladies' gallery, a sea of hats and head-
scarves. Some girls that I recognised; Tamara Cohen smiling at
me. Mum's friends: Jake's mum, Jacob's mum. But my mother
wasn't there, for the first time that I could remember. She was
resting at home.

I took a deep breath. I seized the book. I ignored my dry
mouth, my rumbling stomach, the headache crackling behind
my eyes.

I started at the beginning of the list of sins. And I prayed, like
I'd never prayed before. Mostly I prayed for my mum. But I
spared a little bit of time to pray that this growing fascination
with Ethan that was taking up more and more of my head, that
I'd find a way to get rid of it.

Chapter 31

Kitty

Amsterdam

'So, you and Theo, what's the story?' said Alice.

'We're just friends,' I said, giving her a big smile that hinted at much more.

'Yeah, but what sort of friends?' Alice narrowed her eyes at me.

'Friends with potential,' I told her.

We'd started going swimming together, Alice, Lucy and me. Twice a week at the Zuiderbad, a red-brick building next to the Rijksmuseum. From the outside it could have been an office or a school, but inside was an old-fashioned swimming pool, complete with changing booths and mosaics of dolphins. We'd done thirty lengths and were relaxing in a small warm pool, infused with rosemary and eucalyptus.

'Really?' said Alice. 'I would have thought you'd prefer that Ethan guy.'

'Ethan?'

'Because he's so, you know ...'

'Rude? Abrupt?'

'He's just Dutch. They say what they think. You've got to get used to it. He's gorgeous. He seems keen on you.'

'I'd like to get to know him better,' said Lucy. 'He seems deep and mysterious. I saw him rollerblading in the Vondelpark the other day, looking all moody, like Heathcliff or someone.'

'Heathcliff roams around on the Yorkshire moors,' I said, 'he doesn't ever strap wheels on his feet.'

'Yes, but Ethan's got that wild, untamed look about him. I think it's the long hair.'

All this talk of Ethan was a little annoying. 'Theo's writing a book,' I boasted. 'But he doesn't talk about it, so don't tell him I told you.'

'Theo's very cute too,' said Alice. 'You've done well, girl. Eye candy and brains. I suppose I just thought that you wouldn't go for a Londoner, having just escaped from the Gloomy Metropolis.'

'The what?'

'My name for London. Honestly, I can't believe I lived there for a whole year. It's all traffic jams and broken-down buses.'

It was true that the sheer speed and ease of getting around Amsterdam was still amazing to me, months after we'd moved.

'And the tube!' she went on. 'The one and only place where you pay to sniff other people's sweaty pits and get groped doing it.'

'Oh, it's not that bad. I'm sure Tokyo is more crowded, isn't it, Lucy?'

'Tell me one thing you miss about London, apart from family and friends,' Alice persisted.

'The supermarkets ...' I said. Dirk van de Broek, our nearest supermarket chain, was a bit limited, although it was entertaining that the name translated as Dirk of the Pants. On the other hand, we didn't go there too often, as we bought all our fresh food at the market. 'The ... um ... the theatre.'

'How often did you go?'

'Not much, but it was nice to know it was there.'

'So, go home three times a year for a theatre weekend.'

'Also, vinegar on chips.'

'I love mayo.'

'Custard.'

'Try *vla*. It comes in cartons and it's exactly like cold custard, except there are more flavours. Including butterscotch.'

'Ooh. Mmm. OK, well, English, I suppose. Being able to listen to people talking on the bus.'

'Just work harder at your Dutch.'

'*Ja, klopt.*' I hoped sarcasm translated into Dutch. *Klopt* was my favourite word of the moment. It meant ringing, like a bell, but was used just to mean 'of course'. Ethan said it all the time.

'But anyway, Theo being a Londoner is something I like about him. He's Topshop and custard and vinegar on chips and Channel 4 and the entire English language.'

'Bless! Have you told him that?'

'Well, no, we're just taking things slowly at the moment. Keeping it light.'

'But you'd like to be more serious? Are you in lurrrve?' Lucy used a silly voice and rolled her eyes, but she was watching me carefully, and I couldn't lie. Luckily the warm pool meant I was already pink in the face. I laughed and said, 'Oh yeah, it's true love!' and hoped they'd take it as a joke.

'I'm looking forward to my party,' said Lucy. 'Lots of cool guys there for you and me to pick from, Alice.'

I pressed her for more details of the party. Her father was going away, and so was Saskia, the glamorous actress he lived with. Lucy had the whole flat to herself. She was going to invite everyone she knew in Amsterdam.

'Give me Ethan's number, so I can invite him,' she said. 'If you don't want him for yourself, maybe I'll have a go.'

'He's bisexual,' I said, thinking it would put her off, but not sure why I wanted to do that.

'That's incredibly sexy, isn't it?' said Alice.

'Is it?'

'I think so,' she said.

'Ooh, yes, dead sexy,' said Lucy. 'Very on trend too.'

'Oh, right, well, I'll give you his number then,' I said, wondering why I felt so reluctant. It wasn't that I wanted Ethan for myself, after all. Maybe I was just being protective to my friends. I wouldn't want Ethan messing around with their emotional well-being.

'It's the night before the Sinterklaas parade,' said Alice. 'You're coming to my protest, aren't you?'

'You can rely on me,' I assured her. 'I can't believe they still do the blacking-up thing in the twenty-first century. I mean, it's so obviously offensive.'

I was already planning my strategy for the party. A knockout dress, Lucy to do my make-up. Heels ... except I'd have to be careful not to tower over Theo. Heels to kick off. Perfume that smelled of musk and roses. A look to inspire love. I might not want to admit it to my friends, but I was pretty sure that I was in love.

If love means thinking about someone all the time and feeling special whenever you're with them, if it means little buzzes of electricity making you shiver when you kiss, if it meant listening to every word they say with a hyper-awareness so you can replay the whole conversation when you're on your own, then I was in love. If love means caring about someone so much that it makes you want to cry when they're not smiling, feeling sick with excitement in the mornings because you're going to see them at college, feeling like half a person when you're not together, then I was completely and absolutely and utterly in love with Theo.

I just had to get us to the point where I knew he felt like that about me too. Sometimes I thought he did – when we kissed, when we walked along a canal holding hands, when he bought me hot chocolate in the park and I saw him watching me from the kiosk queue. And he had walked all the way from Amstelveen to the Pijp just to see me on Rosh Hashanah.

But I didn't really know the person I loved. I didn't know the truth about his past, I didn't know how he felt in the present. Did he love this teacher? Did she even exist? Sometimes I felt scared that he still loved her, and sometimes I hated her for seducing him. I wanted to find out her name and address and do something violent, something threatening, something to punish her for what she'd done to my boyfriend. If she had. If she even existed.

I knew these thoughts were crazy and wrong, but I treasured them. If I felt this strongly, it must be love – because what else could it be? Look at Heathcliff and Cathy. They loved each other so much that it destroyed them. Love has to be passionate, it has to include fear and hate and longing. Love isn't soft or easy, it's not just having a good time with a friend. Love means suffering as well as ecstasy. Love is overwhelming or it is nothing.

Theo had to feel it too. It was just a matter of time before he admitted it.

Chapter 32

Kitty

Amsterdam

The dress was perfect. In it, I felt like a different person. Not just Amsterdam Kitty, brave and independent, in charge of my destiny. But Super Amsterdam Kitty. Glamorous. Special. A woman, not a girl.

A dress to launch a million selfies.

The girls applauded when they saw me. 'So gorgeous!' said Lucy. 'Where did you get it?'

I told them about a little vintage shop I'd found near our flat. It looked like a jumble sale, but once you saw past the piles of musty tat, there were brilliant bargains to be found.

Lucy styled my hair for me, only burning the skin on my neck once. Then she applied my make-up, refusing to let me look in the mirror while she brushed my face with deft strokes. I thought back to Martine at my going away party. It felt as though years had passed.

'Look up to the ceiling ... now keep your eyes there ... OK ...

keep still …' It felt like years before she said, 'OK, you can look,' and waved a mirror in front of my face. I blinked. My eyes were smoky and dramatic. My hair fell in shiny ringlets. She'd swapped my red lipstick for something soft and pink.

'I know it's not what you're used to, but you look fabulous,' she said. 'Let the eyes do the talking.'

I blinked doubtfully at the mirror. I looked softer, more feminine, than usual. Mum would like this look, but was it really me? I took a quick picture and pinged it off to Rachel on Snapchat. She replied, seconds later, with a picture of her upturned thumb.

We went downstairs to the living room. Lucy had bought huge bouquets of white and violet flowers, and arranged them in silver vases. She lit tea lights in turquoise and amethyst-coloured candleholders, which glowed softly as she dimmed the main lights. We pushed the leather sofas against the wall, laid out the drinks on the dining table, and debated whether to leave the balcony door open or closed. It was cold, but we knew the room would get hot and smoky, so we decided to leave the door ajar.

Then Lucy put on some music and opened a bottle of fizzy white wine – possibly champagne; she said it was her dad's and he'd never notice – and we drank and laughed and conquered that nervy feeling that you get at the beginning of a party when you don't know whether anyone else will bother to come.

But they did come, loads of them, people that Alice and I had never met. Americans and Canadians and Indians and Ghanaians, French, German, Spanish and Dutch. Ethan turned up with Bart and Rosa, and he raised his eyebrows at me when he saw the dress.

'You look very beautiful,' he said, without even a hint of banter.

'Thanks, virtual-brother. You look very beautiful too.'

He did as well, in a black T-shirt and faded jeans, his hair loose, falling down past his shoulders.

'And you don't smell of the stables,' I added.

'I took my annual bath,' he said.

'Congratulations!'

He laughed at me. I'd never seen Ethan in such a good mood.

'Did you hear from your mum?' he asked. Mum and Paul had gone to Paris for the weekend. It was a big deal and she was concerned about leaving me, but I'd promised her that I'd stay over at Lucy's for the whole weekend.

'Yes, she says the hotel's very nice and they're having a great time. Did you hear from Paul?'

'Yes, similar.' His eyes scanned the crowd. 'Theo's not here tonight?'

'Oh, he'll be here later. Soon, I think. He had to have dinner with his cousins.' Theo had been a bit dubious about whether he'd be able to get to the party at all, it being a Friday night and his cousins being dead religious, but I'd pointed out that they couldn't actually stop him, and he said that he'd do his best.

'*Goed zo.*' Ethan hesitated and I thought he was about to say something else, but then Lucy tugged my arm, and introduced me to a girl she'd known at the British School, and he turned back to his friends.

Theo was one of the last to arrive. He found me in the kitchen, talking to Jane and Finn.

'Hey.' His hand grazed the back of my dress. 'You look amazing.'

I was cross that we'd met when I was under the glare of the fluorescent strip. Seriously bad lighting for my new makeover.

'Hey ... you OK?'

Theo had been back from London a week or so now, but I hadn't seen so much of him. I'd been wondering if he'd seen her, the teacher, back in London. Maybe he'd told her that it was over. Maybe he'd realised that he loved me, not her. I searched for a clue in his face, but he just looked the same as usual.

'I'm good,' he said. We smiled at each other and I relaxed. Everything was going to be fine. I lifted my phone high up in front of us, and we grinned for the obligatory party selfie. I sent it flying off to my followers. Look at us, Instagram! Young, loved-up and having fun!

The living room was loud with music and people, and thick with smoke. Someone handed Theo a joint, and he inhaled. 'You don't mind, do you?' he said to me.

'Not as long as I don't have any.'

'Are you OK with all the smoke?'

'We could go out on the balcony,' I said.

'Won't you be cold?'

'No, I'm too hot.'

There were a couple of kids out on the balcony, but they went inside when we came out. Maybe we disturbed their private time, I didn't care. All I cared about was Theo and me and the magical effect that absence and a party dress woud have on our relationship.

We sat for a bit, while he smoked his joint and I sipped my champagne. My third glass. Lucy had opened a few more bottles. Her dad must be either very absent-minded or very forgiving.

I moved in for a kiss. But maybe the new make-up was a mistake, because he seemed more tentative than before, somehow cautious. The kiss didn't last long at all.

'Are you OK? We haven't really talked since you got back from London.'

Theo ran his hands through his hair. 'Yeah, I know, I'm sorry. Sukkot, you know. I had a load of classwork to catch up with. And London was heavy.'

'Did it make you homesick, going back?'

'Not really homesick. Actually, I'm relieved to be back.' That sounded good. He was relieved to be back with me, the one he loved.

'How's your mum?'

'The same. Not well.'

I took his hand. 'I'm sorry. Still no idea what's wrong with her?'

He shrugged. 'That's what they say.'

He seemed distracted, a bit down. It must have been difficult, breaking up with someone you'd felt passionately in love with.

'Theo, is everything all right?'

He sighed. 'It's all a bit complicated.'

This was it. This was the moment. I was ready. He was going

to tell me about his teacher, confide in me, explain how she'd screwed up his life, how that made him scared to try again.

And I'd be loving and understanding and healing, giving him hope for the future.

'You can tell me,' I said. 'You can tell me anything.'

He looked away. 'I don't know where to start,' he said.

The balcony door sprang open, with a burst of noise and smoke. Ethan stood there, beer in hand. I glared at him, but he ignored me.

'Hey, *Tay-o*,' he said to Theo. I'd forgotten he used that Dutch pronunciation.

'Hey,' said Theo.

'Can we talk sometime? Sorry, Kits.'

'Catch you later?' said Theo.

'OK. See you.' He didn't even bother to shut the door. I gave it a prod with my foot, and we were alone again.

'He's so annoying!' I said. 'You know, he's capable of being quite nice, on rare occasions.'

'Is he?'

I didn't want to waste time talking about Ethan. I moved closer to Theo and took his hand again.

'What were you going to tell me?'

He sighed. 'I don't know.'

I took his hand. 'You can tell me anything,' I said again, 'you know that. Look, I know we've been having fun and stuff, but maybe it's something more serious than that.'

He said something, so quietly that I couldn't hear him over the buzz of the party behind us.

'It's more than a coincidence that we met like this,' I said. 'Don't you think so?'

'Yeah ... I don't know. What is coincidence, anyway?'

I didn't want to be sidetracked into some philosophical conversation about the nature of coincidence. Lucy had put a few candles out on the balcony table, and I admired the way they glowed like jewels, casting purple and blue-green light on our intertwined hands. In fact, if I could get the setting right, it would make a gorgeous, romantic picture. But it might ruin the moment if I got my phone out.

'It's when two people meet, and they're meant for each other,' I said. 'Like you and me. I mean, what are the odds that we both came from north London on the same day, and we ended up meeting here? It's meant to be.'

I thought he might kiss me then. I squeezed his hand a little tighter. But he didn't move, and after a bit he removed his hand.

'Look, Kitty, I need to say something.'

This was it. The truth at last. I held my breath.

'I never really told you about this, but last year I really screwed up because I fell in love with someone I shouldn't have ...'

His voice trailed off. We sat in silence for a few moments. So it was true. Everything was true. Poor Theo.

I couldn't stop myself. 'Look, Theo, you can tell me. Actually my sister happened to mention that you'd had a few problems at home.'

He frowned. 'Your sister?'

'Yeah, Rachel; she was in sixth-form with your brother, you know ...'

'My brother told your sister about me?'

'No ... I mean, I don't think it was him who told her. I think she just heard some rumours.'

His eyes were wide with shock.

'Your sister gossiped about me? You know about Sophie? You always knew?'

'No ... I mean, I didn't know for sure. She didn't have any actual details.'

'And you never asked me?'

'I thought you'd be upset ... and you are upset ... and I'm sorry ... ' My voice was all wobbly. This wasn't how the conversation was meant to go at all. 'I'm really sorry. You must have known that people were talking about you.'

'Yes, but ... not you ... not here ... Jesus!'

'Theo! I didn't mean it that way! I just meant ... I understand. I'm here for you.'

He looked at me, like he didn't recognise me. As though I was someone else completely. Not even a friend. An enemy. Someone he hated.

'Have you told everyone?' he asked. 'Alice? Lucy?'

'No ... no, really, Theo. You've got it all wrong.'

'I can't believe you knew.'

'It didn't matter! It didn't put me off because I really like you! And it can't have meant that much to you because why did you start seeing me?'

'Because ... I don't know. I was trying to forget her.'

'And did it work? Are you still in love with her?'

He gazed into my eyes. I felt all tingly just looking at his face.

'No,' he said. 'I'm not in love with her at all. I don't even know why I thought I liked her.'

Maybe it was the relief of hearing those beautiful words. Maybe it was the champagne. Maybe it was because all I wanted was to feel his arms around me. My heart was full and I couldn't hold back my feelings any more. I said it.

'I love you, Theo.'

Chapter 33

Theo

Amsterdam

I didn't even hear her at first. I didn't fully take in that she'd said ... that she felt ...

'You what?' I said, stupidly, and then she turned away, and I said, 'No ... I mean ... thank you ... I just don't know what to say.'

'I didn't mean to say that,' she said. 'I just mean that you can trust me. I care.'

One minute I was trying to avoid hurting her feelings, the next I was furious with her. It was a big nasty mess, and all I wanted to do was get away. It didn't help that she'd somehow changed the way she looked – soft and vulnerable, instead of strong and confident. It also didn't help that I was well aware that I was in the wrong, not her. I was the one with secrets.

'I thought we were just, you know, YOLO,' I said, deliberately casual.

'We were ... we are ... I'm not putting any pressure on you.'

'I can't cope with anything heavy right now,' I said.

Her hands were in fists, pressed to her mouth. She mumbled something through them.

'I'm sorry, Kitty, OK? I probably should have told you ages ago. I wish I could just be your boyfriend, because my life would be so much easier, so much simpler, if that were ... if we ...'

'I don't want you to be with me because it's "easier" or "simpler". I thought you liked me!'

'I do like you!'

'If you had all these doubts, why didn't you mention them before?'

I couldn't lie any more, even to myself. Kitty was great, I liked her a lot, and I definitely fancied her. But it wasn't enough.

'I've been trying to work out how I feel. The thing is, I wanted it to work with you, I really did. I really enjoy your company and I think you're great. But I don't love you ... not like that. Not enough. It wouldn't be right for me to get seriously involved with you, when ... you know ...'

Tears leaked out of the corners of her eyes. I felt dreadful.

'Um ... are you OK?'

'I'm fine, thank you.' She flicked her tears away, blinking rapidly. Her voice was little more than a growl. 'I'm absolutely not interested in anything else you've got to say. I'm disappointed that you thought it was OK to use me like this, but that's up to you, that's your problem. Not mine.'

'Look, I never made you any promises—'

'There's more than one way to make promises,' she said. 'Stay away from me, Theo.'

She stood up, swaying slightly on her heels. She towered over me, like an Amazonian warrior woman. And then she was gone, pushing the door open, so the noise and the smoke hit me like a slap in the face, and then pulling it closed behind her.

I stayed outside for a good five minutes, dithering about whether I should follow her. Then a load of American kids joined me on the balcony, and I went back inside. It'd been cold outside and my hands were numb.

Kitty was nowhere to be seen. I scanned the room, but with no luck. So I went upstairs to see if the party had spread to the rest of this enormous flat. One floor up, a gaggle of kids was sitting and talking. Two floors up, everything was dark and quiet. One door closed, another door open.

'Theo.'

I stumbled forward, startled, through the open door. Ethan was sitting on a window seat, alone in the dark, a can of Heineken open beside him.

'What are you doing here?' I asked him, peering to see in the dark. Was he really all alone? Waiting for someone? *For me?*

'I'm just resting. Want a drink?'

'I'm not sure,' I said.

'Parties are tiring,' he said. 'All those people. You look a bit ...'

'What?'

'A bit like you did the other day in the Vondelpark.'

'Oh.' Somehow, without really knowing how, I found myself sitting next to Ethan.

'Better?' He leaned towards me. 'What's going on, Theo?'

'What ... what do you mean?'

'Well, you know ... I mean, I'm not imagining it, am I?'

I closed my eyes. My head swam, with weed and alcohol and shame and desire. I didn't even know who I was any more.

'No,' I said. 'You're not imagining anything.'

Chapter 34

Kitty

Amsterdam

As soon as I walked out on Theo, I realised that I'd screwed it all up. I kicked off my shoes and dashed up two flights of stairs to Lucy's room, pulling the door shut behind me and fumbling with the latch.

First, I'd told him that I knew all the gossip about him. Anyone would have been upset. Second, I'd told him I loved him, when before I'd insisted that we were just keeping things casual. Third, I'd given him a hard time for not loving me back, when I had no right to expect any such thing.

I cried for a while, working my way through a box of tissues, gulping down my disappointment and hurt feelings. But then I started thinking.

I'd been honest and true and hadn't said anything to be ashamed of. And why shouldn't he fall in love with me? I was at least as loveable as he was. Huh.

It was painful to admit but I'd been living in a fantasy world.

Possibly all was not lost with Theo, but I'd have to swallow my pride and have a proper talk with him. In the meantime, it wouldn't hurt at all to go back to the party, and make him jealous by seeming really unconcerned and carefree.

I looked at my face in Lucy's mirror. My make-up was in ruins, my eyes were swollen and my nose was pink. But Lucy had eye drops and cover-up and foundation. I reworked my face, back to something more like my everyday Amsterdam look. A dark-red smile. Mascara reapplied. Deep breaths. *You can do this, Kitty. It's not the end of the world.*

There was a whole flat full of people down there, and I was going to smile and laugh and dance, and talk. Ethan was there, too. I'd helped him out when he needed to repel an ex. Now maybe he'd help me, by dancing with me, making me look as though I couldn't care less about Theo. What had he said? Theo wasn't right for me? I might even tell him that he'd been correct.

I opened the door to Lucy's bedroom, and was about to go down the steep stairs, when I caught a glimpse of some movement in the room opposite. Just a couple, I thought. Just two people kissing. And then my eyes adjusted to the gloom and I realised who it was.

Oh my God.

My eyes could not take in what I was seeing. Ethan, his hair falling over his face, his arm cradling the shoulder of ... Theo. Definitely Theo. There was no question about it at all.

I didn't say a word. I didn't stop. I rushed down the stairs, slipping and sliding in the carpet on my stockinged feet. I didn't stop to put my shoes on. I emerged out of the front door, and started running. I needed to get as far away from ... whatever I'd seen ... as far away as I could.

I ran south for about ten minutes, past the shops, across one main road, on to a bridge across a canal, before I stopped. My feet were killing me. And my heart was thumping like a drum in my chest, faster and faster, an awful rhythm that scared me, slowed me, made me dizzy with fear.

It didn't feel right. I didn't feel right. I was gasping for air, head bursting, hot and cold and flashing lights.

I had to get help, I realised, but my phone was back at Lucy's. I knew the Amsterdam Hilton, just across the bridge, was my best chance of finding people, but the bridge meant going up a slope, and then there was a car park to walk through. On the other hand, all the houses next to the canal were dark and silent.

I made it to the brow of the bridge and then leaned on the wall, clutching my chest.

It was deadly quiet, and the night air was sparkling, and I felt sad and stupid and alone. And my heart was thundering so loud, I couldn't hear anything else.

PART 3: After

Chapter 35

Theo

Amsterdam

Ethan calls the hospitals. Nothing. No girl answering to Kitty's description. 'That's got to be good news,' says Alice, but all I can see is Kitty fainting and falling into a canal … in front of a tram … lying in an alleyway somewhere. Maybe she's been kidnapped by people-traffickers? Anything could have happened and my imagination is not helping at all.

We draw up a list of people to phone. The longer the list, the later we can put off phoning Kitty's mum. Alice comes over, and we call our friends from college. Ethan calls the Dutch kids he invited to the party. Lucy takes the others, her friends from the British and International Schools.

Alice touches my hand. 'Come with me,' she whispers, and we tiptoe out of the kitchen. There's a small front room and she opens the door. Inside is a desk, an office chair, a low, squashy armchair, and about a hundred books.

She commandeers the office chair, so I have to lower myself

gingerly into the armchair, which feels so unstable that I doubt I'm ever going to be able to get out of it.

'What do you know?' she asks. She's not smiling.

'What do you mean? Nothing! If I knew anything, I'd say so.'

'OK, let me put it another way. What happened between you and Kitty last night? Something sure did.'

'What do you mean?' I was playing for time and she knew it.

'Well, there were the two of you – a really sweet couple. And there was Kitty looking gorgeous.'

'Yes ... she was ...'

'And you disappear out on to the balcony for ages. And then Kitty comes back, and she looks upset. I would've talked to her, but she went upstairs. And then you go upstairs too, so I think, great, it's all on track. And I think, way to go, girl, you think you're being all subtle and discreet, but I know what you're up to ...'

'But ...'

'And later on I heard her coming down the stairs again and I thought she was crying. I was going to go after her, but it was just too damn crowded.'

'I didn't do anything to her,' I say, but my voice sounds weak and uncertain.

'You better not have hurt her.' Alice's expression is fierce. 'What are you hiding, Theo?'

'Nothing! Nothing happened! Look, we're wasting time. We should phone the police.'

Back in the kitchen, Ethan's opened another beer. He gives us a quick, suspicious glance as we come into the room, and then looks away.

Lucy finishes another phone call. 'OK, well, that was Su-Min from the International School and she says she saw someone in a dress that sounds like Kitty's going downstairs at about one a.m. And she doesn't remember seeing her come back upstairs. And I can't find anyone who remembers seeing her after that.'

'Alice says she was crying. Did anyone see her crying?' I say, because I don't want Alice to jump in and claim that I made Kitty cry or something like that.

'One of my friends said there was a girl ... an emotional girl ...' says Ethan, slowly. 'He also said that she'd had a drink and was dancing.'

'But was it definitely Kitty?'

He shrugs. 'It was a party. There were lots of girls and lots of drinking. I mean, any one of them could have been emotional.'

'Kitty's really distinctive-looking though,' says Lucy. 'People remember her.'

'British people remember her,' said Ethan, 'because you think she's tall. The Dutch and Americans not so much. Kitty is just another pretty girl to them.'

'You don't have to be so callous.' Alice glares at Ethan.

Ethan looks surprised. 'I'm just explaining to you why no one remembers her.'

'Do you think we should ring Kitty's mum?' says Lucy. 'I'm getting freaked out here, that she's disappeared from my party and my dad's away and I don't want anyone blaming me if something ... if she's got into some trouble. I don't think there was any serious drugs action, but what if she took a tab?'

'She wouldn't do that,' I tell her. 'Kitty's very careful about her health.' But I can't help thinking about the time I had to rush her to hospital, and how she begged me not to tell anyone about it.

We agree that Lucy and Alice will go back and check Lucy's apartment one last time. Maybe Kitty is waiting in a café nearby. If she doesn't turn up then Ethan will call Kitty's mum, interrupting the romantic weekend in Paris. 'We can't put it off any longer,' says Alice. 'Kitty's mum needs to know.'

So they go. And I'm all alone with Ethan.

Chapter 36

Theo

Amsterdam

'Theo,' he says, 'don't beat yourself up. It's going to be OK. There are hundreds of places that Kitty could be.'

I shake my head. 'If anything's happened to her, it's my fault. I upset her. She said I used her. And I suppose I did.'

'How so?'

'Well ... at first, she was a way of not thinking about Sophie. A distraction. I mean, I liked her a lot, of course, you couldn't not like Kitty ... But she felt more strongly than I did.'

'She said it was nothing serious, you and her. I asked her.'

'You did?' Despite my worry over Kitty, this admission from Ethan makes me smile. As it's totally inappropriate to be smiling in the circumstances, I try and stop myself by biting my lip, but the sides of my mouth won't stop curving upwards and, when I glance at him, I see he's smiling too.

'I wasn't going to do anything if she said it was serious

between you two. I mean, I wasn't even sure you'd be interested ... I could've asked you I suppose, how you felt about her, but I didn't want to say the wrong thing. You might've thought I was being weird or something. '

I feel incredibly pleased that Ethan has lost his cool, bantering drawl completely, and sounds much less sure of himself than usual. It gives me courage.

'I wasn't sure either. I mean, I knew there was something, but I didn't want to think about it. I didn't need the complication of thinking about whether I was gay or not.'

'You don't have to stick a label on yourself. I don't.'

'I know. I mean, it's just that I wasn't even bi-curious before ...'

Ethan snorts.

'OK, maybe I was, but it was kind of a secret from myself, if that makes sense.'

'Everyone is bi-curious. It's just that not everyone acts on it. That's what I think, anyway.'

'I don't know,' I say. 'I don't know what was going on with Kitty either. I mean, she told you we weren't serious, but then she told me ... something else.'

'I thought you were just ... What would you call it? Kissing friends? Like me and Rosa sometimes.'

Instantly I feel horribly jealous of this Rosa. But then I remember that she was at the party last night and he wasn't with her, he was with me.

'I didn't think we were serious. I just liked Kitty and she liked me too, and, you know ...' My voice trails off. I didn't think I'd done anything wrong with Kitty, not really. I never thought she'd fall in love with me. 'I'm just bad at relationships.'

'Everyone's bad at relationships,' says Ethan. 'Even the ones who think they've found the love of their life; mostly it's bullshit. Who stays together any more?'

'My parents,' I say. 'My cousins. OK, they are newlyweds, but you can see they adore each other.'

'The ones you live with? That must be fun. Well, maybe your family is good at love. Mine isn't. My parents split up when I was a baby and I never got a step parent who stayed around.'

'Is it true, what you said, you've never been in love?' I'm curious about every little thing about Ethan. I've spent the last month not even admitting to myself how much I like him, and all it's seemed to do is make me even more interested. Besides, talking to him helps me avoid thinking about where Kitty might be.

'It's true. But people have fallen in love with me, and that's quite . . . ' He hesitates. 'Quite a lonely place.'

'You just don't believe in love at all?' It's pathetic, asking this, but I am quite desperate – for him to say that this time might be different, that I am special, and that he sees something in me that he never saw in anyone before. After all, it is such a big leap for me to admit that I like a boy – and what I feel for Ethan is more than liking – that surely he must feel something similar? Something life-changing and important, something like love.

He hesitates. He's smiling again, though. 'You want some big statement from me, when all I see is how you go from person to person? From Sophie to Kitty to me?'

'Just ... I don't know ... I don't want this to be casual. I don't think I do casual. If there is a this.'

'I hope there is a this,' he said. 'And I hope it's something not too casual, but you know. Not too scary either.' Then he scratches his head and says, 'But I don't know how good I am at loving someone. I warn you. Even my mom thinks I'm cold and selfish.'

'Your mum said that?'

'She thinks I should be like her and want to save the world.'

'She must want you to be happy?'

'I suppose so.'

Despite everything, the rows and being sent away, I never once doubted that my parents adored me.

'I'm sure she loves you,' I say. 'I mean, why wouldn't she?'

'Now you're just flattering me.' He smiles so I know he's teasing.

'I just ... I want to know why you ...' I can't even say it.

'Why did I kiss you? Is that what you're asking?'

'Sort of.' I feel exposed, like an overturned turtle, legs waving in the air.

'Because I wanted to. I wanted to a lot. And I thought you wanted to.'

'How did you know I wanted to?'

'Oh, there I was, sitting all alone in a dark room, and you come and sit right next to me, almost touching, and you put your head like this,' he demonstrates, 'and really, it would have been rude not to.'

I shake my head. 'I didn't even realise,' I say. 'I didn't know.'

'You've got to pay more attention to your own feelings.'

'I'm scared.'

He moves closer to me, so our thighs are touching, side by side at the kitchen table.

'Would it help if I told you that I'm scared too?'

'I don't know.'

'I am scared too. And I have wanted this for a long time ... at least, it feels like a long time ...'

His voice trails off, and his breath is hot on my cheek. I turn my face to his, and taste him again, the salty, beery softness of his lips. And I've forgotten everything, forgotten all the restrictions and boundaries and limits, and who I ever thought I was.

My phone rings in my pocket. I leave it. It rings again. *Kitty?* I remember why I'm here, like a bucket of ice water over my head. I pull myself away and answer.

It's Lucy. 'She's not here, Theo. You need to call her mum.'

Chapter 37

Theo

Amsterdam

'What do you mean you couldn't get hold of her?' It's eight a.m. and Lucy and Alice are on Ethan's doorstep.

'My dad's phone is just going to voicemail,' says Ethan. 'I've left a message at the hotel, but they haven't rung me. I think they're too loved-up to bother with us.'

'Did you say it was urgent?' demands Alice.

'Yes, obviously. I phoned three times.'

We'd stayed up until two a.m., until Ethan said, 'Look, he's clearly turned off his phone. Should I call Lucy? Or the police? Or shall we wait until the morning?'

I'd dithered. Surely we should speak to Kitty's mum before starting a police hunt? Maybe Alice's parents could help us out? We'd look completely stupid if we made a big drama in the early hours and then Kitty turned up absolutely fine the next morning, having gone off with a friend or something.

'What could the police actually do right now?' I'd asked. 'Let's wait until the morning.'

We were upstairs by then, in the living room, watching old movies. I must have fallen asleep at some point, because when I woke up I was lying on the sofa, covered by a duvet, and Ethan was making coffee in the kitchen.

I'd sneaked over to the hole in the ceiling to watch him – I couldn't help myself. He seemed fine. Kitty must have phoned, I thought. Everything was all right.

Then I climbed down the stairs and asked him, and he said that no, he hadn't heard anything at all from anyone. 'Called my dad again, but his phone's switched off.' Two minutes later, just as my mouth went dry and I began to feel sick, the doorbell rang.

Alice and Lucy exchange glances.

'Are you telling the truth?' says Lucy. 'It just seems weird that they wouldn't pick up at all.'

Ethan rolls his eyes. 'Why would I lie about this? Maybe I should just call the police?'

'You need to get hold of her mum! She'll know what to do.' Lucy sounds a bit panicky. 'You definitely can't call the police first. Her mum would be so upset.'

Ethan says, 'She'll be upset whatever, if Kitty's really disappeared.'

'You're so cold,' Lucy tells him. 'You just don't care.'

'Don't tell me how I feel.'

Alice sits down at the kitchen table, and glares at me as though she's an interrogator and I'm a prisoner of war. 'We've got a few questions for you two. We think we know why Kitty's disappeared.'

Lucy joins in. 'I got a call back from Hidemasa, one of the guys from the International School.'

'Yeah?' Ethan doesn't sit down. Instead he leans against the kitchen top, deliberately casual.

'Turns out it wasn't Kitty who had the secret boyfriend.'

'I don't think ...' My head is throbbing again. I've gone all cold and clammy; I'm terrified that Kitty is dead.

'No,' says Lucy. 'You didn't think, did you?'

My heart is pounding. Ethan says, 'I'm calling the police right now. This is just wasting time.'

'No, don't do that,' says Alice. 'I want Theo to admit it first.'

'Admit what?' I say, but I'm just playing for time.

'Hidemasa told us he saw the two of you having a snog. Why would you do that to her?'

I think I'm going to be sick.

'I didn't do it to her ...' I mumble. 'It wasn't about her.'

Ethan's watching me. His face is completely expressionless.

'I wasn't expecting ... it wasn't something I'd *planned* ...'

'She must've been in a complete state. She must've been so upset. How come you didn't even mention this last night?'

I feel so guilty that I can't even look at them.

'I'm sorry,' I say. 'I'm really sorry. It's all my fault. Whatever's happened to Kitty, it's down to me.'

'It'd serve you right if we posted this all over Facebook,' said Lucy.

'No – please don't—' I say, hopelessly.

'Why shouldn't we?'

The thought of everyone I know hearing about me kissing Ethan makes me feel like I'm going to vomit. Just as I'd added some of my London friends to my new account as well.

'It's just that I'm not ... I've never ... my family ...'

'Look, this is not your fault, Theo.' Ethan's voice is cold. 'Don't kid yourself. I was screwing around with you because it entertained me to mess with your little relationship with Kitty. I wanted to break you up. And it worked. I didn't know Kitty would go off in a tantrum.'

'What are you talking about?' demands Alice.

'Kitty and Theo, I decided to break them up. I could have done it the easy way – by going for Kitty – but I set myself more of a challenge. I didn't think she'd disappear though.'

'Why would you want to do that?' says Alice. 'Talk about twisted!'

'That's the kind of guy I am,' he says. 'Twisted. Mean. I can't bear to see anyone happy, I just have to step in and spoil it for them. Now why don't you kids run along? I'm sure Kitty will turn up eventually.'

Alice looks as disgusted as if we'd dressed up as Zwarte Piet. 'How could you? Kitty didn't deserve that!'

'Poor Kitty!' says Lucy. 'Poor Theo,' she adds, as an after-thought.

I don't understand what's going on. This is not the Ethan that I thought I was getting to know. This is not someone I could love. No one could love this person.

Blood is drumming in my ears. He lied to me. He used me.

He didn't mean anything he said or did. And kissing him, touching him, trusting him ... suddenly it feels dirty and wrong.

'You bastard,' I say, getting up from my chair. I can't bear to look at him.

'Theo, wait—' he says, but it's still that coldly amused voice.

'Screw you,' I say, heading for the front door. Lucy and Alice follow me out. I'm almost sorry that Ethan stays where he is. I'd like an excuse to hit and kick him, to get rid of any confusion, any memories that are still caught up in his game.

Lucy and Alice catch up with me at the tram stop. 'Theo! Theo! Stop! Are you OK?'

Alice flings her arms around me. 'We're sorry! We gave you a hard time and it was all the fault of that ... that pig!'

The girls seem to have forgiven me completely. What's more, they seem to have forgotten Kitty.

I pull my hand back. 'Look, thanks for your support and everything, but we need to call the police. We should have done it ages ago. Kitty could be kidnapped, or ill, anything could have happened to her. How can she have disappeared into thin air?' I get out my phone. 'Does anyone know what number I call?' I force myself to say the unsayable. 'She could be dead.'

'Lucy,' says Alice, 'it's not fair. We need to tell him.'

A tram is rumbling towards us. 'What?' I say. 'Tell me what?'

The tram stops. We get on, and sit down. I briefly remember my bike, tied up outside Ethan's house.

'Kitty ...' says Alice, and stops.

Lucy takes a deep breath. 'She's not dead, Theo. We know exactly where she is.'

Chapter 38

Kitty

Newcastle

The look on my sister's face is priceless.

'Kitty? What the actual—? What are you doing here?'

I'm shivering at the front door of her student residence. Rachel has come down to let me in, wearing a bright-green onesie and fake Uggs.

'Can't I come in? I'll explain everything.'

Rachel hesitates. 'I, um ... Well, yes. But stay very quiet.'

We go upstairs and into her room, and immediately I see why she was stalling. There's someone long, male and dark-haired in her bed, fast asleep, snoring gently. His jeans are folded neatly on her chair. His glasses – designer, black-rimmed – are on her bedside table. A leather jacket is hanging up on the back of her door.

From which I deduce that this isn't the first time he's slept in her bed. It's all too tidy. This is no student one-night stand.

We mime a conversation as she pulls on jeans and a hoodie.

She offers me a jumper and I pull it on gratefully. I gesticulate excitedly at the boyfriend, with 'who, what, when?' hand movements, along with popping eyes and open mouth. Rachel replies silently with an innocent playing-it-down grimace, followed by a wry, *OK, I do really like him* smile. She scribbles a note and leaves it on the pillow, next to his nose, and we let ourselves out of the room, run down the stairs and leave the student accommodation block.

I don't say anything until we are outside on the street. It feels strange to see English shop signs. No offence to Newcastle, but everything seems a bit dull and dreary.

'Oh my God!' I exclaim, momentarily forgetting my own dramas. 'Who is he? Why didn't you tell me?'

'I was going to tell you. Just wanted to, you know ... see how it went. Take things slowly. We were talking about coming to Amsterdam to surprise you.'

'What is he studying? What's his name? Are you in love?'

'Never mind all that. You'll meet him later. What are you doing here? Why didn't you tell me you were coming? You look completely wrecked.'

'Oh, well, thank you, Ray.'

'I mean it! Last time I saw you ... I mean, your picture ... you were all glammed-up for a party. Now you look like you've joined the army.'

'Huh,' I say. 'I'm never getting glammed-up again. Never bothering. My life is a disaster.'

She opens the door to a greasy spoon café. 'Breakfast,' she says. 'And you can tell me all about it.'

Over scrambled eggs and toast I spill out my story. The conversation on the balcony with Theo. Deciding that I was OK, I could cope. Then seeing The Kiss. The devastating, life-changing, heart breaking kiss.

'It was worse, Rachel, because I was, you know, coping. I was all right. And then I realised that he probably never fancied me at all ... he was deceiving me ...'

'Deceiving himself, it sounds like,' says Rachel. 'The little rat.'

'Oh, he's not a rat. Ethan's the rat. Except he's not really a rat either. It's me ... I'm just stupid. I screwed everything up. I was too busy taking pictures of us looking like a pretty couple, making up love stories about us, that I didn't even realise what was going on.'

'Do you think he was cheating on you with this Ethan, before the party? Was that what he was telling you?'

I try and remember our conversation.

'I don't know ... I don't think so. Maybe.'

She digs into her bag. 'Here you are. Good thing one of us always carries some emergency tissues. Eat the eggs. Drink the tea. Let me butter you some toast.'

Watching Rachel expertly dab Marmite and cut my toast into fingers makes me feel a lot better.

'I thought I was going to die! I went running out of the party, and my heart started pounding, and I sort of fainted ...'

'Oh, Kitty. You idiot.'

'Me? Why am I an idiot?'

'Your health is way more important than two stupid boys kissing.'

'I'm going to come and live here. There must be a sixth-form college I could go to. Mum can do the Amsterdam thing on her own. She's all loved up with Paul anyway.'

Rachel looks slightly alarmed. 'Where would you live? Some bedsit?'

I'd totally assumed we'd share a flat. I must've looked a bit disappointed, because she came and sat next to me and gave me a hug. 'It'll be OK. If you want to come to Newcastle we'll make it work.'

I sniff. 'I have to. I'm never going back to Amsterdam. I hate it there.'

'No, you don't.'

'Yes, I do.'

'No, you don't. Look at all your pictures. Look at AmsterKit and all your followers. You love Amsterdam. You'll probably live there all your life.'

'Not now I've been completely humiliated!'

'What's humiliating?'

'My boyfriend's left me for another boy!'

Rachel offers me another tissue. 'Don't you think you might just ever so slightly be overreacting?'

'How would you feel if your first proper boyfriend didn't just reject you, he rejected your entire sex?'

'Well, I probably wouldn't see it quite like that.'

My voice wobbles dangerously. 'Wh-what do you mean?'

'Well, first I'd feel quite flattered that someone who is possibly gay, but probably bi, had shown a massive interest in me in the first place. And second, it wouldn't be my fault if he eventually realised that he was actually gay. And third, it might be that he hadn't really meant to kiss this Ethan person, he was just a bit sad and drunk and stoned. I mean, these things happen. And the boy's clearly confused.'

'They do? He is?'

'Absolutely. And mostly no one ever finds out. You were just in the wrong place at the wrong time. But sometime soon you'll be in the right place at the right time. Karma. Coincidence. Call it what you want. Grandma would have said that he wasn't your *beshayrt*. It wasn't meant to be. Put it down to experience, and move on.'

I do feel better, even though I don't believe in the *beshayrt* business, comforting though it is to think that the angels might be busy finding my perfect partner.

'My friend Dina, she went out with a guy for two years before he left her for the captain of the rugby team. Turned out they'd been conducting a secret affair for six months. Dina was the Unwitting Beard.'

'The what?'

'Beard being a word meaning fake date, used by gay people to pretend they aren't. Dina never realised. So, Unwitting Beard. It sounds to me, though, that this Theo didn't even realise he needed a beard, so you weren't. You were more of a Potential Moustache.'

'You are talking drivel. And you don't know anything about Theo. He might have planned this on purpose to hurt me!' Even as I said it I knew this was nonsense, but the drama made me feel slightly better.

Rachel's trying not to smile. 'Really? If I were you, I wouldn't rush to think the worst of people. I'd think, I am Kitty, I am magnificent, and any stupid boy who hurts me is going to have to grovel to get back in my favour.'

I'm beginning to feel slightly better.

'Repeat after me: "I am Kitty. I am magnificent …"'

'I am not going to repeat after you. Talk about cringe.'

'Well, remember it, OK? You're my little sister and I love you, and no one's going to hurt you.'

'I love you too.'

'I'd feel better if I knew what was going on. Like, have they been seeing each other behind my back for ages?'

'Ah,' says Rachel. 'Well, I might be able to help you there.'

Chapter 39

Theo

Amsterdam

'Kitty's in Newcastle, with her sister,' says Alice.

'She's in *Newcastle*?'

'She got the ferry last night. We thought – she thought – we'd teach you and Ethan a lesson. We didn't know it was all his fault, Theo.'

My head is spinning.

'I've spent all day and most of the night thinking that Kitty is dead, and you knew where she was all the time?'

'Um, sorry,' says Lucy.

'We thought you'd been two-timing her,' says Alice.

I'm totally relieved about Kitty, but also so angry that I can hardly see. My fury is fuelled by guilt, because Ethan and I *had* been out for a few drinks in the week before the party. But nothing happened. We were just talking about stuff, like my book and his films. Sure, I should have made more of an effort to see Kitty as well. It wasn't really two-timing. I wasn't even certain that Ethan was gay or bi or whether we were just mates.

I didn't know what I wanted him to be.

I didn't know that he was just tricking me, and so were Kitty, Lucy and Alice.

'I can't believe you did that!' I say.

'We're sorry!'

'Leave me alone!'

'Look, we're sorry, OK? Come on. Here's our stop.'

I follow the girls off the tram, because I need more answers.

'What if we'd called the police?' I demand.

'We were trying to get you to call Kitty's mum, because she knew Kitty was OK, and going to Newcastle, and we thought you'd be embarrassed. That's all we wanted.'

'Oh, yeah, right, I can't see anything going wrong with that plan.'

'Getting arrested spoiled it. It meant that we lost hours.'

'I can't believe that you ... that *Kitty* ...'

Lucy sighs. 'Come back to the flat, Theo. I'll make you breakfast and try and explain what happened.' I'm torn between wanting to storm off, and needing to know what happened. Curiosity wins, and I follow them into the flat, where she warms up some croissants and makes hot chocolate.

'So, what happened? I demand.

'Kitty went running out of the flat. Lucy noticed her going downstairs, so we followed her. But she was running, so we didn't catch her up until we got to the bridge.'

'She was in a total state, gasping for breath. We were really worried. And she didn't have her shoes on.' Lucy looks at me accusingly. 'And it was all down to her having seen you two kissing.'

'Oh, so it wasn't some random Japanese guy?'

'No. It was Kitty. She was completely devastated.'

'So we took her to the Hilton Hotel for a drink, because we didn't want there to be any danger of her seeing either of you. And then Lucy used her dad's credit card so Kitty could stay there for the night. Actually I stayed there too, so she wouldn't be on her own.'

'When you went out for your morning coffee I sneaked out with Kitty's bag and stuff, and took it to the hotel. She and Alice had been talking.'

'We were up all night!' said Alice. 'We decided it was essential that she didn't rush into a confrontation with the two of you. I totally backed her in that. So she rang her mum and explained that she wanted to go and see her sister in Newcastle and her mum was fine with that, so we booked her onto the night ferry.'

'So ... she was in Amsterdam all day?' My head is spinning.

'She got a taxi back to her flat.' Lucy looked a bit embarrassed. 'And then we thought it wouldn't do you and Ethan any harm to get a little bit worried about where Kitty was.'

'So we persuaded her to leave her bag with us.'

'But the bag had everything in it! Her keys ... her clothes ...'

'Yes. But she took all that and then we sort of filled it again. The only things in that bag that are really hers are the phone and the knitting. We didn't trust her with the phone, because we thought she shouldn't even try and call you for at least 24 hours.'

I couldn't believe what I was hearing. 'What about the knitting? Did you think she was going to do herself an injury with
it or something?'

They looked at each other. 'Lucy took it out of the bag before
she went to the hotel,' said Alice, 'because we thought you'd
believe us if we had her knitting. Kitty was so distressed she
didn't even realise. That's how much you upset her, Theo! You
made her forget her knitting!'

'That's like fraud! You faked her disappearance!' A tiny part of
me was grateful that Kitty didn't seem to have instigated the
conspiracy – but she must have realised that I'd worry about her.
Unless she thought that Alice and Lucy would explain where
she was.

'It just felt like a good idea at the time,' Alice has the grace to
look a bit ashamed of herself. 'We were really angry with both
of you. And Lucy did give her a spare phone, so she wasn't completely unable to communicate.'

'At least you found out what an evil person Ethan was, before
you got involved with him.' Lucy hugs me. 'Honestly, Theo,
you've had a lucky escape.'

'Don't make out that this was actually a good idea!' I tell her.
'You need to learn to mind your own business. Who appointed
you as the Relationship Police?'

'We were just upset for Kitty! We're her friends! And we
didn't think it would go on this long. We thought you'd ring her
mum after the parade and then you'd feel really stupid when
she said everything was OK.'

'Yeah, well, next time keep your noses out!' And for the

second time in one morning I have the satisfaction of stamping out of someone's front door and slamming it behind me. Not much satisfaction, I have to admit.

I get the tram back towards Ethan's house, so I can retrieve my bike and then start walking along the riverside. I'll insist I have to go back to London. I've finished with Sophie; there is no reason for my family to keep me away. I never want to see Ethan or Kitty again. Amsterdam is finished for me.

Love only causes pain. I'm going to tear up my manuscript and rewrite my book, write out all the love and romance. We are all better off on our own. Love hurts. Love is a battlefield.

Then I realise that I'm just reciting the titles of cheesy old songs. I'm not even original in my misery. My phone rings and, instead of checking who it is, I'm stupid enough to answer.

'Yes?' I bark.

'Theo? Are you OK?'

'Simon? Is everything all right? Mum?'

'She's a bit better. I think they're planning to come and see you soon.'

I'm nearly at Ethan's house. There's a small playground at the street corner and I find a bench to sit on, looking out over the river. It's cold, and I'm shivering a bit.

'She's better? Really?'

'You ought to talk to them, Theo. Anyway, how are things with you?'

There's something strange about the way Simon says this. He's trying to hurry me off the subject too quickly.

'Simon, do you know something that I don't know?'

'Probably loads of things.'

I don't usually give him easy openers like that. This time I don't care.

'No ... I mean, about Mum. Do you know something ... maybe no one told me because I was away ...'

'You need to ask them, not me.' Simon sounds distinctly shifty. 'I'm not even at home right now. You ring them, Theo. It wouldn't kill you.'

'Look, I'm having a really bad day, so if you've just phoned up to patronise me, you can piss off.'

'Ah, well, that's why I rang you.'

'What?'

'Because I thought you might be having a bad day.'

'What are you, Mystic Simon all of a sudden?'

'What's going on, Theo? Come on. You can tell me. Just tell me what's going on.'

'Oh, nothing,' I say. 'Nothing.'

'It doesn't sound like nothing.'

I've never talked much to Simon. But then I've never felt as lonely as this before.

'All my friends lied to me, and made me look like an idiot, and I thought I liked someone, but they were lying too.'

'So, the teacher thing? That's all finished?'

'The teacher thing?' I spend a second thinking about Sophie. There are no good memories left. I just see her grim face, telling me I'm history.

'Oh, that's well finished. Over. Forgotten. She dumped me.'

Simon makes a noise that I think might be a sigh of relief.

'OK, so that's good. I know it's difficult, but you must see that you're better off without her.'

'Everything's a whole load more complicated. And I don't have any friends any more.'

'Theo, you do have friends. All the guys in London, all your friends, they're always asking about you ...'

'Huh,' I say. 'I mean my friends here.'

'So, who's been lying to you? And why?'

'I don't know why.' I think about what Ethan said. 'For fun, maybe? To make me look stupid.'

'What about Kitty?' asks Simon. I nearly drop my phone.

'How did you know about Kitty? Did Mum tell you?'

'Yeah ... sort of ...'

'Yeah, well, Kitty and I are over. And she's been lying to me too.'

'So, um, have you been seeing someone else?'

I go all cold inside. Simon knows. He knows about Ethan. I can tell from the tone of his voice, which is nervous, interested and ... somehow ... informed.

'What the actual hell, Simon?'

'What?'

'What? You tell me what? Why are you snooping around and asking me stuff?'

'I'm ... OK, I do know something. Sort of. Not any details.'

I use the rudest word that I know.

'It's just ... Look, Rachel and I were friends for ages before you met her sister.'

Rachel? Oh yeah, Kitty's sister. 'You were at school together. So what?'

'So, she messaged me when it turned out that her sister was in Amsterdam as well as you, and we've kind of been seeing each other the last few weeks, and I'm in Newcastle right now, because that's where Rachel's at uni and Kitty turned up this morning.'

'What did she tell you?' My voice doesn't really convey how shocked and angry I'm feeling right now. It just shakes a little at the end of the sentence.

'Nothing, really – just that she thought you'd been two-timing her with someone else.'

'Did she say who?'

Simon doesn't say anything, which means, yes, she did.

'Well, you can tell Kitty to leave me alone. She can play stupid tricks on someone else. And I am not seeing anyone else, and I am never going to get involved with anyone ever again, and you can all piss off and mind your own business.'

I end the call before he can answer. How dare Kitty out me to my brother? What next, some tell-all Tumblr post?

'You're here! Did you come back for your bike?'

I look up. Ethan's standing over me, impossibly tall. He's got a smirk on his face.

'I've got something to tell you,' he says.

Anger explodes like a bomb in my brain. 'Go away!' I yell, jumping to my feet and shoving him away as hard as I can.

Chapter 40

Theo

Amsterdam

Ethan hurtles away from me, arms flailing, speeding towards the river. He grabs at a tree branch to steady himself, loses his balance altogether, slams against the trunk, goes crashing to the ground and stays there. He's only a few centimetres from the water's edge.

I can't understand what's happened until I see that he's wearing rollerblades. That's why he seemed so tall. I am beyond stupid.

I approach him cautiously.

'Are you OK?' Dumb question. He's clearly not OK, in fact he's lying on the ground, clutching his arm. Tears are pouring down his face, which is covered in grit and sand. Blood dribbles down his chin as though he were an injured vampire.

My anger drains away. I feel sick at the damage that I've done.

'I'm so sorry ... I didn't know you were on skates ...'

Ethan takes a deep, shuddering breath. 'My arm,' he says. 'My arm.'

'I'll call an ambulance.' Maybe I should call the police too, and report myself for assault. Then they can lock me up for the second time in two days and, ideally, deport me.

'It's broken,' he says. His eyes look a bit vacant; I think he must be in shock. He's shivering so much that his teeth are chattering. 'It hurts. It's broken.'

I take charge, unstrapping his skates, taking off my jumper and draping it around his shoulders. 'Can you get up?'

He shakes his head, no, and forces himself to speak. 'Not yet. Give me ... a minute.'

'OK. I'm really sorry ...'

He stares at me. 'She's safe. Kitty's in England. My dad rang back.'

'I know. They tricked us, the girls. They tricked us, like you tricked me.'

He doesn't seem to understand. His eyes blink as he tries to process his thoughts. He says something that I can't hear properly. Not far, it sounds like. It was not far.

Not far to England?

He's leaning against the tree. I sit down next to him, because I'm scared he's going to pass out and roll right into the river. I try and brush the sand off his face, but he winces, so I stop.

'It hurts,' he says. 'It hurts. My head ... my arm.'

I pull out my phone to call an ambulance. Of course, the battery's dead.

'Mieke,' he says. 'Please. Call Mieke.'

'Who? I don't know her number,' I say, and then I realise that his phone has fallen out of his pocket and is lying next to him. I find this Mieke's number and call. An old girlfriend, maybe?

'*Dag, met Mieke,*' she says. 'Ethan?'

'Um, Mieke, this is Theo; I'm Ethan's friend ... sort of ... and we need your help.'

'How so? Is Ethan all right?'

'He's hurt ... he fell over on his skates ... I think he's concussed and he might have broken his arm.'

'Where are you? I'll come right away! Where is his father?'

'He's in Paris,' I tell her. 'I think we need an ambulance.'

'Oh, Ethan,' she says. 'Can I talk to him?'

I put the phone to Ethan's ear and listen to her fussing over him. He only says a few words. His eyes keep fluttering shut, and I'm worried he's about to pass out.

At last she stops talking and I take the phone back. She asks me where we are, and I explain. 'Don't worry, Theo,' she says. 'I will call the ambulance and I'll be with you very soon. Thank you for looking after him.'

'I didn't mean ... It wasn't ...'

'Let me call them now,' she says, and she's gone. Ethan's head is drooping and he's so near the river's edge that I have to gently move him away. The pain wakes him up, and he groans out loud.

'She's coming ... and the ambulance ...' I say, and Ethan grimaces.

'Kitty ... she's OK ...' he says again, and I nod and say, 'I know, Alice and Lucy told me.' He doesn't seem to hear me. 'But she's OK ... I didn't want you to worry ...' Then he turns his head away and vomits all down his front, and that must have hurt his arm or something, because he starts crying again, and all I can do is use my jumper to wipe some of the puke away.

'It's all right,' I say, 'don't cry, they're going to come soon; I know it hurts, I'm so sorry.'

His eyes are flickering again now, and I know enough about concussion to realise that I have to keep him awake, I have to keep him talking. I hold his hand, shaking it uselessly.

He opens his eyes wide. 'Kitty,' he says. And then he's talking in Dutch and I'm straining to hear, and I don't understand it anyway.

'Ik hou van jouw. Het was niet waar.'

I hear you? It was not far?

All I care about is trying to keep him awake and away from the water.

'It's OK,' I say. 'Just stay awake.'

Someone's at my side. An older woman, with spiky hair and dark-rimmed glasses and a bright-red raincoat. 'Theo?' she asks. 'I'm Mieke. Ah, Ethan, *schaatje.* Be brave now. The ambulance is on its way.'

I watch Mieke sit down next to Ethan, and how he tries to smile for her. She strokes his hair and talks to him in Dutch, and I wonder if she's a kind of substitute mother for him, or whether he'd prefer his real mum to be here.

And I wish my mum was here now, or we were in London so I could go home and give her a hug.

Then the ambulance arrives, and the paramedics take over. I back away as fast as I can, until I can hardly see the little bunch of people at the side of the Amstel River.

Chapter 41

Kitty

Amsterdam

Knitting is a bit like being the general of an army, without having to kill anyone. Control, order, no arguments in the ranks. Even if things go wrong, you can always unravel and start again. Plus there's a rhythm to it, which I find soothing. One stitch after another. It's meditation for hands.

That's what I've been doing. Knitting, knitting, knitting. Hospitals make me nervous, whether we're in London or Amsterdam.

We're waiting to see the specialist who did all the tests last week. Mum insisted once she heard how I'd virtually collapsed on the bridge after the party. 'Thank God Alice and Lucy came after you,' she said. 'I wish you'd rung me. You should've gone straight to the hospital.'

'Well, we didn't,' I said.

I felt horribly guilty about my trip to Newcastle. I'd never meant the boys to get so scared. That is, it had occurred to me that they might worry a bit, but I assumed that Lucy and Alice would give them a bit of a scare and then tell them. Actually I didn't much care if they were freaked out. After all, I'd had the shock of my life.

The only bad moment was when Theo knocked at my door and called to me when I was getting changed in the flat in the morning.

I almost opened the door, abandoned the whole Operation Evacuation before I'd even got on the ferry. But then I remembered the way his body was relaxed against Ethan's, his eyes closed, the way Ethan's hand gently cradled Theo's head, and I froze, still and cold as a snowman.

It wasn't our fault that Mum and Paul hadn't answered Ethan's phone calls, meaning that the boys went on worrying longer than we'd expected. And we were totally not responsible for Ethan's mysterious concussion and broken arm, which no one had really explained.

Every day I see Theo's miserable face at college, and I feel terrible. I'm totally not over him, and I want to apologise ... comfort him ... But every day I remember. He isn't sad about me. It was Ethan who had upset him. Lucy and Alice had told me what Ethan said. I could hardly believe that anyone could be so evil that they'd just kiss someone else's boyfriend for the fun of breaking them up.

'Kitty Levy,' calls the nurse, and we go in to see the doctor. He shakes our hands, and invites us to sit down.

I'm so used to doctors saying that everything's fine, that nothing needs to be done, that it takes a moment to grasp that this isn't happening this time. He's showing us charts and explaining what they mean. I can't hear him. There's a roaring noise in my ears, the thunder of fear.

'So, a pacemaker is really the only sensible way forward?' says Mum, and he launches into an explanation of why and how, and what it'll look like ('a small lump, just here', gesturing towards my left boob), and how it'll jump start my unreliable interior engine, should it go flat.

Afterwards, we don't go for our usual celebration in a café. Mum calls a taxi and we go straight home. I keep the tears back until we're safely in our flat.

She hugs me. 'Oh, Kitty! Sweetheart! It'll be OK! It's really quite a minor operation.'

'I don't want an operation!' Now I've started crying, I can't stop. 'I don't want a lump on my chest!'

'Kitty, darling ...'

'It'll look horrible!'

Mum takes my hands. 'No, it won't. And so what if it does? It'll keep you alive, and that is all that counts.'

'No one will ever want me!' I'm being a drama queen, I know, but I can't seem to stop. All the pain of the last few weeks seems to be pouring out – literally – in tears and snot and I'm even feeling a bit sick, because the sobs are making me hiccup.

'Oh, Kitty. That's nonsense. Tell you what, why don't you call Theo? He might cheer you up.'

'Mum!' I wail even louder. 'I'm not talking to Theo! He's not talking to me!'

Alice and Lucy had tried to persuade me that everything was

Ethan's fault. I hated him, but I still blamed Theo. He didn't have to fall for Ethan's scheming.

'And neither of you are talking to Ethan. I know. I just don't understand why. I can't keep up with you. Paul says he's utterly miserable.'

'He's not utterly miserable, he's utterly horrible!'

'Oh, Kitty. The poor boy. He needs his friends.'

'Well, I'm never going to be one of them.'

'I wish you'd explain.'

'Never.'

'Never say never.'

'It's none of your business!' I summon all my strength, grab my knitting and the box of tissues and stomp off to my room.

She gives me half an hour to recover, during which time I manage to stop crying, redo my mascara and knit a few rows of the scarf that was meant to be for Theo, but is now for me. Then Mum taps at the bedroom door, and tries to entice me out with a cup of hot chocolate.

'I'm fine. I don't need babying,' I say.

'I went out specially to buy marshmallows ...'

'Oh, all right.' I'm grumpy, but slightly comforted by her efforts to make me feel better.

'It's Sinterklaas Eve tonight,' says Mum. 'Shall we put out your shoe?'

'You what?'

'If you put out your shoe then Sinterklaas will bring you presents.'

'How old do you think I am, six?'

'Well, I just thought it would be nice to follow a local custom.'

'Sinterklaas is a deeply racist symbol of Western imperialism,' I point out.

'Well … that's how some people interpret it. It's kind of cute, though. The Dutch write little poems to each other. I could write one for you. *I love my daughter, Kitty. She's clever and she's pretty.*'

I snort. 'I am not putting out my shoe.'

'I don't know why you have to be so grumpy all the time.'

'Huh,' I say. 'I'm Skyping Rachel.'

Rachel's annoyingly upbeat about the whole thing. 'It's great news!' she says. 'All that worry you've been carrying around! Not to mention all that worry that I've been carrying around. I don't want to lose my little sister.'

'Huh,' I say. 'It's a sign. My heart is unreliable. I'm never going to trust it again.'

'Nonsense! This is a physical problem, not a metaphorical one.'

'Rachel, this is huge!'

'Look, why don't you make it up with Theo? Simon says he's really down too.'

'Never,' I say, as firmly as possible.

'Oh, come on. It's going to be so awkward when Simon and I come and visit.'

'I'll cope.'

'Just mark it down to experience and move on,' coaxes Rachel. 'Look, if you'd just let me tell Mum about it. I know she's worried.'

It's all very well for her, I think, once we've finished talking.

Rachel flits from one casual relationship to another, and now she's in love she thinks that everything's going to be great for ever. Forever and ever. Well, that's because she is shallow. And lucky.

She even had the cheek to suggest that the coincidence of me and Theo meeting in Amsterdam meant that she and Simon were meant to be together.

My only comfort is that it probably won't last with this Simon (if he's anything like his brother) and then she'll be sorry. She'll be heartbroken like me but even that won't make me happy because I'm going to be miserable for the rest of my miserable life, which will now go on for ever and ever, thanks to Doctor van Pacemaker. Thanks for nothing.

Chapter 42

Kitty

Amsterdam

Mum knocks at my door. 'Come on, darling, you can't gloom around in here all day. I'll take you out to dinner.'

The air's so cold that I can see my breath puffing out in front of me. Amsterdam looks different, veiled by a sprinkling of snow. Still pretty, still picture-perfect, still begging to be framed and copied and admired. But my phone stays in my pocket. I've hardly posted on Instagram for weeks.

We get the tram into town, and Mum leads the way along the Herengracht, to the Utrechtestraat. I'm too miserable to admire the gorgeous shops we pass along the way. 'Here we are,' she says, ringing the bell of an Indonesian restaurant. I'm just wondering why she's chosen this one in particular, when the door opens and I see two people sitting at a table for four.

I go into reverse as quickly as I can, cannoning into Mum and the waitress.

'What's going on? Why are they here?'

'Because Paul is important to me, so you and Ethan are going to have to get over whatever it is.'

'But – he's—'

'He's had a tough time too, Kitty. Arm broken in two places.'

'I don't care!' I say, but Paul has seen us, and he's standing up and there's no way of getting out of this without actually running out on to the street.

'I hate you!' I hiss at Mum, and then Paul is giving her a hug, and trying to hug me too, except I step swiftly backwards, landing on the waitress's toe.

Ethan must have seen all this, and I'd have expected an amused smile, but instead his face is blank. As we approach, he ducks his head down, staring at his hands. His right arm is in plaster from elbow to wrist. He looks terrible. His eyes are puffy, with dark shadows underneath. His skin is coloured with bruises fading yellow and green.

'Well!' says Paul. 'How nice to get together!' His faux-cheerfulness makes me wince, and despite myself I glance sideways at Ethan to share the moment. But he doesn't catch my eye. He might be feeling ashamed of himself, but I doubt it.

'How are you, Ethan?' asks Mum. 'Not much longer in plaster?'

I wait for Ethan's sarcastic reply. Will he ignore her, or make some stupid joke, or …?

'Three more weeks,' he says. His voice is soft, almost croaky. As though he hasn't used it much, recently.

'How did you get on at the hospital this morning, Kitty?' asks Paul. 'Everything all right, I hope?'

Mum adopts the tone that Rachel and I call the Voice of Optimism.

'Well, it turns out that the doctors here think that Kitty should have a pacemaker fitted. Just a precaution, you know. And it'll be marvellous because Kitty will be able to be so much more confident, won't you, love, and not worry all the time, and it's really a very small procedure, not like heart surgery at all.'

Ethan's eyes widen, and I have the satisfaction of seeing that he is quite shocked to hear this. I almost wish that I'd had a heart attack when I saw him kissing Theo because that would have punished him for his appalling behaviour. Except I'd probably have died, which would be very harsh on Mum.

'It is surgery and it does involve the heart,' I say, fingers itching for my knitting. 'So it is heart surgery.'

'A pacemaker is a wonderful thing when you think about it,' says Paul. 'If you think of your body as an orchestra, it's like putting a top conductor in charge.'

Mum beams at him. 'That's a beautiful image, darling. Something to think about, Kitty.'

I'm trying not to be rude. 'Yes, but conducting an orchestra doesn't involve cutting into my flesh and inserting ironware!'

'Not really ironware, sweetheart: a life-saving, high tech invention that will make sure your heart doesn't misbehave.' Mum pats my hand.

I hide behind my menu, hyper-aware of Ethan next to me, staring into space, not even pretending to be interested. Of course he wouldn't care about my heart. He actually hates me.

Paul is asking more about the operation – when, where, will

I have to stay overnight? Mum answers for me and I study the menu as though I'm revising for an exam in Indonesian food. Chicken in coconut sauce sounds OK, and that's what I order. Ethan just shrugs when it's his turn, and Paul orders something for him. 'Do you think you can manage that with your left hand?' he asks, and again I wait for the sarcasm. Nothing. Ethan just nods.

I can't bear it. He's turned himself into some sort of victim, when he's actually the one to blame for everything. It was pure karma that he fell over and broke his arm.

So I say, 'What's the matter with you, Ethan? You've gone very quiet.'

He looks me in the eye for the first time. 'I broke my arm,' he says. 'That's what's wrong with me.'

'Seems like you broke your mouth too,' I say. 'Although maybe that's not a bad thing. Now you've got a broken arm, perhaps it'll slow you down a bit. You can't manipulate people for fun.'

'If you're having an operation you won't be able to manipulate people either,' he replies. 'For fun or whatever.'

'I didn't do it for fun!' I explode. 'I did it to teach you a lesson! You and Theo!'

'Kitty—' says Mum, but I am unstoppable.

'Next thing you'll be telling me you broke up my relationship for my own good!'

'I'm not telling you anything,' he says. Then he shrugs, which makes me want to hit him. 'There's no point trying to talk,' he says. 'Believe what you want. It's probably true. Anyway, you told me it wasn't serious, you and Theo, so I don't know what you're making a big fuss about.'

'You what?' I am beyond outraged. 'You asked me if I was serious about Theo! You never said "Do you mind if I make a move?"'

'I didn't know for sure that's what I was going to do,' he mumbles, refusing to look at me and pleating his napkin between his long fingers.

'Well that's what you're supposed to do when you're about to steal someone else's boyfriend!' I know my voice is too loud, and I can feel other people's voices hushing as they turn to see who is shouting, but I can't stop myself.

'Kitty! Ethan!' says Mum, 'What's going on? People are looking!'

'Nothing,' I mutter. Ethan doesn't even acknowledge the question.

'Ethan?' says Paul. 'What have you done to upset Kitty?'

'Mind your own business,' Ethan growls.

The chicken in coconut sauce has arrived and it smells delicious and I'm hungry, but there's a principle at stake. 'I'm not eating with him. He's just a … a nasty person … and I don't see why I should be forced to have anything to do with him. Sorry. I'm going.'

I stand up, but Ethan's standing up too.

'I'll go,' he says. 'I can't eat anyway.' He turns to Paul. 'I told you this was a bad idea. Sit down, Kitty, I'm going.'

'No, *I'm* going!'

'It's not necessary.'

'Shut up, both of you,' says Paul. 'Stop behaving like babies.'

We're both as shocked as each other.

'Yes, sit down,' says Mum. 'And either tell us what this is all about, or be quiet and eat your food.'

I feel a bit ridiculous standing there, and so I sit down. So does Ethan.

'Right,' says Paul. 'So, what's it to be? Who wants to start?'

'I don't want to talk about it,' I say. 'And I don't think Ethan does either.'

'No,' he says. 'It's all too complicated.'

'It's not exactly complicated,' I say, irritated by the way he refuses to admit that anything is his fault. 'It's simple. I had a boyfriend and Ethan decided to nick him. Just for the fun of breaking us up.'

'Oh, Ethan –' says Paul.

'Oh, Kitty –' says Mum.

At last, Ethan seems defeated. 'I can't do all this,' he says. 'I'm just crap with people. Just leave me alone, OK?' He pushes his chair back, and strides out of the restaurant, almost bashing into a waitress in his hurry to leave us behind.

'I'd better go after him,' says Paul. 'I'm so sorry.'

Left alone, Mum and I help ourselves to tiny amounts of food. It tastes like mouthfuls of pebbles, and I can hardly swallow it.

'Oh Kitty,' she says. 'What a horrible mess. You should have told me, darling.'

I sniff. 'It's OK. Look, you have a good time with Paul, that's fine, but don't expect me to spend time with Ethan, OK? I hate him.'

Mum blinks a few times, 'It's not that easy, sweetie.'

'What do you mean?'

'Well ... we weren't going to tell you until Rachel comes to stay ... but Paul proposed when we were in Paris. We're getting married, darling. Ethan's going to be your brother.'

Chapter 43

Theo

Amsterdam

I think about calling Ethan and finding out if he's OK, but I just can't do it. Not even a text. I feel terrible about his broken arm, and I wake up at night from dreams where he falls over the river's edge. But I can't forget what he said, what he did. I still feel dirty and used. And I'm completely confused about whether the feelings I had for him were real and is so what they mean.

College is pretty horrible now I'm not talking to Kitty or Alice or Lucy, and I escape as early as I can. Especially today, which is Sinterklaas Eve, and everyone is invited over to Finn's house for a politically correct, Zwarte-Piet-free celebration. He asked me if I wanted to come, but I made an excuse. And actually Chalex did make a big point of asking me to be home early.

The house smells of apple and spice and Chani offers me a cup of tea and some pepernoten warm from the oven. A few years ago, I'd have laughed my head off at the idea of biscuits called pepper nuts. Now, it barely amuses me.

'Alex will be back soon,' she says. I can hear the excitement in her voice, and it makes me smile. You can't dislike Alex and Chani, they are both such good, nice people, and they've done so much to welcome me. It's not their fault that everything has gone wrong.

'I'm surprised you celebrate Sinterklaas,' I say, 'it being a saint's day and all that.'

'Oh, it's a Dutch thing, not a Christian one,' she says. 'It's such fun; we loved it when we were kids.' She sings me a little song: '*Zwarte Piet, wiede wiede wiet; Ik hoor je wel, maar ik zie je niet.*'

'What does it mean?' I ask, thinking about how Alice would go mad.

'The first bit is just nonsense, and then it says, "I hear you but I don't see you." But I used to sing "Ik hou je wel," which means, "I love you," because I loved Zwarte Piet so much. I think lots of others did too.'

My mind goes back to Ethan lying on the ground next to the canal, trying to talk to me in Dutch. I hear you, he said. I hear you, Theo. Or was he saying something else? It couldn't be ... could it?

'Chani, I heard something the other day, which I didn't understand. What does it mean, *het was niet waar*? Not far? Not fair?'

'It was not true,' she corrects me. 'Waar means true.'

Not true? He was telling me that something wasn't true?

I'm on my feet. 'Chani, I can't stay. I've got to go. I'm really sorry.'

'No, Theo, you can't go!' she says. Then we hear Alex's key at the door. 'Ah, here they are!'

I hear them first. The rumble of my dad's voice, Alex's cheerful chatter. Then, another voice. 'Theo? Where are you, darling?'

Am I hallucinating? My mum looks the same – still thin, still pale – but she seems completely different. She's smiling, she's got that busy, energetic feel about her again, I can tell just from the way she's standing there, looking at me, arms out wide.

'Theo!' she says, and I run to hug her. She even smells different, of perfume and make-up. She smells like Mum. She doesn't smell strange and ill any more.

'Good surprise, eh?' says Dad, clapping me on the shoulder.

'I didn't think you were well enough to travel – but you look great. Why didn't you tell me?'

Mum lets me go. 'I think you've grown, Theo, in just a few weeks! Thank you so much, Chani, for taking care of him so well.'

'We didn't want to tell you we were coming just in case we had to call it off,' says Dad. 'Your mother's a lot better, but I have to keep an eye on her, just the same.'

I'm amazed. 'So, what … how … Did you just get better? Did they work out what was wrong with you?'

'Why don't you show me your room?' says Mum. 'That's all right, isn't it, Chani? Then I can tell you all about it.'

'There are a lot of stairs,' I say, doubtfully.

'I'll take it slowly.'

Dad stays downstairs, talking to Chalex, about the business, the family, Arsenal. I lead the way upstairs slowly, but Mum's more than able to manage, even the last bit, which is pretty much a ladder, although she has to sit down on my bed to get her breath back.

'Are you OK? I can get Dad.'

'I'm fine,' she says. 'Just out of practice after months of doing next to nothing.' She pats the bed next to her. 'Come and sit down, Theo, I've got something to say to you.'

I sit down, slightly reluctantly. It's going to be about Sophie, I'm sure. Simon will have told her that it's all over. What else has he said? Does she know about Ethan?

'Look, Mum, about Sophie ...' I say.

She pats my hand.

'I know it's important, but that's not what I want to talk to you about. This is more important, Theo.'

OK, she knows about Ethan. I'm going to have to explain somehow.

'Mum, I don't know what Simon told you, but I'm not actually gay. I don't think so anyway. It was just a kiss, and it turns out ... well, I'm not sure ... but that was all it was ... I mean, I might be gay but it's not actually an ongoing thing at the moment.'

As coming-out speeches go, this is clearly the most pathetic in the history of gay pride, especially as she doesn't seem to have understood one word of it.

'Sorry ... what are you telling me?'

'I kissed a guy,' I say, miserably. 'And I liked it.'

Mum looks like she's trying not to cry. But she's smiling at me at the same time.

'Isn't that a song?'

'Not exactly.'

'Will you be upset with me, Theo, darling, if I say that I'm not very surprised? That your dad and I always thought there was a possibility ... ?'

I could not be more stunned if she'd pulled a mallet out of her bag and bopped me over the head.

'But ... I didn't know ... '

'Maybe you didn't admit it to yourself,' she says.

Who would have thought my mum would know so much about me?

'Being different is difficult in our world,' she says. 'Everyone's handed a template for life. For some people, like Alex and Chani, it seems to come easily. But it's not for everyone.'

'I ... but ... how did you know? What did you know?'

'Oh, tiny things when you were growing up,' she says. 'And you always reminded me very much of my Uncle Lou.'

My great-uncle Lou died a few years ago. He had a wife, three children, eight grandchildren and one great-grand-daughter. He had a season ticket for Tottenham and he'd built up a business in women's underwear. I mean selling women's underwear, not wearing it. As far as I know.

'But he was married,' I say, feebly, and she says, 'He came from a different generation, Theo, and he couldn't be the person he wanted to be. No one ever talked about it. But Auntie Ruby knew, and, since he died, she's talked to me about it a little. You don't need to decide anything right now, sweetie, you're still so young. But don't worry about us, about our reaction.'

'I do worry,' I tell her. I'd never realised how much until this moment.

'Well, don't. If we can cope with Jonny becoming a frummer, we can cope with pretty much anything that you do. Within reason.'

'Dad's proud of Jonny.'

'Your dad makes a lot of noise, but eventually he likes to build bridges. If you decide you're gay, I have no doubt he'll come around to it, and start taking part in Pride marches.'

I grin at this idea. It would be typical of Dad, she's right.

'So, Simon did tell us that it's all over with the teacher, with Sophie?'

'Yeah. She finished it.'

'I can't pretend I'm sorry. This person you kissed, he's not your teacher, is he?'

'No. Absolutely not.'

'And will I get to meet him?'

'No,' I say. Then I think back to what Chani just told me. Had I got it all wrong about Ethan? 'I don't know. I need to talk to him. Maybe. One day.'

'Then talk to him. But first, I have something to tell you.'

I force myself to listen.

'I have a confession to make. I've kept a big secret from you. I did have a diagnosis, just a few weeks before your GCSEs. A diagnosis of cancer.'

For a minute I can't breathe. They kept this secret from me? But then I think what's worse, the news, or the secret? The news, obviously.

'You have cancer?' I swallow. 'Are you going to die?'

'I'm in remission now. I'm fine. I've been having chemo for

months. I can tell you all the gory details later, darling, if you want them. The main thing is that the cancer is gone now, and the oncologist says there is a very good chance that it won't come back.'

'You didn't have to keep it a secret from me. I would have ... could have done so much ...'

'I suppose I wanted to protect you. I couldn't bear to think of you worrying. We didn't want you to mess up your exams. And then there was the thing with the teacher ...'

'Mum, you could have told me. I'm not a baby. You told Simon, didn't you? And Jonny?'

'We told them. Simon's found it very difficult indeed. Especially keeping it from you.'

'Huh,' I say. 'I'm sixteen! You could have told me.' *Simon could have told me*, I think.

'I know you're not a baby, Theo, but all of you boys, you're all my babies. Your pain is my pain. I saw the effect it had on Simon, and I wasn't strong enough to tell you as well. It seemed easier to send you here, so that I could have the chemo and you could have a break from everything. I was selfish, I know. Maybe I love you too much.'

I do think they were totally and absolutely wrong, but I sort of understand why they didn't tell me. Anyway, I'm so relieved to see her looking so well that I don't care as much as I might have done.

'You didn't have to protect me.'

'I've had a lot of time to think it through,' she says. 'Remember my father came to England on the Kindertransport? All his family died in the Shoah. He never talked about it to my sisters or me. He kept it to himself because he wanted us to live our lives free from all that pain and sorrow. And perhaps he wanted to avoid the actual talking bit as well. I didn't think I was like him. But I've discovered that I am.'

We never ever talk about Grandpa's past. It's too painful to talk about. So maybe we have a family tradition of keeping secrets? And maybe now Mum and I have acknowledged it, things might change?

But I'm wondering what would have happened if the chemo hadn't worked. If the cancer had won the battle. When would they have told me? At her funeral?

I give her another big hug and she says, 'So we're quits? No more secrets?'

'OK,' I say.

'Do you want to come back to London? Or are you happy here?'

'I don't know. I need to talk to someone, to Ethan ...'

'Let's go downstairs and have the food that Chani's been working hard to make for us. Let's hear all about this Dutch tradition that she wants to tell us about.'

'OK,' I say.

'You take your time to think about what you want to do, whether Amsterdam or London is the best place for you. We'd love to have you at home again. But we'll understand if you decide to stay.'

Chapter 44

Theo

Amsterdam

The next few days are busy. There's college and then I have Mum and Dad to entertain, taking them to the Rijksmuseum, the Van Gogh Museum and accompanying Dad on buying trips to various warehouses full of designer Dutch furniture, which is actually sort of fun.

Ethan's on my mind all the time. I go with Chalex to see my parents off at the airport, and as soon as we get back I cycle over to his house. Surely we can sort things out? I'm almost certain that when he was babbling in Dutch, he was telling me that he'd been lying. That he loved me. It's going to be all right.

I knock at Ethan's door, the one that leads up to his room. No answer. Maybe he can't hear me. So I knock at the other door. Ethan's dad opens it.

'Hello,' he says. 'Theo, isn't it? You came to my workshop. How's the novel going?'

KEREN DAVID

I haven't written a word for weeks. 'It's OK,' I tell him. 'Is Ethan in?'

'I think so. It's good to see you. Mieke tells me that I have a lot to thank you for.'

Is he kidding?

'No, well, I'm sorry about what happened,' I say. 'I didn't know he was wearing skates, you see . . .'

Paul ignores all this. 'Mieke said that if it weren't for you, Ethan could have fallen into the water. I dread to think what might have happened.'

'Yes, but—'

'He's upstairs, I think. Just go and find him. Hopefully it'll cheer him up a bit. I can't get close to him when he's in this mood.'

'Oh, um, right. Well, I'll just . . .'

'It's not easy being a parent. Whatever you do is wrong.'

'OK, well, I'll just . . .'

'I do understand. He can't think that I disapprove. He can sleep with whoever he wants, boys, girls, it's all fine with me.'

I've got my foot on the spiral staircase.

'Um, well, I'll just go and talk to him then.'

'I'm doing my best. I really am. I know there's been a difficult situation with Kitty, but I'm sure it can be resolved . . . And I'm not going to nag him about art school any more. He can fritter away his life as much as he wants, if only he'd just communicate with me and his mother . . .'

I climb as fast as I can. 'Bye,' I call from the top, vowing never to have a conversation with Ethan's dad again.

I have to open a few doors before I find the stairs up to Ethan's attic. I knock at his door a few times before I hear his voice. It doesn't sound very welcoming, but I go in anyway.

Ethan's room isn't tidy like it was the first time I saw it. His bed is unmade; there are piles of clothes on the floor. The window is open, despite the snow drifting down in random gusts, as though a giant child is scattering frozen handfuls. Ethan's sitting in a corner. He stands up, awkwardly holding his arm in front of him. He's got a plaster cast, covered with a blue cloth cover. He's wearing sweatpants and a baggy T-shirt. His hair needs a wash, and he hasn't shaved.

I'm just so happy to see him again and I'm actually trembling because I want to touch him so much.

'Hi,' I say.

'What do you want?' he says. 'Why are you here?'

'I just wanted to ... I worked it out. What you were saying to me.'

'What I was saying to you?'

'When ... by the river. When you were hurt. You were talking to me in Dutch.'

'I don't remember saying anything. I had *hersenschudding*.'

'What's that?'

'I don't know the English word. Brain-shaking.'

'Concussion.'

'That's it. Concussion.' He sits down at his table. 'I was in the hospital. I broke my arm in two places. I can't do anything – cycle, skate, draw, anything.'

He doesn't invite me to sit down, but I do anyway.

'I worked it out,' I say. 'You were telling me that what you said … it wasn't true. You didn't just break Kitty and me up for fun. It wasn't true!'

'*Het was niet waar*,' he says. 'It took you all this time to understand?'

'I didn't take a Dutch class,' I explain, 'because I didn't think I was staying. I didn't think it was worth it.'

'OK,' he says. 'So you finally worked it out. I was lying. I never thought you'd believe it in the first place.'

'Why? Why did you lie?'

'Because I didn't believe the girls' story. They were much more interested in telling us off than finding Kitty. And also … you made it clear … you were ashamed about kissing me. You didn't want anyone to find out. So, I thought I'd make it easier for you.'

'I didn't mean to hurt your feelings.'

'I don't have any feelings. Don't worry about it.'

'I was so angry. I felt … like you'd assaulted me.' I don't want to remember that sick, dirty feeling. 'You'd lied to get me to do stuff that I'd never …'

'I understood,' he says, looking away from me. 'I'm sorry you felt like that.'

'It was only because of what you said.'

'I wanted to tell you that Paul had called. That Kitty was OK. And that it was all a lie. I was so happy to see you, sitting there on that bench. I thought you'd come back to me.'

I'd come back for the bike. I'd felt ashamed of kissing him. I don't know what to say.

'But then you broke my arm,' he continues. 'You didn't even let me speak. And now, weeks later, you finally work out the truth.'

'I didn't mean to hurt you! I didn't realise you were on skates!'

'You didn't wait to find out ...'

'I thought you were laughing at me!'

'You didn't have to hit me! You knew that Kitty was OK, and you never told me!' Ethan's voice is getting louder, and I can see tears in his eyes. He gets up, and walks away from me, staring out of the window, at the whirling snowflakes.

I dare to follow him. 'I didn't hit you. I really didn't. I pushed you. If you hadn't been on skates then you would've been fine.'

'I don't remember anything about it. Just waking up in hospital and you weren't there.'

I put my arms round him and pull him into a hug. 'It's OK,' I say. 'It's taken me ages to work out what happened, but we both know the truth now and it's OK. I really want to make this work.' I kiss the only bit of his face that I can see, his forehead. 'We can get over this. I even told my mum about you.'

For about a minute he relaxes in my arms, and we are heart-to-heart, breath-to-breath together. I know how much he wants me. If a hug can tell you that you're loved, then this is the one.

But then he pulls away from me. 'I think you'd better go.'

'But ... why?'

'I can't do this.'

'Why? I think we can get over this whole thing. I understad now.'

His face is so sad. 'Don't you get it? You hurt me. Physically hurt me. And I don't think I can be with someone who does that. So, however much I like you – and I do like you – I have to say no.'

'No?'

'If I was a girl, and you'd broken my arm, would you expect me to take you back if you just said sorry?'

'No, but – it's different. You're not a girl. And it was an accident.'

He looks at me and he shakes his head. 'No,' he says. 'It doesn't work like that. You'd better go.'

I'm desperate. 'I'm sorry! What can I do to make it up to you? I'm so sorry!'

He turns away from me again. 'Sorry can't take back what happened,' he says.

Chapter 45

Kitty

Amsterdam

Today is the day. Time to get my permanent souvenir from Amsterdam. Other people buy plastic tulips or Van Gogh on a fridge magnet, or – and I have seen this – sweets in the shape of female genitalia. I get a pacemaker.

I used to imagine the inside of my body as looking like a fuse box, with wires and switches, blinking lights and perhaps a twirling meter – a meter running backwards, to the moment of my death. Because that's how I thought it would end. But now, there'll be something inside me to monitor my heart's electrical rhythm. If the beat stops, the pacemaker will spark me back to life again. I'll have a whole episode of *Casualty* under my skin.

It's a good thing, obviously, but I feel all shaky and nervous, as though they're inserting a ticking time bomb instead of a lifesaver. 'You'll have to be buried, not cremated, when the time comes,' says the surgeon, who is tall and blond and has a loud voice that hurts my ears.

'I'm sorry?'

'If you are cremated, there would be an explosion that would take out most of Amsterdam!' he says. Then he laughs a lot. I'm a long way off getting the Dutch sense of humour.

It does make me understand Ethan a bit better though. I wonder if sometimes I thought he was being obnoxious when he was just being Dutch. But being Dutch doesn't excuse total obnoxiousness.

I have a drip attached to my hand and I've taken a tablet that helps me relax and sleep. I suppose I knew that with a local anaesthetic I would be conscious for the operation. I just hadn't thought about what that actually involved.

'The first needle will hurt, probably a great deal,' says the doctor. 'But the medication we've given you will make you drowsy, and you won't feel anything. You can watch what's happening inside you on a screen, if you want?'

I shudder. 'No, thank you.'

'It's interesting, Kitty,' says Mum. 'When will you ever have the chance again to see something like this?'

I glare at her. 'Never, hopefully.'

'Lots of people choose not to watch,' says the doctor. 'Now ... try and relax.'

I can't think of anything less relaxing than sitting on a bed with a load of people looking at my chest area, which is only covered up by a flimsy hospital robe. The nurse has put up a screen thing under my chin, so I can't see what's going on, and now the needle is going in, and it's just as painful as he said.

Mum squeezes my hand. 'It's OK, sweetheart. Just relax.'

I'm about to protest, but I'm finding it difficult to line up my brain and my mouth. I'm tired without being sleepy. The room is hot, full of shadows and whispers, and all I can feel is funny, tugging touches here and there behind the screen.

'This is a good thing, Kitty,' says the surgeon, except it's not the surgeon any more. His mask has gone and instead he has a stubbly beard, and I'm squinting because his blurry face looks slightly familiar.

'Don't you recognise me?' His face is sad.

'You're my dad!' I think it, because my mouth isn't working, and he seems to understand because he laughs out loud, that big booming laugh which is the only thing I properly remember about my dad. His laugh bounces off the walls and echoes in my ears. It drowns out the muttered Dutch that drifts in the air.

'At least you haven't forgotten me!'

'I'm never going to forget you,' I think, and now I'm feeling very small and we're on the sofa in our old home and the carpet is swirly, and there are flowers on the wall, and we're watching matchstick men kicking a ball.

'I told you every day of your life,' he says, 'that I love you, Kitty Levy. I love you now and I'll love you for ever. And you take that love with you, wherever you make your home.'

'I love you too,' I'm thinking, 'I wish you wouldn't go,' and then his face is shrinking and distorting and I'm trembling and crying, and I feel Mum shaking my arm and the surgeon is back to being a tall, blond, Dutch giant, and he's saying, 'That's it. Everything's done. That wasn't so difficult, was it?'

I can't feel my body at all. The screen has disappeared and my gown is back in place and a nurse is pulling a blanket over me. If I look down, I can see there's a dressing just where my left bra strap should be.

'We're going to leave you to rest now. You're still hooked up to all the machines, and Isabelle will come and check you often.'

Mum's talking to me, but I'm not listening really, just thinking about my dad and how if he'd known about his heart, if he'd had this operation, then he would still be here, and Mum and I wouldn't have come to Amsterdam, and I'd never have met Theo or Ethan.

I close my eyes, and Dad's voice is back, just in my head this time, just singing to me like he used to when I was a baby. A lullaby that his mum sang to him, and her mum sang to her. I know that because my grandma used to sing it after he'd died.

And somehow I can hear her voice too, and I'm sleepy and pain-free and nowhere in time or space, just floating peacefully with my new reliable heart.

Chapter 46

Kitty

Amsterdam

I look in the mirror. 'I am Kitty,' I tell myself. 'I am magnificent.'

I don't feel magnificent. I haven't got any make-up on, and my hair is a mess. Mum's gone out with Paul, and I've promised to tidy up, because she's invited a few friends over to watch the fireworks from our balcony. New Year's Eve in Amsterdam is all about fireworks, it seems. People started letting off firecrackers in the street mid-afternoon. It sounds like a war zone round here and it's only five o'clock.

It's one of the bonuses of being Jewish that we get two goes at New Year, new starts, resolutions, the lot. The autumn one has been rubbish so far, so I'm pinning my hopes on this one. I have no real resolutions, except to stop falling for boys who like boys.

I wash and dry my hair, put on jeans and a black jumper. I even slick on a bit of lip-gloss and mascara and try the mirror thing again. 'I am Kitty,' I say. 'I am magnificent!'

The flat is full of cards and flowers, but the operation was more than a week ago, so now the flowers are drooping and some of them are brown, and the water's gone stale and smelly. I throw out the stinky ones, and combine anything worth keeping. Then I hoover and tidy up, and open a window to let in a blast of cold air. More firecrackers. Maybe it is gunfire. Maybe there's been a coup, and some fringe militia has taken over Amsterdam and we're doomed, all doomed . . .

The doorbell buzzes and I answer, hoping it's not one of Mum's friends because then I'll have to be polite and talk to them until she gets back. It's not. 'Hey! It's us! Let us in!' Alice and Lucy burst into the flat and engulf me in a group hug.

'Woo! Kitty! You look great!'

'We'd have come before, but your mum said you needed a bit of peace and quiet. But you're OK now, aren't you? Don't worry; we're not going to drag you out. We thought we'd bring the party to you.'

'Oh . . . well . . . I don't know.' I make a face. 'I'm a bit off parties.'

'Not a real party, just a few friends, eating pizza, watching the fireworks,' says Lucy. 'I'm so happy you're OK! I was scared, with you having open heart surgery!'

'It wasn't open heart surgery,' I scoff. 'I wasn't even under general anaesthetic. They just put in this thing . . . look . . . here.'

I show them the dressing over the faint bump. They give a good show of pretending to be impressed. 'It's cool! It's different! You'll have a story to tell!'

'A story to tell to anyone who sees me without any clothes?'

'Exactly! And you'll have a scar!'

'Ugh. Who wants a scar?' The wound is healing, and it's itchy rather than painful. But I hate it when Mum changes the dressing, because who wants to see massive stitches eating into your flesh?

'Scars are uber-sexy!' says Lucy. 'If I were you, I'd tell people I'd been shot.'

'Saved by your bra strap!'

'Oh, stop it,' I say. I'm laughing but there are tears in my eyes. 'I'm never going to get involved with anyone ever again. No one's seeing this scar.'

'Oh, Kitty!' Alice puts her arm round me.

'I know how you feel,' says Lucy. 'It's tough being on your own when you've just come out of a relationship.'

'Oh, well, I didn't really have a relationship with Theo,' I say bravely, and then realise that tears are dripping down my nose. 'I'm sorry. I just cry randomly all the time since the operation.'

The girls hug me again, give me tissues and make me hot chocolate.

'A boyfriend,' says Alice, 'should be like the sprinkles on top of an ice cream. A nice extra, but something that you can do without.'

'Sprinkles,' says Lucy, 'but not the cone. Never the cone. You shouldn't feel incomplete if he's not there.'

'But if there's no cone, won't I just melt all over the place?' I say, doubtfully. 'Assuming I'm the ice cream.'

'Ah,' says Alice. 'That's where the bowl comes in.'

We all start giggling.

'What or who is the bowl?'

'All your family and friends, that's the bowl. Me and Lucy, we are the bowl. We are *your* bowl, Kitty! You don't need a cone! And some lovely sprinkles will come along when the time is right.'

'Or a cherry,' says Lucy.

'As long as he's not a flake,' I say, and we all laugh so much that I'm nearly crying again.

'So,' says Lucy, recovering first, 'you're going to be just fine.'

'I was always fine on my own before,' I say. 'It's just ... I liked that romance thing. That feeling of being the heroine in a love story, you know? But actually Theo didn't really want a heroine after all.'

'This is not a love story,' says Alice. 'This is the story of your life. You don't need any hero apart from yourself.'

'And your bowl-shaped friends,' says Lucy. 'Anyway, you are in love. I've never seen anyone fall for a place like you've fallen for Amsterdam.'

I do love Amsterdam, it is true. I love the houses and the canals, the New Year *oliebollen* – sugar-coated doughnuts – and the little baby pancakes. I love cycling around the park, and walking on the streets. I love the way the roads are paved with bricks that look like someone's knitted them in herringbone. I love the dolls' houses in the Rijksmuseum. If I never fall in love again, I'll still be happy as long as I'm living in such a cool place.

Plus, spring is coming. I've got a balcony planted out with pots full of bulbs. I'm looking forward to seeing fields of tulips. And, even better, taking pictures of them.

'I'm fine!' I say. 'Who needs sprinkles anyway?'

The door bell buzzes again. I'm irritated. Why does Mum never remember her key?

'Who is it?' I ask into the intercom.

A disembodied voice. 'It's me. Theo. Can we talk?'

I turn round to Lucy and Alice, who nod and smile.

'Er, OK. I'll let you in.' I click the door release.

Then we dance around, in an excited panic.

'We'll go!' says Alice. 'No, we'll go into your bedroom. Or out on the balcony?'

'You'll freeze!'

'We'll go then.' There's a knock at the door. 'Too late! Come on, Lu!' And they disappear into my bedroom.

I open the door and there he is. Just as gorgeous as ever. If he asked me to get back together, I'd forget everything.

No, I wouldn't.

'Um, Kitty, how are you? I heard you had your operation.'

'I'm recovering,' I say, stepping out of the flat and shutting the door behind me.

'What are you doing? Can't I come in?'

'No. Two reasons. First, Alice and Lucy are in my bedroom and they'll hear every word we say. And second, we need to talk to Ethan as well.'

Chapter 47

Theo

Amsterdam

I follow her into the lift, protesting as she texts.

'I don't want to see Ethan ... there's no point ... I just wanted to talk to you. Before I go back to London.'

'I heard you were leaving,' she says. She's looking different again. Paler, weaker, less carefully put together.

'Are you sure you're OK?'

'I'm not meant to leave the flat. But we won't go far.'

'Ethan won't even want to talk to me.'

'He doesn't want to talk to me either. But he will.'

I swallow. 'You're not going to do something like filming it for your vlog, are you?'

She raises her eyebrows. 'Would I do a thing like that?'

I don't know. It seems to me that someone who could pretend they were missing for a whole day could do almost anything.

Outside in the square, she says, 'Where's your bike?'

'I didn't bring it. I came on the tram. It's a bit icy.' I feel slightly pathetic saying this, because, sure, it's icy and the snow is still thick in the Vondelpark, but real Amsterdammers don't let a little bit of black ice put them off cycling.

'OK. Never mind.' And she sends off another text, waits for an answer and then says, 'We'll wait in the café. Or you could ride my bike, and I'll sit on the back?'

I try to imagine explaining to her mum how her bike skidded on ice into a canal. 'No, we can go to the café. But I don't think Ethan will want to ...'

'Shut up,' she says.

'Oh. OK.'

We sit down and order a mint tea for her and a coffee for me, and I ask her about her operation. Her scar is tiny, apparently, but she's got a small lump near her shoulder. 'It's my bionic bit,' she says. 'It's going to set off airport security all over the world.'

I might have known she'd take heart surgery in her stride.

'Look,' she says, 'I've got something to say, and I need to say it to you and Ethan together. I don't care what's going on with you two. At least I do care, but—'

'Kitty?' I stop her.

We look up. Ethan's standing at the door to the café. He's looking better than when I last saw him, his bruises have faded, his cast is off, he's washed his hair and he's wearing a blue shirt that really suits him. *He's better off without me* is the only conclusion I can come to.

'Hey, Ethan,' says Kitty.

Ethan comes over to our table, but stays standing. 'I didn't know he was going to be here.'

'Look, sit down,' she says. 'I've got something to say to both of you. I'm pretty tired after the operation and I can't be bothered with having long conversations.'

Clearly Kitty and Ethan have made it up. I suppose it's because his dad is getting married to her mum. I got the news from Simon. 'It's sort of weird that I'm going to be invited to your ex-girlfriend's mum's wedding,' was how he put it, 'especially when it's to your ex-boyfriend's dad. At least I'll get to meet everyone you snogged in Amsterdam. Unless there's stuff you're not telling me?'

'I thought you hated me,' says Ethan, sitting down. 'You've got to stop manipulating people, *susje*.'

Oh. So they haven't made up after all. I find my voice. 'Why did you come, if you thought she hated you?'

'She texted me, said I had to come over and talk to her, something urgent. I didn't realise. I suppose I should have guessed. Did you plan it together?'

'No,' I retort, stung by his tone. 'I came to say goodbye to Kitty. I'm leaving Amsterdam. I wasn't expecting to see you.'

He doesn't react at all, just nods and says, 'Yeah, I suppose that's the best thing.' His eyes are cold and he's speaking in that bantering drawl again. 'You were right. It would've been a waste of time for you to learn Dutch.'

'Stop it,' says Kitty.

'Yeah, well, I've got stuff to do,' says Ethan. 'So, if we're finished?'

'No!' Kitty bangs her hand down on the table. 'I need to say something. I am sorry. I shouldn't have just disappeared off to Newcastle and tried to make you feel guilty. It was a bad thing to do. Whatever you'd done, it was wrong of me.'

'I'm sorry too,' I say. 'I messed you around, Kitty. I was just a bit confused, but I should have been more honest with you.'

'Ethan?' says Kitty.

I think he's going to leave, or make some sneering wisecrack, but he doesn't. He runs his fingers through his hair and says, 'Kitty, I should have told you I was interested in Theo. I was trying to be subtle, but that was stupid of me. I was way too British.'

'Yes, but what about what Alice and Lucy told me? That you deliberately tried to break us up?'

'That wasn't true,' I say, and Ethan looks at me with a half-smile. Could he possibly be grateful?

'It was a lie,' he tells her. 'It was a story. I had my reasons; I was all mixed up. But I didn't do anything on purpose to hurt you. I may have misread things ... but I do care about you, *susje*. It was horrible when you disappeared.'

Her smile is dazzling. 'Truly, it was a lie? Because I didn't like seeing you two kiss, but it's worse if it was just a fake kiss.'

Time for me to speak up. 'I should have told you, Kitty, I'm sorry. I didn't even realise myself how I felt. It wasn't until I saw Ethan ... I didn't know ...'

'So you two – it's OK now? Now Ethan's said he was lying?'

Ethan shakes his head. 'Could you be with someone who broke your arm, Kitty?' His voice is strained. 'I wish it could be different, but I can't do that.'

'Oh! Theo, you did that?'

'I didn't mean to. Kitty … Ethan … please believe me.' And I explain about the push and the skates and the tree, and then she looks from me to Ethan, and he looks away.

'It's just such a shame,' she says, 'if Theo goes back to London and you two never have a chance to make up.'

Ethan reaches out and holds her hand. 'We all got hurt in the end. It's OK. We'll live.' He looks at me properly for the first time.

'How are you?'

'I'm OK,' I say. Then, 'Well, I'm not really. I screwed everything up. That's why I'm going back to London.'

'It's a shame to go in the winter,' he says. 'Amsterdam is better in the spring and summer. Flowers and stuff. You never got to see them.'

'I can't just stay for the sake of some tulips.'

Kitty pats my arm. 'You should stay. Even if it's just until the summer. It'll mess up your exams, leaving now.'

'I haven't got any friends. Everyone hates me.' I know I'm sounding as gloomy as Eeyore, but it's all true.

Kitty's still holding Ethan's hand. Now she grabs mine too. 'Can't we all be friends? We're obviously rubbish at falling in love with each other, but we could have a go at being friends. Couldn't we?'

How can I be friends with Ethan? I can't even see him

without wanting to touch him. It's actually killing me, just sitting here at the table with him.

'We could try,' he says, slowly. 'It's a starting point anyway.'

'Theo?' asks Kitty.

I'm trying to work out what's going on in Ethan's head. Has he forgiven me? Is there hope? Whatever, it seems to me that this is my best chance.

'Friends,' I say. 'And maybe I don't have to leave right away.' My mum had already told me she'd understand if I wanted to stay. 'It sounds like there's unfinished business in Amsterdam,' is what she'd said.

'Yay!' says Kitty. 'Go us! Friends. OK, ground rules. No kissing.'

'No lying,' I say. 'No secrets.'

'No violence,' says Ethan. His eyes meet mine, finally. There's a hint of a smile in them. 'No broken limbs.'

'But we might need to renegotiate some of the rules at some point,' I say. 'I mean there might be an essential secret, for example.'

'We'll see about that if it happens' says Kitty. 'And now you are going to come upstairs and make up with Alice and Lucy too.'

Chapter 48

Kitty

Amsterdam

It turns into quite a New Year's Eve party. We order in pizza and open bottles of wine and people keep on coming in. Mum's friends from work, Paul's workshop writers. And some of our friends from college as well.

Mieke arrives with a tall woman who looks vaguely familiar. She's got blonde hair cut short, and bright blue eyes. I'm just trying to think where I know her from when Mieke introduces her. 'This is Melinda, Kitty. Ethan's mum.'

'Oh! I thought you were in Afghanistan!'

'I just got in yesterday.' She smiles at me. 'It feels as though I'm on another planet.'

'Oh, wow, I can imagine. I mean, I can sort of imagine.'

'It's difficult to explain what it's actually like out there. That's why I went into this kind of work. It wasn't enough to raise money or support good causes from home.'

I'm trying not to stare. There's just something about her, something fascinating that makes everyone else seem a little bit

smaller and greyer. Beauty, sure, but also a sort of aura of good-
ness.

'It's lovely to meet you, Kitty,' she says. 'I've been hearing all
about your operation. That's quite something to go through at
your age. How are you feeling?'

'I'm OK,' I say. 'A bit tired.'

'You take care now. They say it's a small thing, an operation
like that, but it can knock you sideways. Now, how are we going
to go along? I think I'm going to pretend I'm your auntie. After
all, you're going to be Ethan's stepsister.'

'Oh, well, Ethan and I are friends really,' I say, casting a
glance over to the corner where Theo and Ethan are sitting.
They're not touching, they're not kissing, but the way that
they're talking – leaning in on each other, laughing, listening
intently – makes me wonder just how our three-way vow of
friendship is going to develop.

'I'm so glad of it.' She follows my gaze. 'Ethan needs good
friends, and I can tell you're a friend worth having.'

I'm completely tongue-tied.

'I've been trying to persuade him to do a year volunteering in
Africa; I know just the right scheme, but he's so resistant. So
closed. I sometimes worry that he's actually agoraphobic. He
hardly seems to leave the house.'

'Oh no, he goes out all the time,' I say. 'Cycling and
rollerblading and stuff. It's just his arm that's making it difficult
at the moment.'

'He's wasting his life,' she says. 'But I'm sure he'll find his
purpose one day.'

'Um, yes,' I say. 'You know, I'd be really interested in that Africa scheme. Not for now, but for when I finish my exams.'

She tells me she'll send me the details, and adds, 'I'll have to try and be back for the wedding. Won't that be exciting?'

I am super-excited about the wedding, now that I've made peace with Ethan. I was born to be a wedding planner. My head is full of bridesmaid's dresses (polka dots? 50s style?) and bouquets (lily of the valley, with tiny pink rosebuds), and I'm wondering if we can hire a party boat. Ethan will know. In fact he might be a superb collaborator. I might start a tumblr called 'Daughter of the Bride'. It could be awesome.

I'll have to ask Mum what she makes of Melinda, and whether she was even planning to invite her, but right now I'm just pleased that everything's sort of calmed down and nothing feels passionate and dramatic and life-changing any more.

I'm an independent scoop of ice cream in a crystal bowl, I think. That would make a nice picture. But then I consider how easily crystal is broken and I change my mind. I'm stem ginger ice cream in a stoneware bowl.

Alice is arguing politics with the young guy from the bookstore where Paul does his workshops, but she's debating in a jokey way that makes it clear that she likes him. Lucy is chatting to Mike, who's an intern at Mum's office. I'm pouring wine and handing out bowls of tortilla chips and wondering if we ought to order in more pizza. My mind is buzzing with thoughts of Africa ... travelling ... the wedding ... doing things that, in the past, my dodgy heart prevented me from even thinking about. I'm bubbling with excitement. I can do anything I want.

I don't notice that Theo and Ethan have got up from their exclusive corner and come to find me.

'So, you met my mom?' says Ethan, taking a handful of tortilla chips.

'Yeah, she's lovely.'

'A living angel, hey? You can see why I'm a disappointment.'

'You're not a disappointment,' I say. 'Stop it.'

He gives me a half-hug. 'I am,' he says, 'but maybe there's hope for me.'

'My brother's arriving tomorrow,' says Theo. 'He's totally in love with your sister, Kitty. I hope she's going to be kind to him. He's not that bright, you know, but basically he's a good person.'

'She's completely potty about him,' I tell him. 'We'll probably have two family weddings this year.' It was going to be all kinds of weird having Rachel and Simon staying with us, but now I'd made peace with Theo I thought I could cope.

'Then I'll be your step-brother and Theo will be your brother-in-law,' says Ethan. 'I did warn you about family relationships.'

I know him well enough now that I just roll my eyes and say, 'You wait till you meet Rachel. She's always wanted a younger brother to crush underfoot.'

'Come on,' says Theo, 'it's time to go and watch the fireworks. There's not going to be room on the balcony unless we bag our place now.'

So we all squeeze outside, Alice and Lucy and Ethan and Theo and me. And we count down the minutes to midnight and watch as the sky bursts with colour. I'm trying to take pictures, but after a few shots I put down the camera.

Sometimes, you can't hide behind a lens. Sometimes you have to live the moment, instead of capturing it in a frame.

I'm going to think bigger than Instagram. I'm going to knit a map of Amsterdam, with dolphins and mermaids and glimmering fish. I'm going to cover a bicycle completely in knitting, and decorate it with models of clogs and windmills and Sinterklaas and cheese. I'm looking forward to spring and tulips and an event called King's Day when everyone parties and sells their old clothes and stuff on the streets. I'm going to be so busy, so creative, that anyone interested in falling in love with me is going to have to persuade me that they're worth spending time on.

I am Kitty and I am magnificent, says a voice in my head.

And right now, as the clock strikes twelve and the sky explodes, I believe every word.

Acknowledgements

*Met hartelijke dank/*With heartfelt thanks:

In Amsterdam: Cindy, John and Liam Yianni; Debbie Noble and Ann Maher, Cato and Milo Fordham, whose house I stole for Ethan. Plus everyone who helped with Dutch, Hebrew and Yiddish (never again) on Facebook.

In the UK: Valerie Kampmeier, Fiona Dunbar, Inbali Iserles, Keris Stainton, Emma Cravitz, Lee Weatherly, Lydia Syson, Avital Nathan and Amanda Swift. Also Phoebe Moss and Gila Sheldon, for ice cream wisdom.

My wonderful agent, Jenny Savill, and her colleagues at Andrew Nurnberg Associates.

The ever-patient and understanding Karen Ball and the brilliant team at Atom: Becca, Kate and Emma – and Sarah and Olivia for the final stages.

Catherine Wightman, who bid generously in the Authors for the Philippines auction to include the name of her daughter in this book. I hope Alice likes Alice!

Cristina and everyone at Sable d'Or in Crouch End, where most of this book was written.

The Sisters, the Thinkers, the Friends and Nicky, Yvette and Laura. Hilary Totterman, first partner in creativity, and Anna Longman who made it all happen.

Frank-Jan de Leeuw for offering my husband a job in Amsterdam in 1998. Barend Toet, Kate Russell, Floris Leeuwenberg and all my colleagues at The Cover Story 2004-7. All my expat friends and everyone at the International School of Amsterdam 1999-2007. You made Amsterdam feel like home.

Xavi Maddison for taking photographs of Amsterdam through Kitty's eyes, for the AmsterKit tumblr.

Mum and Dad, Alun, Deborah, Jeremy, Josh, Avital and Eliana. Mum, I hope you will like the finished version better than the first draft.

Laurence, Phoebe and Judah. *Ik hou van jullie allemaal zo veel. Van Londen naar Amsterdam en terug.*